IF YOU LOVED ME

Angela slid her hand into his. Her unexpected gesture of support comforted him. His fingers closed around her hand, feeling the calluses that shouldn't be there. Something prompted him to bring her hand to his mouth. He placed a light kiss on her knuckle, marveling at how small and vulnerable her hand looked wrapped in his larger one.

Ransom watched her watch him.

The pupils of her eyes widened infinitesimally while her lips parted. Her mouth might speak of divorce, but her body responded to his touch. He didn't remember the particulars of their one night together, but the sensual memory of her eager participation tugged at him.

He welcomed their physical attraction. Craved it. They were locked in a situation beyond their control, but that at least would make life bearable . . .

Ransom's Bride

Ginger Hanson

ZEBRA BOOKS
Kensington Publishing Corp.
http://www.kensingtonbooks.com

ZEBRA BOOKS are published by

Kensington Publishing Corp.
850 Third Avenue
New York, NY 10022

All Kensington titles, imprints and distributed lines are available at special quantity discounts for bulk purchases for sales promotion, premiums, fund-raising, educational or institutional use.

Special book excerpts or customized printings can also be created to fit specific needs. For details, write or phone the office of the Kensington Special Sales Manager: Kensington Publishing Corp., 850 Third Avenue, New York, NY 10022. Attn. Special Sales Department. Phone: 1-800-221-2647.

Zebra and the Z logo Reg. U.S. Pat. & TM Off.

First Printing: April 2004
10 9 8 7 6 5 4 3 2 1

Printed in the United States of America

To Jean Southwell, librarian extraordinaire.
Thank you.

Chapter 1

"Sabrina?"

The familiar voice jolted Angela Stapleton out of her reverie. The sad moment in the family cemetery shattered into joy. Ransom Champion? Alive? Before she could turn, a pair of strong hands twirled her into an embrace.

To her surprised delight, he kissed her. When his mouth swallowed her husky squeal, she rose on her toes to meet him. In the split second before her eyes fluttered shut, she stared into a pair of aquamarine eyes. Then, she closed her eyes, unwilling to see his shocked expression when he realized he kissed the wrong sister. Until he did, she wanted to soak up every sensation of her first kiss.

Her first kiss.

Given by the last man she ever expected to kiss her, but the only man she had ever dreamed of kissing her.

Their bodies touched from chest to thigh. She wondered if he could feel the galloping pace of her heartbeat. Wonderful sensations pooled in her abdomen and she wanted to melt into him. He smelled of cool sunshine, wood smoke, and horse, but underneath the outdoorsy mix was his scent and it made her dizzy with wanting him. She had not known a man's beard could be that soft against her face.

A dog growled at the same moment Ransom pulled his mouth free. She couldn't stop her body from following his retreat the merest of inches. Her hands lifted in protest, she wanted to grab his head and hold his mouth against hers.

She didn't.

She dropped her hands to her sides and opened her eyes.

White teeth flashed in a grin she thought never to see again.

"Looks like I made a mistake."

He still gripped her shoulders. Angela didn't think she could be any happier than at this moment. Ransom Champion was alive. She smiled back at him.

"Don't expect me to apologize, little one. Returning soldiers are allowed some liberties."

"We thought you were dead." Angela's smile got bigger and happier. Her eyes drank in the sight of him. Sure, he looked awful because the war had etched its way across his body, leaving a gaunt stranger in its place. But he was alive! Standing before her, a flesh and blood man. Her heart soared with happiness.

"The Yankees tried, but I guess I'm a hard man to kill."

Thin. Bearded. War ragged. Was that a scar running along his right cheek?

"I see your trusty guardian survived the war," he said.

The man who reached down to ruffle Jackson's ears bore little resemblance to the dashing cavalry officer Sabrina had sent to war. Of his handsome

Confederate uniform, only a threadbare gray frock coat, worn down cavalry boots, and slouch hat remained. His poorly mended blue trousers hovered several inches above his boots. A calico shirt that looked like peppermint candy peeked between the gaps caused by the missing buttons on his frock coat.

The Yankees had ordered all the CSA buttons cut off uniforms. For some men that meant no buttons on the only coats they had left.

He looked as patched together as the renewed Union.

Damp February air flowed across her face, cooling her flushed skin. Less than a week earlier, a freezing cold had chased away the unusually mild winter. Now patches of snow clung in tree shadowed hollows, fighting for survival after Sunday night's rain.

She pulled her shawl closer and hunched into its warmth, corralling the urge to run her hands over his shoulders and down his arms. She wanted to feel his body beneath her fingertips. To press her hands against his chest and feel the beat of his heart.

Jackson pushed his large body between them, forcing them farther apart. The dog lifted his upper lip to expose a set of yellowed, but sharp teeth. He growled again.

"Don't you remember me, boy?"

"He remembers you. He'd be hanging off your throat if he didn't." Angela dropped to her knees and wrapped her arms around the dog's neck. Hugging Jackson kept her hands off Ransom's body. Her bonnet, knocked askew by his exuberant embrace, dangled against her shoulder blades by two frayed green ribbons. Since she didn't trust her shaking hands to right it, she ignored the bonnet and hid her fingers in Jackson's soft fur.

The dog accepted her attention as his due, but his soulful brown eyes never left Ransom's face.

"The last time I saw that dress and hat, Sabrina wore them." Ransom glanced around the small graveyard as if expecting Sabrina to come out from behind the nearest tree. "I'm afraid I mistook you for your sister."

Oh my! Angela dug her fingers into Jackson's neck. The dog whined.

She eased her grip. How would Ransom know about Sabrina? There had been no reason to tell him, because they thought he was dead. Panic welled in her heart. She wasn't sure she had the strength to tell him. Not yet. She smoothed her hand down Jackson's chest, searching for some way to postpone the inevitable.

"I can't believe you're here. Everyone said you'd been killed." She bit off her babbling words, wondering if he noticed her anxiety, hoping he'd attribute it to shock.

"I'm sure Colonel Truesdail didn't expect me to live."

His small smile did funny things to her chest.

"But I survived." He shrugged.

His dismissal of his survival ignited a tiny ray of anger. If he'd told them he was alive, she wouldn't be in this untenable situation of having to tell him about Sabrina.

"Why didn't you write and let us know you weren't dead?" She'd gone from babbling to waspish.

"I would have, but the Feds took me to an island so far south, I could throw a rock and hit Cuba. My captors didn't encourage letter writing."

She sensed memories beneath his clipped recital that she doubted he would ever share.

"Then one day late last summer, they threw me in

a boat, took me to the Florida coast, and left me. No money. No food. No way to get word to Sabrina I was alive."

His brusque description erased the last vestige of her irritation. "I'm sorry, I didn't mean to imply—"

"You didn't." He brushed aside her apology, "I've come for Sabrina. It's past time I took her to Texas."

"Ah yes, Texas." Angela knew Ransom's plans because she'd been his correspondent until his presumed death two years earlier. From the first letter, she regretted agreeing to Sabrina's scheme. Writing to a man while pretending to be someone else smacked of unforgivable deceit, but refusal had been impossible. Sabrina so seldom begged for anything.

And her argument had been excellent. She had horrible penmanship and it would have been embarrassing for Ransom to see how poorly she wrote. Angela agreed to write the letters Sabrina dictated. All too soon, Sabrina grew bored with a romance conducted via sporadic letters, and Angela became Ransom's correspondent.

Although she enjoyed writing him, she never intended to fall in love. Nor had she realized the depth of her affection until they received word of his death. No one knew how much she resented her sister's immediate search for another man to ease her supposed grief. A search that led to her own death.

"Your aunt said Sabrina was down here."

Ransom's casual announcement brought Angela scrambling to her feet. "Aunt Julia said Sabrina was down here?" Her voice cracked on "here."

"Has something happened to her?" Her borderline hysteria swung his gaze from its cursory search of the small cemetery. He stepped toward her, his brows drawn in worry. "Tell me, now! Where's Sabrina?"

She stood between him and Sabrina. He hadn't noticed the fresh grave to the side of her father's resting place. Unable to stop the tears that welled into her eyes, she stepped aside.

His body tensed as he read the inscription Angela knew by heart:

Sabrina Sue Stapleton
April 12, 1842–January 10, 1866
Beloved daughter and sister

"No! No!" He stepped backward, shaking his head. "I did not survive the war to have Sabrina die."

His words ripped through Angela's soul. She wanted to pull his rigid body into the warmth of her embrace, but she no longer existed for him. He had entered his own hell. The woman he loved had died weeks before his safe return. Their future lay buried in the cold Tennessee ground.

As quickly as he had appeared, Ransom disappeared. The small wrought iron gate clanged shut behind him. Within moments, she heard the fading hoofbeats of his horse.

Angela's legs buckled and she sank to the ground. Her hand slid to the locket she wore around her neck. Pulling out the flat oval case, she opened it. Twin miniature portraits peered back at her. Sabrina on one side. Ransom on the other. Sabrina forever young and beautiful. Ransom forever handsome in his gray uniform.

Why don't you keep the locket, sister dear. You can pretend you're in love with Ransom when you answer his letters.

Before she died, Sabrina had made Angela promise on the locket she would never tell anyone the truth about her death. The promise had been easy to make, because Angela believed the only man who would be hurt by the truth was dead.

Snapping the locket shut, she dropped it back between her breasts. Jackson flopped to the ground beside her, resting his heavy head on her thigh.

"He would've been miserable married to her." She stroked the dog's wide brow. "Sabrina wanted to live at Champion's Crest, drink champagne, go to parties and flirt with good-looking men. Be the wife of a wealthy planter." Her hand stilled and she stared at the tombstone. "She didn't see his dream."

Jackson sighed and settled himself more comfortably.

"She had no intention of going to Texas. If she'd only read his letters, she would have understood how much he loved Texas."

The glade her father had chosen so many years ago to bury his first wife and their stillborn child seemed lonely now rather than peaceful. Jackson shifted his head beneath her hand to remind her he needed petting.

She massaged his ears. She had never expected to be faced with telling Ransom that Sabrina was dead. It would be a long time before she forgot the bitter despair in his eyes.

"He doesn't know what unhappiness awaited him had he married her. Now, he can grieve, let time mend his heart and then find a better woman to share his life in Texas."

Although the thought of Ransom married to any woman pained her, there was a measure of relief in knowing he would not be her brother-in-law.

Jackson raised his head and stared intently toward the house. Then he lumbered to his feet and met a lanky adolescent at the edge of the cemetery.

Angela smiled a greeting. "Are you looking for me, Tommy?"

"You all right, Miz Angela? I saw Major Champion fly outa here like the devil were achasin' him. And that broken down old horse he was ariding, why he'll be lucky if it goes a mile without dying. Nothing like that purty horse he rode off to war on."

"I'm all right, but I'm afraid Major Champion does feel as if the devil has conspired against him."

Tommy scuffed his boots in last year's leaves. "I reckon you done tole him about Miz Sabrina?"

"Yes, I told him." She slipped the once fashionable leghorn bonnet off and smoothed her hair.

"Do you reckon he'll be back? 'Cause I thought I'd ask him 'iffen I could go to Texas with him. Don't ya think he might want some company?" Eager green eyes pleaded for a positive response. "It's a long way to Texas, ain't it?"

"Oh yes, it's a long way to Texas." Unsure how to answer Tommy's real question, she settled her bonnet on her head and tied the ribbons.

She knew Tommy saw Texas as a land of opportunity. For many Southerners, it was the only state large enough to comfortably hold both Rebels and Yankees. But Texas also contained Indians.

Sabrina had relished telling her stories about the savage Indians, who killed and scalped. Oh, she didn't come out and say Angela had these tendencies, but she implied that Angela's genteel behavior didn't make up for blood she had inherited from a half-breed Cherokee father.

Angela pushed herself to her feet and shook out her skirts. Jackson nosed around the leaves at her feet, his huffing snorts gently scattering winter's debris. She hated to deflate Tommy's dream, but she could put off it off no longer.

"I'm afraid you won't get a chance to ask Major Champion if he'd like company." She tried for a brisk tone, but failed miserably. "With Sabrina dead, Ransom has no reason to return."

Chapter 2

Four hours later, Ransom plodded back up the wide porch steps. It seemed strange to visit the Stapleton home and not have dozens of people greeting him. Many of them had been patients, because Sabrina's father had been the only doctor for miles around. Some of the visitors had been young men eager to court Sabrina.

He rapped on the weathered door.

Within moments, he heard footsteps in the hallway. They wouldn't belong to Sabrina. A wave of despair washed over him. He couldn't believe she was dead. Dreams of a future with her on his ranch in Texas had kept him alive during five years of war and imprisonment and the long trek home.

Angela opened the door.

He pulled the battered hat off his head and stared into her soft gray eyes. "How did she die?"

Without a word, she opened the door wider, stepped back and waited for him to enter. When he walked past her, he breathed the tantalizing scent of jasmine. It had been one of the clues that slammed the truth into his consciousness when he kissed her earlier that afternoon. Sabrina favored rose scents.

Had favored.

His step faltered. Angela walked past him. He took

a steadying breath, then followed her to her father's office.

He stopped on the threshold, shock penetrating the dull haze of grief. Dr. Stapleton's office no longer existed as he remembered it. Gone were the bottles, books, papers, microscope and other paraphernalia of the medical profession. A lone, straight backed chair faced the large library desk, probably deemed too old and too large to steal.

A black leather case sat in the middle of the desktop. The solitary reminder of a once thriving practice.

Angela stopped beside the desk, reaching out to run her fingers across the leather case. "Captain Andrews brought this with him when he came home. He said Father asked him to make sure I got it if anything happened to him."

"I was sorry to hear of your father's death. The Army lost a good man with his passing."

"Thank you." She looked around the room as if realizing how stark it must seem to someone who had not watched the soldiers strip it bare. "I apologize for bringing you here, but I thought you might wish privacy. We put most of the furniture in the dining room."

"This is fine. Please." He touched her arm and motioned toward the chair. "Be seated."

He paced the small room, wondering if he really wanted to hear the details of Sabrina's death. She had believed him dead. Had she married? He couldn't bear to think of his beautiful Sabrina with another man.

"Did she marry?"

Angela was in the midst of seating herself. From the way her head jerked up, he knew his question caught her by surprise.

"Marry?" Her voice held an odd edge and she averted her gaze. "Well, not exactly. She had become engaged, but the gentleman died in a hunting accident."

A selfish feeling of relief flowed over him. "Poor Sabrina. She must have thought the Fates conspired against her."

"That is a good description."

For the second time that day, Ransom wondered if Angela had any idea of how the sultry low timbre of her voice and its deep Southern accent affected him.

Then, the merest of smiles curved her generous mouth.

Hot, hungry, unexpected need slammed into him. He never should have kissed her. Six years of considering her a little sister wiped out with one kiss.

Cold, miserable, righteous guilt exploded need into a thousand pieces. He had returned to find out how Sabrina died. It shamed him to think he asked about her while lusting after her sister.

"I need to know how she died."

She rubbed her hands on her skirt, running them up and down her thighs as if she were trying to cleanse them. He found it odd she would not look at him.

"Early in January, Sabrina got caught in a bad storm. It was windy, the day cold. She was chilled by the time she got home. A fever followed. It went to her lungs . . ."

Angela's husky-honey voice dwindled into silence.

Ransom gripped the edge of Dr. Stapleton's desk. He felt as old and worn out as the desk that had survived the arduous trip by wagon from Georgia thirty years ago.

Guilt crushed his soul. "I should have married her."

"You tried twice. It isn't your fault the Yankees were

impossible to dislodge from this area. And what if you had married her and left her a widow with a child?"

"You sound like the excuses I wrote in my letters."

To his surprise, she blushed slightly. "Sabrina sometimes shared parts of your letters with us. We were starved for news during the war. The Yankees closed our book publishers and controlled the newspapers."

"I was a fool. Better risk death for a few hours together as man and wife rather than have none." Bitterness racked his voice. "I should have tried harder, but I had some foolish notion I shouldn't marry her if I couldn't protect her. And how could I protect her when the Yankees controlled her home and mine?"

Angela's skirts rustled as she crossed the room. She paused near him, but didn't touch him. He looked into her soft gray eyes. They invited him to tell her what he had told no other, because they promised she could help make things better. And so he told the truth about himself.

"There was so much death, it didn't seem likely I'd survive the war. I told myself how much harder it'd be on Sabrina if I left her a widow with a child. Better for her to be unmarried and childless, why she could marry a Yankee if need be."

Ransom knew he should stop Angela when she refilled his glass. It had been a long time since he had had such good whiskey.

"You should have seen Aunt Julia and me. There we were, behind the barn, in the middle of the night, pouring most of father's whiskey on the ground."

He watched the flow of amber liquid as it dissipated the rainbows created in the crystal by the flickering candlelight.

"We heard the Yankees were in Nashville. Well, sober Yankees would be bad enough to face. We certainly didn't want to deal with drunk Yankees."

Angela placed the decanter on the sideboard. He watched her resume her seat, trying to remember how he got from her father's office to the dining room. He had bathed and shaved. He wore a clean shirt and his trousers and frock coat had been brushed.

His fingers played across the unfamiliar texture of his smooth cheeks. It had been months since he last shaved.

The almost forgotten smell of Kentucky bourbon curled into his soul when he sipped the whiskey Angela had unearthed from her father's hidden stock. It slid easily down his throat and dulled his senses, chasing away the flit of Sabrina's skirts that he saw behind every door.

"I haven't been good company for you and Mrs. Kramer tonight."

"We invited you to dinner to insure you ate something, not to be entertained. We've had several weeks to adjust to a loss that is cruelly fresh for you."

"Dessert." Julia Kramer came into the dining room and set a pie in the middle of the table.

His stomach should have welcomed the sweet end to the first decent meal he'd eaten in months. Instead, it lurched at the idea of mixing apple pie with whiskey.

"I think you have outdone yourself on this one, dear." The older woman smiled at Angela as she picked up a silver knife. "In celebration of his safe return, I think Major Champion needs a large piece of apple pie."

He didn't have the heart to refuse Mrs. Kramer's

offer. "It appears your pie making talents have improved since last time I was here, little one."

"Now Major Champion, you know her pies always tasted good. They just didn't look too good. At least, Angela learned her way around a kitchen. Sabrina—"

"You give me too much credit, Aunt Julia."

Angela's interruption of Mrs. Kramer's criticism swung a pair of stricken brown eyes to Ransom. She held out a plate of apple pie. "I didn't mean to say anything unkind about Sabrina . . ." Her voice trailed away.

He took the pie as well as the apology. "Death doesn't change how a person lived her life. We all know Sabrina had no desire to learn housekeeping chores."

The spicy scent of cooked apples and browned crust curled into his nose. His first bite confirmed what he suspected; apple pie did not sit well with whiskey. But he couldn't refuse their food any more than he could refuse Dr. Stapleton's whiskey. He almost wished he wasn't seeking the oblivion of drink.

"You know you're welcome to remain here for a few days if you wish," Angela's aunt said. "If you choose to continue your journey tomorrow, we won't regard it as anything more than a son's eagerness to see his family. I can only imagine your mother's happiness when she learns she didn't lose two sons."

If his mother knew the truth about how his younger brother died, she might not be the welcoming matriarch Mrs. Kramer expected. Ransom shoved that memory away; it was enough he had to deal with Sabrina's death.

Angela watched Ransom weave his way up the wide staircase, fumble with the doorknob to her father's old bedroom, and stumble out of sight. Then she returned to the dining room where she collected a load of dishes and carried them to the back porch.

She and Aunt Julia had rigged up a place to wash dishes on a corner of the porch after the detached kitchen was destroyed by a group of bushwhackers. Sabrina's cries had brought help before the fire spread, and Angela knew their location on the edge of town had saved the house.

"Poor man." Aunt Julia straightened from her position over the dishpan.

Angela stacked china and silverware on the scratched table near her aunt's elbow. "His grief will pass. He would've been more miserable if he married her."

"Angela!"

"Ransom is correct. Death doesn't change a person. Sabrina didn't want to go to Texas even though she knew he had his heart set on ranching. How could they have been happy?"

"I know you find it difficult to forgive Sabrina for neglecting him and taking up with the Yankee officers. But Ransom doesn't know what she did, any more than he knows you wrote him. He thinks those letters came from her and he loves the Sabrina you created."

Angela grabbed a drying cloth. "It's just as well he will be leaving in the morning. I doubt I could maintain his illusion very long."

She picked up a damp plate and gave it an angry swipe. Aunt Julia might know Sabrina had wheedled Angela into writing Ransom. She might also know Sabrina had flirted with every male in the vicinity after her engagement—young, old, Confederate, or Yankee—but she didn't know Sabrina had gone farther than flirting with Nicholas Stevens.

Sabrina had found out she was pregnant the week before Nicholas died. The handsome young Yankee soldier-turned-carpetbagger who had survived the war, had not survived being thrown from his horse.

"If you wipe on that plate much longer, you'll wear the glaze right off the china."

"Sorry." Angela grabbed a good reason for her anxiety. "I keep worrying about medical school. I fear they won't accept a Southern woman at a Pennsylvania school."

"Now Angela, the war's over. And Tennessee was full of Unionists. How are those people to know you supported the Confederacy?"

"You're right. My money is as good as anyone else's. And I doubt women are beating down their doors to become doctors."

"You'll begin a new life in Pennsylvania and Ransom will begin a new life in Texas."

Angela took the wet plate her aunt handed her.

"He'll have his memories of Sabrina and you'll know you eased his life during the war."

Bowing her head over the plate, she scrubbed it dry and wondered why her aunt's words distressed her. She'd known for years Ransom belonged to Sabrina. Her sister's death didn't change anything. Through her letters, Angela had created a Sabrina worthy of Ransom and she doubted if he'd ever be able to love another woman. In truth, she pitied any woman who tried to capture his heart.

While she daydreamed, Aunt Julia picked up the dishpan and headed to the back steps. "And you'll probably never see him again."

Why did her aunt's pronouncement, spoken with such practical firmness, spiral sadness into Angela's soul? Every chatty word coming from her aunt's lips was true.

* * *

With the dishes cleaned, dried and stored, Angela and her aunt returned to the dining room which had become the heart of the house. Two rocking chairs placed in front of the fire awaited them. They had moved what remained of the downstairs furniture into this room. The pieces were the odds and ends left after repeated raids of the Yankees, Rebels, servants or bushwhackers.

Neither Angela nor her aunt complained; they had a roof over their heads. Many of their friends and relatives hadn't been so fortunate. Angela was saddest over the loss of her father's medical library. She doubted if any of the men involved in that day's work were even literate.

"Shall I read another chapter before we go to bed?" She picked up the tattered copy of Walter Scott's *Ivanhoe* that Julia's friend, Mr. Stillman, had lent them.

"I would enjoy hearing more of the story. Mr. Stillman told me yesterday the Bigelow sisters are anxious to read it." Julia pulled a petticoat from her mending basket. A soft smile curved her lips as she bent over her work. "Mr. Stillman says we may take as long as we wish to read the book, but I know they will pester him to death until he brings it. I told him we were nearing the end."

As Angela read about Ivanhoe, Rowena, and Rebecca, she tried to forget about the man who slept in her father's bedroom. Upon finishing the chapter, she looked up to catch her aunt stifling a yawn.

"Dear me," her aunt smiled. "I can't keep my eyes open."

Angela placed the ribbon marker in the book and closed it. "We should probably retire. I imagine Ransom will want to make an early start. If he's lucky, Rosie will lay some eggs tomorrow morning."

"As long as Jackson doesn't chase a rabbit through the chicken coop."

Angela grinned. "You seemed to enjoy having rabbit stew as much as Jackson did yesterday."

Julia folded the petticoat. "I'll get up early and make a fresh batch of biscuits. Ransom will need some food to take with him." She put the petticoat, her needle and thread back into her mending basket. "Are you coming to bed?"

"In a few minutes. I'll bank the fire." Unspoken was her promise to check the doors and windows. While the war had taught them their home was not a safe haven, peace had not yet brought civil order. Two months from the anniversary of surrender, and reports of sporadic acts of violence still peppered the newspapers. The county still reeled from Judge Smart's recent murder.

"Perhaps I will sleep more soundly with a man in the house," her aunt said. She paused by Angela's chair to kiss her goodnight. "Rest well, dear."

Angela stroked her aunt's hand where it rested on her shoulder. "Soon, we'll be in Philadelphia." She tilted her head back to look up at her aunt. "I doubt we shall have to worry about lawless brigands there."

Aunt Julia opened her mouth as if to say something, then smiled. She squeezed Angela's hand briefly before going upstairs.

Angela pushed her toe against the floor and relaxed into the rocking chair. Philadelphia. Medical college. The challenge of becoming a doctor would eradicate thoughts of Ransom.

Her father had given his life to the Confederacy, but he'd invested funds in England to ensure his family's fortunes after the war. She was not wealthy, but she could afford school. Then she would return to Gallatin and establish a practice to care for women.

Moments later, Angela went from room to room, checking windows, doors and fireplaces. As she walked back through the dining room, the amber glow of whiskey beckoned her. She set her candle on the sideboard, reached for the decanter, and poured herself a dollop. With the glass beneath her nose, she breathed in its rich fumes. The scent made her think of her father, cigars, and the rumble of masculine voices late at night.

Closing her mind on the nostalgic memories, she sipped the whiskey. The fiery liquor seared its way across her tongue, down her esophagus, and into her stomach. She squeezed her eyes tight against the unexpected rush of tears and waited for the whiskey burn to ease. By the time she set the glass on the silver tray, the whiskey effect tingled all the way to her toes and a hazy good feeling settled on her.

Gliding up the stairs, she snuffed out the candles in the sconces she had lit earlier in the evening. During the war, lamp oil had become nonexistent while the price of candles had gone sky high. She found it hard to believe some Northern cities had been lit with gaslights.

In her bed chamber, she stripped off her clothes and pulled a cambric night rail over her head. When she tried to tie the faded lilac ribbons, one of them tore off in her hand. She stared at it, then tossed it on her bow front chest of drawers. She was in no mood to go downstairs for a needle and thread.

From across the room, her diary beckoned and she answered its quiet pull. Picking up the slender book, she stroked its leather binding. War shortages had taught her to keep her entries brief. Pen in hand, she wrote *February 20, 1866. Ransom Champion is alive.* She read what she wrote, then closed the diary.

She wanted to write down the sweet joy of finding herself in his embrace. And oh, so many other feelings, but she didn't. She turned her back on her diary and undid her braids. Thick strands of wavy black hair tumbled free to her waist. She picked up her hair brush, pleased as she always was, to hold something her mother had used. If her father hadn't insisted they bury most of their silver before he left for the battlefront, her mother's brush, comb and mirror set would have become Yankee plunder.

She pulled the brush through her wavy hair. It didn't take long to brush the waves away. Her tainted Indian blood kept her straight black hair from ever becoming the riot of golden curls that had blessed Sabrina's head.

Yet another difference between Sabrina the illusion and Angela the reality.

Chapter 3

Ransom hated his dreams.

They took him into the carnage of a battlefield littered with bodies: his brother, his friends, his comrades-in-arms, his enemies. Confederate soldiers, Union soldiers. Corpses stacked a dozen men high and stretching as far as the eye could see.

Death surrounded him. The familiar stench of war's rotting waste filled the air while the incessant cries for water hung over a field hazed with smoke from the thousands of guns that had been fired.

He hated the feeling of frustration, the raw sweat dampening his body, the frantic pounding of his heart.

But mostly, he hated the fear that tainted his mouth.

For he had feared death, until it had become such an hourly companion he found himself sometimes fearing he would live.

He fought to push away the shackles of his dream, but it dragged him into the midst of battle.

"Watch the trees to your right, men! Damn, they're everywhere." His throat felt raw and hoarse from yelling.

A thick fog shrouded the battlefield, its drifting tendrils first hiding, then exposing the soldiers.

For every bluecoated enemy he killed, another took his place. Perspiration mixed with blood and slicked his hands. He tossed aside his empty gun and pulled his saber free.

"Hush, Ransom. It's all right."

The soft words wove their way into his dream. The enemy vanished. Ransom stood alone in the clearing. His heart pounded while his lungs grabbed air. Body tensed, he searched the clearing for the enemy.

"You're safe now. There's no need to fight."

"Sabrina?" He turned toward the voice.

As dreams do, everything shifted. The sun burned away the fog and soldiers, revealing a wooded glade. A warm breeze filled with the scent of roses rustled the leaves of the nearby maple tree.

"The war is over, Ransom. Go back to sleep."

"Is that you, Sabrina?" He needed to feel her warm body.

A flicker of movement caught his eye. Sabrina walked toward him; the folds of her nightdress swirled with enticing promise. The sun's rays danced in strands of curly blonde hair that flowed to the small of a dainty back his fingers ached to touch.

He smiled, opened his arms, and she ran into them.

She pillowed her head on his chest, fitting her soft curves into the lean contours hammered into his body by months of subsistence living. His labored breathing eased; the fear faded. She felt so good in his arms. He relaxed, letting this dream rule his senses and dismissing the battlefield nightmare.

"I'm here, Ransom. Everything will be all right."

Her husky voice grabbed his gut and wouldn't let go.

"I'm so hungry for you." He wove his fingers through her hair, unleashing a hint of jasmine. The dichotomy failed to stop his sigh of contentment. He kissed her.

Oddly, she tasted faintly of whiskey.

"Ah, sweet darling Sabrina." He murmured the words against the moist softness of her lips. When he tried to push his tongue into her mouth, she mewed her resistance. Her coyness startled him. Sabrina had been kissing boys behind the church since she was twelve. If his fiancée knew anything, it was how to kiss.

"Trust me," he whispered against her mouth.

He felt her mouth soften on a gentle sigh.

"Good girl." He slipped the tip of his tongue between her lips and licked the inside of her lower lip.

She surrendered with a muffled gasp of pleasure.

With care, he eased her down onto the sweet summer grass and planted small kisses along her jaw. When he reached her ear, he ran his tongue around the outer rim. Then he tasted her ear. She melted against him.

His hands had not been idle. He slipped his right hand inside her night rail. At his touch, her body stiffened. If it hadn't been a dream, he might have eased his hand free, but it was his dream and he wanted her.

"It's all right, darling." He licked her ear lobe.

She relaxed. He caressed her breast. Sweet Jesu, how long had it been since he filled his hand with the full ripeness of a woman's breast?

"Oh sweetheart, I need you so badly."

His other hand glided over her rib cage to rest lightly on her hips. He didn't like the barrier of her night rail so he tugged it above her thighs. Now he could touch skin.

His fingers played across puckered skin on her right thigh. Scars? On his flawlessly perfect Sabrina?

She shivered and now his fingers stroked smooth skin. Reassured, his hunger drowned his questions.

His fingers found what they sought in the juncture of her legs.

"Ransom!"

Her legs clamped around his hand.

"Don't worry, sweetheart. Trust me."

Her muscles remained rigid. He moved a finger and breathed softly in her ear. "I love you, sweetheart. Please. I need all of you.

Her legs fell open. He gently rubbed her, reveling in the wet response. He was as hard and ready as she was soft and moist.

"Touch me." A thread of command wove through his plea. He took her unresisting hand and guided it to his groin. When her cool fingers curved around his shaft, he nearly exploded.

"Oh my."

Her soft exclamation stirred the hair on his temple. Her hand crept downward in exploration, cupping him, testing his weight. He gritted his teeth. It had been a long time since he had felt the gentle hands of a woman anywhere on his body.

Nuzzling aside the neck of her night rail, he closed his mouth over a nipple. She seemed to shrink back away for a split-second, but he had no time to puzzle over her reaction because she arched her back and pushed her breast into his mouth.

He reached his limit. Either he exploded on her stomach or inside her. Those same muscles that had clenched in fear, now clenched in excitement. He tangled his fingers in her hair and leaned down to possess her mouth as he eased himself into her wet, tight warmth.

She moved against him with an eagerness that sharpened his own urgency. God help him, he had no control left. His release came on his second thrust.

"Sabrina, my love!"

Ransom's guttural cry as he collapsed on top of her, snapped Angela into reality.

Dear God, what had she done?

She had copulated with her deceased sister's fiance.

No. Impossible.

Horrified, she stared at the dark blond head pressed against her breasts while her brain spewed medical explanations at her. Facts and illustrations had not prepared her for the act or the feelings it involved.

She tried to shove him away, but couldn't budge him. Nor could she think with him sprawled across her. Their arms and chests touched, their legs intertwined. Her body hummed with unfamiliar sensations at every point of contact and blocked rational thought.

How she had prided herself on her professionalism. Not once in all the months she worked for her father before illness sent her home had she been anything other than a nurse.

But no other patient had been Ransom.

And this patient had tempted her with something she never thought to possess.

Her careening thoughts slowed because she couldn't breathe with his weight on her chest. She wiggled, then froze when he murmured something. His large hand sought and found her left breast. Then, his breathing slowed into the deeper cadence of sleep and he nestled closer to her.

She turned, unable to resist inhaling the scent of

him. The wonderful melting sensation that had caused all her problems flooded her body. Heat fanned out from where they touched to warm every inch of her body. She wanted to rub herself along him like a cat, marking him with her scent.

Had she gone mad? She closed her mind to the memory, tried to mentally pull away, but the sensations filled her thoughts. His raspy cheek sliding along her neck. His tongue in her ear. More heat pooled in her abdomen. She craved his touch down there. She felt incomplete, but didn't know why.

And would never know why. Their coupling had been an accident. He thought he bedded Sabrina. No matter how much her heart ached at the misconception, it was better he think their encounter a dream.

She must not be in his bed when he awoke.

Another wiggle and she shifted his weight from her chest enough to breathe. Something warm trickled down the insides of her thighs.

She would not dwell on what she had done—or the consequences. No dry medical book could have prepared her for the overwhelming emotional and physical responses that drove rational thought from her mind.

She would not think about it, she would wait for him to roll off her.

Then, she would slip out of his bed and return to her room. He would never know about tonight.

"Sabrina."

Something nuzzled the hair at Angela's neck. She swatted at it, resentful of being chased from the soft cocoon of sleep and a most delightful dream about

Ransom. His hands and mouth had been doing the most shocking things to her body.

"My darling, Sabrina."

The words tickled in her ear, dragging her toward wakefulness while a warm hand slid over her arm to cup her breast. Angela's eyes snapped open. She could feel a fully aroused, naked male body curved against her heels, her calves, her thighs, her buttocks, and the length of her back. A mouth pressed kisses on her neck.

Memories of the previous night slammed her into consciousness.

Hellfire and damnation! She had fallen asleep in Ransom's bed.

"Hmmmmm, you smell wonderful . . . wonderful . . . different. Like jasmine?"

She knew the moment he opened his eyes. He untangled his fingers from her hair, grabbed her by the shoulder, and turned her over. She stared up into a pair of startled aquamarine eyes.

"Angela!"

He jumped out of the bed. "What in blue blazes are you doing in my bed?" In his agitation he didn't seem to realize he was nude.

Angela couldn't help but notice because when she pushed herself up on her elbow, her eyes were level with the middle of his body. Neither the illustrations in her father's medical books nor her months spent nursing soldiers had prepared her for what she saw.

"Oh my." Right before her eyes, he was getting larger. Suddenly, she better understood what had happened last night.

"Sweet Jesu!" Ransom ripped the quilt from the bed and wrapped it around his waist. "Good Lord, woman. Have you no shame?"

He stalked away from the bed, turning when he

had put the width of the room between them. "What are you doing in my bed?"

"It's not what you think." She shrank against the scarred walnut headboard and pulled the bed linens to her neck.

"You have no idea what I think. But right now all I want is an explanation. Why are you in my bed?"

She had never seen him angry. Her throat squeezed shut around her explanation.

"I'm waiting."

"Y-you cried out."

His eyebrows rose in disbelief.

But he made no move toward her. Relief seeped into her brain. His anger wasn't going to translate itself into physical violence. The vise tightening her throat eased. She took a steadying breath. "I came to see what was wrong."

His scowl darkened.

Dear God, why had she fallen asleep? "I tried to wake you. To calm you. You were fighting . . ."

Her trailing explanation erased the scowl and his eyebrows lowered.

"I must have had a nightmare." One hand held the quilt to his waist; the other ran through his disheveled hair. His gaze snapped back to her. "That fails to explain why you're in my bed now."

She grabbed the simplest answer. "You wouldn't let me go."

He shook his head and took a step backward. "Tell me nothing happened."

Now was her chance to lie. To claim nothing happened. If he knew he took her virginity, he would do the honorable thing and insist they marry. The idea tempted her, but it would condemn them both to a lifetime of misery. She had no choice but to lie.

"I assure you, nothing—"

"I don't believe you." He crossed the room and jerked the bed linens out of her hands. Ignoring her gasp, he pushed her night rail up her right thigh to reveal a patchwork of faded scars.

And then she remembered his touch of the previous night and his hesitation when his fingers encountered the scars.

"It was you." He released her gown as if it were afire. "I wasn't dreaming."

"Ugly scars, aren't they?" Her voice was high, tight with nervousness. "I tried to make my horse take one too many fences. Actually,"—she tugged her gown back into place—"it was a fence and a creek. I landed in a tangle of dead brush. Father was furious." Her hands shook, but she grabbed the bed linens and pulled them back up to her neck.

Now that she'd started talking, she didn't seem able to stop. "I don't know which was worse, listening to him rant and rave or having him sew me together. He swore I'd be the death of him, if I didn't kill myself first. After I broke my arm, he decided it was a good thing I had a doctor for a father if I was going to persist in injuring myself."

"Dammit, Angela! Why didn't you stop me?"

The roar of his question cut off her nervous monologue. Anger flared to life. She wasn't going to take all the blame for their predicament.

"Stop you? How could I stop you? You outweigh me and you're stronger than I." She refused to admit aloud that his hands and mouth had sucked all resistance from her body.

"How could this have happened?" Now he paced the room in earnest. The gaily colored quilt flapped around his long legs. "My God, I'm your sister's fiancé. I love Sabrina."

"I know."

Her quiet agreement stopped his pacing and brought him back to the bed. He sank onto its edge, rested his elbows on his knees, and dropped his head in his hands. Silence clung to the room, alleviated only by the chirping of birds awakening outside the window.

Angela stared at his bent head. She longed to reach out and touch him, but if she touched him, she might never let him go.

"We'll have to marry."

His muffled words shattered the silence.

She had to put some distance between herself and temptation. Slipping out of bed, she went to the French door leading to the rear gallery. The wood floor was cool on her bare feet. She pushed aside the aging drapes that would need replacing when she and Aunt Julia returned from Pennsylvania.

Below her, the dawn shed a forgiving light over a once-prosperous land. Gray mist masked the damage wrought by three years of Federal occupation determined to bring her beloved Middle Tennessee to its knees.

Peace brought its own brand of suffering.

Oaths of allegiance, blame for the President's assassination, lawlessness . . . sometimes she was glad her father hadn't lived to see the devastation of his homeland.

Her gaze swung to the back yard and Jackson's wagging tail. He stood beside a man in the shadows of the elm tree. If Jackson saw him as a friend there was no cause to be alarmed. But who was it? She leaned closer to the door, squinted her eyes and studied the man.

"It can't be!" She opened the door, started out and then remembered she wore nothing more than her night rail. "I'll be right down."

* * *

Ransom raised his head in time to see Angela run to the bed, toss back the covers, and rummage around until she found her shawl.

"We'll finish this discussion later." She flung the words and her shawl over her shoulder. The shawl's fringe shimmied down her back to end in a vee inches above her waist. Her night rail, made transparent from age and repeated washing, followed the enticing curve of her buttocks. And if that wasn't enough to distract a man, her black hair flowed over shawl and night rail, swaying with each step she took.

He licked his lips and the taste of her haunted his memory.

Then she was gone. A wisp of lilac ribbon floated to the floor to mark where she had stood. He picked it up, crumpling the fragile fabric in his hand.

He wanted her. When all was said and done, he wanted Sabrina's sister. Even at this moment, his body was hard for her.

Her bare feet made little noise in the hallway, but he thought she went to her room. A moment later he heard the solid tap of shoes on the stairs.

He reached the French door in time to see her cloaked figure run across the yard and into the arms of another man. The man's hat brim shadowed his face, making identification impossible. Ransom's mouth curled around a snarl. His reaction surprised him and he didn't like it any more than he liked seeing another man touch Angela.

Soft but explicit curses tumbled from his mouth as he tossed the quilt to the bed and reached for his trousers. Then he paused, reached for the bed linens and jerked them loose. The faint musk of sex and jasmine wafted from the bed, but he saw no signs of deflowered virginity. Did Angela's lack of tears and recriminations mean it had not been her first sexual encounter?

Rather than offer him relief, the thought enraged him.

He shoved his feet into his boots and his arms into his shirt. Buttoning trousers and shirt, he followed Angela.

By the time he reached the open back door, the happy greeting had disintegrated into an argument. There was nothing lover like in their exchange, which pleased him.

They stood in the middle of the yard. Angela had her back to the door, but he had a clear view of the visitor, who had tipped his hat back on his head. It was his old friend Fletcher Darring.

Jackson sat beside Angela, ears cocked as he watched the man facing his mistress. Her hand rested on his head.

Ransom paused inside the doorway.

"You've got no choice, Angie darling." Fletcher took her by the shoulders, ignoring a warning growl from Jackson. "Archibald Seyler is not a man to be trifled with. Max and Quincy are dead. Do you hear me? Dead. Seyler is out to destroy anyone who worked with me during the war and you're on his list."

"Pooh, I didn't do that much. Why would anyone want to hurt me because of a few messages I carried for you?"

Jackson growled a little louder and showed a few inches of teeth. Fletcher frowned at the dog, but released Angela.

"I don't think Seyler is discriminating between those who worked for me a little and those who worked for me a lot, Angie darling."

"Things might be a little chaotic right now, but we have laws. Archibald Seyler can't go around killing people."

"If they're former Rebels, he can." Fletcher tugged off his hat and brushed it against his thigh in frustration. "You know the mood of the men running the state. Our governor didn't earn the nickname 'Bloody Brownlow' from passing out cigars."

"But why bother with me?"

"I'm sorry, Angie darling, but you're a former Confederate spy. The Unionists blame us for the war and won't be happy until all Confederates are dead. My God, some of them wanted to hang General Lee."

As far as Ransom could tell, Fletcher's arguments served only to stiffen Angela's ramrod spine.

"I'm taking Billie D'Angelo to New York tomorrow." Fletcher assumed a coaxing tone. "I want you to come with us. After I get her settled, you can decide where you want to go and I'll take you. You can go to California with me, if you want."

If she had still been barefoot, Ransom was sure her toes would have dug into the ground.

"Thank you for the offer, but I can't go to California."

"It doesn't have to be California—"

"I will be attending the Female Medical College of Pennsylvania in the fall."

Ransom wondered if his expression reflected the same shock he saw on Fletcher's face. From all appearances, the former spy master's ability to mask his emotions had gotten rusty in the last year.

"Medical school?"

"Lectures begin in October. My aunt and I will leave Gallatin in September to seek lodgings near the school. As you can see, California is out of the question."

"That's a wonderful ambition, Angie darling."

Ransom admired Fletcher's quick recovery.

"And," Fletcher added, "I'll bet everyone in town knows about it."

Ransom waited for Angela to figure out what Fletcher meant.

Her stance relaxed the merest bit and she tilted her head to the side. "Why would I make a secret out of going away to school?"

"That's the problem, Angie darling. Your plans aren't a secret. You can't wait around Gallatin for school to start and you can't go to Pennsylvania early. Not with everyone knowing your plans and Seyler after you."

"I'm not afraid of this man."

Fletcher stepped closer to Angela, ignoring Jackson's raised fur and low-pitched growl. "Then you're a fool, Angie darling. And I never took you for a fool."

The sun rose over the horizon, chasing away the dull gray of dawn. Angela's shoulders dipped the tiniest bit as she digested Fletcher's words.

"I'm not saying never go to medical school." A conciliatory tone edged Fletcher's promise. "You just need to disappear for a short time. Get out of Seyler's reach. He won't be in power forever, he's made too many enemies."

"Time!" Angela's head snapped up. Indignation crackled through her body. "If I wait much longer, I'll be too old. First, the war ruined my chance to go to school. Now you say I must again postpone my dream of becoming a doctor because of Mr. Seyler. Well, I won't do it!"

Ransom stared at the woman he was going to marry; he didn't think medical school was in her future.

Somewhere between his room and the yard, she'd wrapped her ebony hair into a knot that nestled on the neck he remembered kissing. He licked his lips where the taste of her skin lingered.

He sauntered onto the porch. "Good morning, Fletcher. I see you survived the war."

"By all that's holy! We were sure Seyler had you killed and thrown in a ditch somewhere." Fletcher shoved his hat back on his head and bounded up the porch steps, one hand extended.

Ransom welcomed his friend's hearty handshake. "Colonel Truesdail's men caught me, not Seyler."

"Thank God."

To Ransom's surprise, Fletcher pulled him into a quick hug that disintegrated into a manly pounding on the back as if reassuring himself Ransom wasn't an illusion.

"They thought they had captured the infamous Fletcher Darring."

Fletcher's broad smile vanished. "What did he do? We got word you were captured, followed by weeks of silence and then someone claimed you had never been captured but killed in a skirmish outside Memphis."

"As you can see," Ransom spread his arms. "I wasn't killed. But your friend Truesdail had a special hell waiting for you—only I got to sample it."

"Why didn't you tell them you weren't the man they sought?"

"I told them who I was. And I wasn't carrying any secret messages so they couldn't hang me for a spy. But I happened to be where Truesdail had been told you would be."

"It would've been me if I haven't been so ill. Damn! Why the devil didn't he release you?"

"Stubbornness?" Ransom shrugged, unable to say

why Truesdail had acted as he did. "He couldn't prove I wasn't you any more than he could prove I was me. On the chance I was you, he sent me to a friend of his who runs a prison for Yankee deserters. Fort Jefferson."

"Fort Jefferson? Off the coast of Florida? Miles from nowhere?" Fletcher's disbelief grew as he pinpointed the location of Fort Jefferson.

"Far enough away that it took months for my release papers to come through. You're lucky Truesdail never captured you; he's a sadistic bastard."

"I'm sorry, Ransom. I had no idea Union troops were waiting for me at that rendezvous. I never should've let you volunteer to do it."

"What's done is done. If the need arises again, I'll remember I don't make a particularly good spy." He nodded toward Angela. "Who threatens her and why?"

"Fletcher worries needlessly." Angela said. "No one has the least bit of interest in me."

"I wouldn't be so quick to dismiss Archibald Seyler as no one," Ransom said.

Her startled expression told him she didn't expect him to recognize Seyler's name.

"Thank you," Fletcher said. "That's what I've been trying to explain to her."

"It sounds as if Ransom faces more danger than I." Angela waved a hand toward Fletcher. "He was mistaken for you. What if it happens again?"

Ransom didn't like the gleam in her eye.

"I think he should go to Texas immediately." she said.

"Angie darling, your attempt to shift the focus of our conversation won't work. We were discussing you." Fletcher shook his head in exasperation. "You can't stay here. I can't leave you unprotected."

"She won't be here and she won't be unprotected."

His flat tone erased the smug expression from Angela's face. She scowled.

"Do you insist we finish our discussion here?"

"It's as good a time as any," he said.

"I cannot marry you." She clutched her cloak tighter and straightened her posture. "I am going to medical school and nothing will change my mind."

"Marry Ransom! What a perfect solution, Angie darling. Did you say he was going to Texas? I doubt Seyler will bother you there." Fletcher slapped Ransom on the back. "You sly dog, grabbing one of the finest women in Tennessee while our backs are turned."

Fletcher's congratulations rained over him, but his friend's pleasure at having found a solution for Angela's problem couldn't eradicate the grief that squeezed Ransom's heart. He wanted to shout aloud he couldn't marry Angela because she was the wrong sister! Oh, Sabrina, how could you die?

"Hellfire and damnation! Stop congratulating him. I am not going to marry Major Champion."

"Angie darling, I don't think you understand how well this solves the problem."

"The war's over." She glared at them both. "There's no reason for Mr. Seyler to bother me. If he does, I shall petition the local authorities."

"Don't be daft, Angie darling." With a quick wink at Ransom, Fletcher jumped off the porch and headed back toward Angela, arguing the whole time. "The local authorities are Yankee soldiers, scalawags, and carpetbaggers. They're Seyler's friends."

"They'll do whatever he wants." Ransom followed Fletcher off the porch. None of their arguments seemed to sway Angela's resolve. He knew what would crush her resistance, but preferred not to speak about last night in front of Fletcher. Their combined presence had already tightened her mouth into a thin line.

"This is good advice, Angie darling. Marry Ransom and you'll be safe."

"You have the sisters confused, Major Darring." Mrs. Kramer's cheerful voice broke into Fletcher's argument.

The foursome in the yard looked in unison at the back door. Tail wagging, Jackson left Angela's side and ran to greet Mrs. Kramer, who smiled at the dog and scratched his ears. She had dressed hastily. A sleeping cap remained perched on her head and she wore a pair of mismatched knitted slippers on her feet.

She looked up from the dog and said, "Ransom was to marry Sabrina, not Angela."

Chapter 4

If Angela hadn't been so distressed by Fletcher's news, she would have laughed at his reaction to her aunt's announcement. It caught him unawares and paralyzed him into silence. A year away from spying seemed to have taken its toll on his glib tongue.

Several heartbeats and he recovered.

"You look as delightful as ever, Mrs. Kramer. I trust you are surviving the peace as well as you survived the war."

Angela welcomed her aunt's intervention. Perhaps the two of them could convince Fletcher she would be safe in Pennsylvania.

"How you do go on, Mr. Darring."

When her aunt twittered like a schoolgirl, Angela's heart sank. Would Fletcher flatter her into joining the opposition?

"I know I'm not dressed decent for company." Aunt Julia patted her nightcap. "But never mind that. I'm sure you're hungry. Why don't y'all come into the house? I'll fix breakfast for everyone."

Angela wanted to race to the back door and bar Fletcher's entry, but she contented herself with tapping her foot angrily on the hard-packed dirt.

"How can I refuse an invitation to dine with the two

prettiest women in Sumner County?" Fletcher climbed the steps and offered his arm to Julia.

"That kind of talking will get you an extra plate of pancakes." Aunt Julia placed her hand on Fletcher's arm as if they strolled into a ballroom and not a shabby house. At the doorway, she called over her shoulder. "Angela dear, go see if Rosie left us some eggs this morning." Then she looked up at Fletcher and said, "Now why on earth do you want Angela to marry Ransom?"

Before Angela could move, two strong arms closed around her. She froze, dismayed by the way her heartbeat quickened at Ransom's touch. His large hands rested on her abdomen. Memories of how he had touched her the previous night slid into her mind. Heat pooled down there.

"He's right, you know."

Ransom's voice came from slightly above her left ear. Delicate shivers danced down her spine. She prayed he would not touch his tongue to her ear. Or that he would.

Appalled that his touch could ignite this barrage of feelings, she concentrated on their conversation. If she were not careful, she would acquiesce to his will.

"No, I don't know Fletcher's right," she said.

"Seyler is a problem," Ransom continued, unperturbed by her denial. "But he's not the reason we will marry."

His right hand stole through the gap in her cloak to stroke her stomach. The thin fabric of her night rail offered no barrier. It was as if he touched her skin. And she wanted more. Her resolve to ignore his touch melted. She jerked it back in the place.

"Seyler is not enough of a problem to make me marry you. And I see no other reason for us to marry." Her legs wanted to buckle; she would not let them.

"There is another reason for us to marry."

"If you're feeling noble and wish to sacrifice your life because of last night, don't." She struggled to argue while his fingers massaged her stomach.

"Do you think they'll allow you to remain in medical school if you are with child?"

"I . . . there are ways . . ." Her voice spiraled into horror. She could not believe those words came from her mouth. They took her out of Ransom's arms into a place where no early morning sun edged its way above the trees. No birds greeted the new day.

Darkness surrounded her. The wind tried to rip her cloak from her shoulders while lightning scored the night sky. It had been a blustery night with the scent of rain heavy in the air. After a grueling ten hours, Old Millie's fever had broken and Angela wanted to sleep in her own bed. Hiram had escorted her most of the way home, but she had urged him to return to his wife when the first raindrops fell.

The rain hit fast, thick, and furious. Her cloak, skirt, and petticoats soon weighed her down. Hoping to find refuge in the vacant servant quarters, she cut across the meadow. About one hundred yards from the quarters, she stumbled over Sabrina, who lay sprawled in a puddle. They had spent the night in a storage room.

A night of blood, tears, and death. Sabrina's attempt to rid herself of Nicholas' baby had killed her. Unable to stanch the flow of blood and baby, Angela had watched the life seep out of her sister.

"For desperate women. But you aren't a desperate woman, are you?" His arms tightened around her.

His question brought her out of the past and into

the cool sunlit morning. She had backed into the cradle of his body and welcomed its warmth.

Was she a desperate woman? If a child stood between her and medical school, would she follow Sabrina's path? She doubted she could take a life.

"No," she admitted quietly, "I'm not a desperate woman. More a cautious one."

"Do you think me so lacking in honor I could sleep with you and walk away?"

"It has nothing to do with honor." She twisted out of his embrace, turning to face him. "It has to do with love. Your love for Sabrina. You ask me to tie myself to the man who loves my sister. It is a path of misery for us both."

The clear morning light intensified the blue in his aquamarine eyes. Their beauty snatched her breath away. When she stared into those cool depths, she had trouble remembering why she didn't want to marry him.

"Perhaps not misery. Perhaps friends caught in an unfortunate situation? I thought we were friends before the war."

"Yes." She thought of the letters they had exchanged. They were better friends than he would ever know. "We're friends."

"Do you want me to say I'm sorry I had a nightmare that brought you to my room?" he asked. "Because I am. I'm sorry for what happened last night."

He stepped closer, crowding her.

"Being sorry won't erase the life we may have created. There are consequences for what we did." He paused. "But last night isn't our only problem."

They also had the problem of Archibald Seyler. She knew the man by reputation, but doubted if all the stories about him were true. On the other hand, his inhumanity to anyone who had supported the Confederacy was well documented.

She would have fought Fletcher and Ransom over medical school, Seyler be damned, if last night hadn't happened. But it had happened.

They may have created a new life.

A layer of fear nestled beneath her bravado. Despite her protests, she realized she had little choice. Until she knew whether or not she was pregnant, she couldn't chance Seyler's wrath. Fear of harm to an unborn child tilted the balance toward marriage. Fear of a broken heart made the decision difficult.

His finger slid beneath her chin and tilted her head upward. She looked into the cool depths of his eyes and wondered if she would ever see affection, laughter, and most of all, love in them.

"Angela Stapleton, will you marry me?"

Could she spend her life with a man who loved Sabrina? Was there no other solution?

"I don't know what to do."

He stared at her for a moment longer, then stepped back. A light morning breeze cooled her skin of his touch.

"It's difficult to make a decision on an empty stomach. Why don't we see if Rosie has been an accommodating hen?"

Ransom sensed a rapport had developed between his old friend and Angela's aunt by the time he and Angela reached the dining room.

"I apologize for bringing Angela to Seyler's attention." Fletcher shoved another chunk of wood into the kitchen range. "Few people knew she helped me during the war."

"She never told me," Mrs. Kramer said. "But she was quite exhausted when she returned home."

"Fletcher exaggerates. What I did pales in comparison to his endeavors."

"Will one of you tell me what Angela did?" Mrs. Kramer thrust an empty bowl at Ransom.

He wanted to second the request. Instead, he transferred the eggs they'd collected from Angela's cloak. Curiosity about Angela's role as a spy had bedeviled him since Fletcher's appearance.

"It would be my pleasure." Fletcher folded his arms and leaned against the pie safe. "Angela is the perfect courier. She possesses an uncanny ability to memorize numbers."

The last egg slid from Ransom's grasp to crack against its former nest mates. Mrs. Kramer rescued the bowl from his clutches. He could tell she didn't understand the scope of her niece's talent, but he did.

"Coded messages with no writing involved?" he asked.

"It was nothing," Angela protested. "Fletcher would write his message in a numeric code. All I did was memorize the numbers and recite them to someone. I only did it a few times. I can't see why Mr. Seyler would be interested in me."

"Angie darling, I've tried to explain to you, the number of messages you carried doesn't interest Seyler. He wants revenge on me. The best revenge he can get is to kill all my former operatives."

"He'll have to kill half the state!" Angela grabbed a much battered coffeepot and headed for the stove. She stopped, turned to face them, her eyes wide with horror. "He means to let you live?"

"Or kill him last," Ransom volunteered. He didn't like frightening Angela, but he'd known men of

Seyler's ilk during the war. Angela wasn't safe here. Last night had made her his responsibility, but he'd have assumed that role without having bedded her, because she was Sabrina's sister.

"I don't intend him to kill anyone else," Fletcher said. "I've contacted everyone I believe Seyler knows about. Max and Quincy only knew the names of certain operatives which means half the state is not in jeopardy. I'm sorry, Angie darling, but Max was your contact."

"But I want to go to Pennsylvania." Angela's full lips pouted like a two-year-old's denied a peppermint treat. "I want to be a doctor and I can't learn how to do that hiding in Texas. I have to go to Pennsylvania. We'll be safe there, won't we, Aunt Julia?"

"Well, ummmmm . . ." Mrs. Kramer busied herself with cracking eggs into a bowl. "Maybe—"

"Don't tell me you think Fletcher is correct!"

"It's not so much Mr. Darring's news, Angela dear . . . it's more I don't want to go to Pennsylvania." Mrs. Kramer's words tumbled out.

The announcement hung in the silent air for a split second. Mrs. Kramer rushed to fill the void.

"I'm sorry, dear. I should have told you sooner, but I didn't know how."

"Not go with me to Pennsylvania."

Ransom's heart melted a drop at the stricken expression on Angela's face. He had postponed his dream for a war, but he had another chance to grab it. Angela's second chance had been ripped from her grasp. Then, to his surprise, a beatific smile lit her face.

"Mr. Stillman has asked you to marry him!" The coffeepot clattered to the stove top and she ran to hug her aunt and the bowl of eggs. "When? I can't believe you didn't tell me!" Joyful tears sheened her beautiful gray eyes.

Ransom marveled at her generous spirit. Her dream had evaporated, but she didn't let bitterness color her pleasure at her aunt's unexpected news.

"Mercy, child. Let me set these eggs down before you crush them."

Ransom rescued the eggs. Mrs. Kramer smiled her gratitude.

"Now, where was I? Oh, yes, he asked me last week. I didn't know how to tell you."

"If I hadn't been selfishly focused on my future, I would have thought of yours." Angela held her aunt at arm's length. "Can you ever forgive me?"

"There's nothing to forgive, dear." Mrs. Kramer patted Angela's cheek. "You needed me. Mr. Stillman understood we must wait until you finished school."

"He's been your dear friend a long time." Angela hugged her aunt again. "He'll make you a good husband. Don't worry about me, I'll think of something."

"Marriage to Ransom would be a good thought." Only Ransom saw Fletcher wink.

"He's right, Angela dear," Mrs. Kramer said. "With this man threatening you, you need someone to protect you. Why don't you marry Ransom, go to Texas and be safe?"

Ransom didn't add his voice to the chorus pressuring Angela. She should be reluctant to marry him, because he could promise only friendship. His heart belonged to Sabrina.

A series of subdued raps on the back door silenced everyone.

"Major Darring?" a voice hissed. "Sir, a word with you."

"It's James. He's one of my men." Fletcher reassured everyone. "I'll be right back."

Ransom trailed him as far as the dining room door.

"My lands," Mrs. Kramer said. "If I don't hurry up and fix breakfast, it will be time for dinner."

The creak of a floorboard told Ransom that Angela had joined him in the doorway. He wanted to drape his arm across her shoulder and give her a reassuring squeeze, but the rigid stance of her body warned him away.

On the porch, Fletcher and James held a quiet but intense conversation. Then Fletcher shook hands with James, watched his contact walk down the steps and mount a horse. The hoof beats faded into silence before Fletcher walked slowly back to them. He took Angela's hand in his.

The expression on Fletcher's face made Ransom edge close to Angela, ready to catch her should she faint.

"I'm sorry, Angie darling. Seyler has gotten an arrest warrant for you."

Chapter 5

Angela ran her fingers across the satin, enjoying the rich smoothness of the skirt's fabric.

"Thank heaven, Sabrina's gown was not suitable material for bandages." Aunt Julia slipped the dress over Angela's head, tugged it into place, and began to fasten the buttons. "It's a little wrinkled, but we haven't time to iron it. Ransom should be back with the Reverend Wallner any minute."

No one knew how much time Angela had, but her aunt wouldn't let her leave Gallatin unmarried.

Angela stared at herself in the cheval glass, fascinated by the sway of the fabric as it settled over the hoop petticoat. Huge skirts might be fashionable in some circles, but they had no place in a hospital ward where they could knock irreplaceable medicine bottles to the floor. Although her nursing career had been cut short by illness, she hadn't found hoop skirts any more suitable for work in a garden. Sometimes she forgot how much her life had changed in the past five years.

She smoothed her callused fingers down her abdomen, caressing the fabric. Her hands hovered over her stomach. Did her body nurture Ransom's child? The possibility pleased her more than she was willing to admit.

"You've lost more weight." Her aunt fussed with the plunging neck line.

"It never plunged on me." Angela plucked at the excess fabric. "And now there's a gap."

"It's just as well you're skinnier than Sabrina, your corset is in tatters. Why didn't you mention it?"

"I thought to buy a new one before I went to school." No matter what her aunt thought, the dress was a poor fit. Sabrina had been built on lusher, shorter lines. Aunt Julia had pinned tucks in the bodice and waist, but there was no time to add length. The dress stopped three inches above the floor.

Although Angela appreciated her aunt's efforts, the dress had looked better on Sabrina. The pale shimmery blue added roses to her sister's cheeks; it gave Angela's complexion an unhealthy hue.

"Perhaps another tuck here. And here." Aunt Julia plucked another pin from the corner of her mouth. "You'll have to walk carefully."

Angela sighed. She'd not often envisioned her wedding, but a beautiful wedding dress had been in the dream. Sabrina's remodeled dress was a cruel reality, reminding her she married her sister's fiancé.

"Stand still," her aunt ordered as she wove another pin into place.

Angela's gaze stole to the battered bow front chest of drawers across the room where the locket rested on its scorched top. It was the only piece of jewelry she had left, but she would go without jewelry rather than wear another reminder of Sabrina.

"If you keep your arms down, I doubt anyone will notice the pins." With a final pat, her aunt stepped back to admire her handiwork. "Turn." Head tilted, she studied the effect. "Very nice. Now where did I put . . .

She bent down and scooped something off the floor.

"Not those," Angela wailed when she saw a pair of dance slippers dangling from her aunt's hand.

"Yes, these."

"How did they escape being stolen? Had I known, I would have left them on the front porch with a note attached saying 'please steal me' when a Yankee patrol visited." She collapsed onto the bed. Then winced when a pin stuck her. "There has to be a woman in the North with feet as small as Sabrina's."

"For an hour or less. You can wear them that long, can't you?"

"Wear them yes, walk in them, no."

The rumble of male voices signaled the return of Ransom and Fletcher with the minister. Panic welled in her aunt's eyes. She lifted her skirt and wiggled her right foot, still encased in mismatched knit slippers.

"I'm not dressed for the wedding!" She scurried from Angela's room, paused to lean over the banister. "We'll be right down," she promised.

"But the shoes. How will I put them on?" Angela questioned an empty room. She looked down toward her feet. Yards of satin and cotton as well as a metal hoop stood between her and them. A woman needed help when she wore all these layers. Slippers in hand, she tiptoed from her room and peered over the banister.

Dare she seek help from Ransom? He was to be her husband in a few moments. And he'd seen her bare feet that morning. A blush heated her cheeks. Her bare feet hadn't been all he saw.

She stopped at the top of the stairs, hoping to see Ransom before anyone saw her. Then he walked into the hall in his freshly brushed gray frock coat and blue trousers. From her higher vintage point, she could see the crisp part in his damp ash blonde hair.

Something alerted him to her presence and he looked up. When his mouth fell open, an unexpected bud of happiness blossomed in her breast.

"I would wed you naked before I would wed you in that dress."

"Wh-what did you say?" She staggered backward a step, the bud of happiness ripped from her chest by his harsh words.

"I refuse to marry you if you wear that dress. Put on something else!"

For one eternal instant Angela stood at the top of the staircase, her hand clutching the banister all that kept her knees from buckling in humiliation. He refused to marry her if she wore the only decent dress in the house? Anger roared into her blood.

"Then I guess the wedding is off." Strength flowed back into her legs. She whirled around and headed for her bedchamber.

Aunt Julia stood in the way, her fingers stilled in their nimble race to button the front of her dress. Wide brown eyes slid from shock to realization.

"Mercy, I forgot. That's the dress Sabrina wore to her engagement party."

"The wedding is off," Angela announced. "He refuses to marry me if I wear this dress. As if I have a wardrobe full of dresses from which to choose." She stormed into her bedchamber, wincing as yet another pin pricked her left arm.

"You gave him a shock, that's all." Her aunt hurried behind her, closing the door. "Remember, it's been less than twenty-four hours since he learned of Sabrina's death. You can't blame him for being upset at seeing you in her dress. I imagine their engagement party is one of his fondest memories."

Every word her aunt spoke was true and shredded Angela's heart. She slumped onto her bed. Did she possess the strength to walk this impossible path?

Her aunt sat beside her and wrapped her arms around Angela as if she were a small child again. "I wouldn't push you into this marriage, if your life wasn't in jeopardy. And if I didn't think you loved Ransom."

"Love Ransom?" Angela's voice squeaked in childish denial, but she wouldn't lift her head from her aunt's shoulder.

"We both know he loves Sabrina, or rather her memory," she continued as if Angela had not spoken. "But believe me, a memory makes a cold bed partner."

Angela's indignation melted. Her aunt seldom spoke of the husband she lost ten years ago, but his portrait hung over the small fireplace in her bedroom. And she'd rescued a small bundle of his letters each time their house had been ransacked.

"Sabrina's loss is fresh, but he needs a living, breathing companion not a memory." Her aunt rubbed Angela's back, soothing her physically as she soothed her with words. "It won't be easy and you can't change his heart overnight, but he'll fall in love with you. Give him time to put Sabrina in the past where she belongs. Remember you'll have his present and future."

Her aunt's commonsense advice eased her anger at Ransom. Perhaps the day would come when Sabrina no longer commanded his heart.

"You could speed the process along if you told him about the letters . . ."

"No." Angela raised her head. "I refuse to shatter his memories of Sabrina." They hadn't been the best of sisters, but she would carry Sabrina's secrets to the grave.

She gave her an aunt a tight hug. "Will you help me remove the pins? I need to find something else to wear to my wedding."

Her oak wardrobe didn't offer many choices. In her zeal for collecting cloth for bandages, she had emptied her home of old clothing and then scoured the county for more. It never occurred to her the Yankees would establish such an effective blockade. As the war continued, fabric became more and more scarce and more and more exorbitant in price.

There had been no new dresses. There had been mending and making do. Her "good" dress had been dyed black when her father died.

"What about your mother's dress?"

Her aunt held up a dress Angela would have cut up for bandages if the fabric had been suitable. Cut along lines popular for an earlier generation, the dress had three flounces trimmed with such wide lace that the dress fabric was invisible.

"You won't be able to wear the hoop in your petticoat." Her aunt fanned the dress across the bed. "What do you think?"

Angela swallowed the truth. The dress was hideous. Its former lilac color had been eradicated by her aunt's experiments. No plant dye had yielded a black for their mourning clothes, and the barége dress fabric and lace trim now sported varying hues of muddy brown.

"A perfect choice," she said. The muddy brown matched her muddy future. "I see no reason for this dress to upset Ransom, do you?"

After her aunt unpinned her and pulled the blue dress over her head, Angela grabbed Sabrina's locket. She fastened it around her neck and then tucked the locket out of sight beneath the high neckline. Moments later she walked past the cheval glass without glancing at herself. Who needed a looking glass? Muddy brown was muddy brown under any light and seen by any eye.

Thank God he'd seen Angela before the wedding. Ransom doubted he would have been able to say marriage vows to any woman dressed in a gown that figured so prominently in his memories of Sabrina. Although he regretted causing Angela distress, he didn't regret ensuring she did not wear Sabrina's dress.

"Word of the wedding has spread." Reverend Wallner peered out the drawing room window. "It appears we'll have plenty of witnesses."

Within moments, Ransom found himself playing host to Angela's friends and neighbors, while Fletcher and Tommy arranged to seat as many of the women as they could. Ransom wished he could exchange places with Fletcher. Then he wouldn't have to endure the congratulations of the same people who had attended his and Sabrina's engagement party.

"Major Champion? How delightful to learn you survived the war." A thickset matron patted his arm.

"It didn't make the Yankees happy." Ransom lifted the pudgy, gloved hand and kissed her knuckles.

A smile lit her broad face.

"You remember my husband, Mr. Carmichael?"

Ransom took the outstretched hand. "I believe we met before the war." He could not mention the engagement party. To his relief, neither did the Carmichaels.

"If you gentlemen will excuse me, I'll go upstairs and see if Angela needs any help."

"Our Angela will be missed." Mr. Carmichael watched his wife climb the staircase. "She has a way with medicine, studied with her father."

Mrs. Carmichael disappeared into the upper hallway.

"His death was a great loss to Gallatin." Mr. Carmichael stuck his hands in his pockets. "Word has it you'll be taking her to Memphis."

He and Fletcher had settled on this lie so he murmured his agreement.

"I guess she'll have to postpone medical school. Probably for the best." The old man rocked back on his heels. "She's a handful now, no telling what ridiculous ideas medical school would put in her head."

"I beg your pardon, sir." Ransom smiled over Mr. Carmichael's head at one of the women seated in the drawing room. "Who will be a handful?"

"Why Angela, of course." Mr. Carmichael pulled out his pocket watch and flipped it open. "Two years without the guidance of a man have given her an unseemly independence." He peered up at Ransom, snapping his watch closed. "No doubt you'll soon bring her to heel."

Ransom wondered how he could politely shed his pompous companion.

"Impetuous. Headstrong. Opinionated. And Dr. Stapleton encouraged her." Mr. Carmichael shook his head, a thick white lock of hair fell on his forehead. He brushed it back. "Unhappily, her father wasn't here to curb her during the war. It's a wonder the Yankees never arrested her."

Ransom glanced toward the stairway, hoping for a sign that Angela was ready. If they didn't get this ceremony under way, Mr. Carmichael's prophesy might come true.

"But who can truly complain about our Angela?"

"Who indeed?" Ransom's sarcasm flew over the shorter man's head.

"She may be impetuous and she may not always display the proper humility for a young woman." Mr. Carmichael nodded at an acquaintance. "But these are minor imperfections when measured against her generous nature and dedication to the Glorious Cause."

Mrs. Carmichael rescued Ransom. "Angela's ready!" She announced as she bustled back down the stairs. When her slippered feet touched the hall floor, she herded them out of the hall.

"You," she pointed at Ransom, "into the drawing room. While you," she grabbed her husband's arm, "are to escort the bride."

At the doorway to the drawing room, Ransom peeked over his shoulder and caught a glimpse of Angela waiting at the top of the stairs. She wore an ugly brown dress. Relief washed over him. He wouldn't face his past while he pledged his future.

"No peeping, Major Champion!" Mrs. Carmichael shooed him into the drawing room. "It's bad luck to see the bride before she walks down the aisle."

Fletcher, who had agreed to be best man, waited with Reverend Wallner at the front of the drawing room. Ransom joined them.

"She's not the sister you wanted," Fletcher whispered, "but she's a fine person. Thank you for taking care of her."

Ransom didn't want to think about what he was doing.

The sound of whispered voices in the hallway terminated his unwelcome moment of trepidation. He joined everyone else in looking toward the doorway, where Mrs. Kramer appeared first. Then he saw Angela. Her gaze fixed on the floor, she let Mr. Carmichael escort her down the makeshift aisle Fletcher and Tommy had created.

All too soon, Angela was beside him. A delicate scent of jasmine hung in the air, reminding him of last night. She clutched a bouquet of silk flowers and a flimsy veil of ivory fluff drifted around her head.

If a man followed the minister's lead, everything was simple in a marriage ceremony. There was no reason to think about what one promised or to wonder why one was promising it to the wrong woman. Ransom found it easier not to look at Angela as he repeated the minister's words and then waited for her to echo all the sentiments.

Or almost all the sentiments.

"Oh my," she whispered suddenly. "Everything happened so quickly we didn't have time to discuss this."

"Discuss what?" Reverend Wallner asked.

"The word 'obey'."

"Discuss 'obey'?" Reverend Wallner's appalled tone rose a notch. "My dear child, I realize you've been without male guidance lately. But I'm sure your father, God bless his soul, would accept my role as fatherly advisor at this important moment in your life."

Ransom recalled Mr. Carmichael's description. Was he about to see a different side of Angela?

Reverend Wallner didn't bother to wait for her response.

"All brides vow to obey their husbands, because it is the husband who knows what is best for the wife." Patriarchal condescension tinged the minister's advice. "A *good* wife accepts this order and submits to her husband's superior counsel."

"Call me a bad wife if you insist, I have no intention of making a promise I can't keep."

Reverend Wallner's aging lips clamped into a tight, thin line of disapproval.

Beside him, Ransom heard Angela take a deep breath. Then she swatted aside the veil.

"I'm truly sorry to deviate from your ceremony, Reverend Wallner, but I cannot in clear conscience promise to obey my husband."

Ransom couldn't resist cocking his head enough to see her face.

The makeshift veil drifted back into her eyes and she shoved it aside with visible annoyance.

"It's a ludicrous promise and I see no reason to have it in the marriage vows. After all, it's not as if I'm a dog who must obey its master." She thrust her chin upward. "I believe marriage to be an equal partnership and if he doesn't have to obey me, then . . ."

He knew why Angela protested the word "obey." She would never be able to keep the vow. In truth, he was marrying a little minx. Physically, she had matured, but he had a good idea that the mischievous young girl who had once challenged him to a horse race and then greased his saddle, lurked close to the surface.

His sense of humor stirred; a smile twitched his lips. There'd been so little cause for laughter these past two years, he'd forgotten how to laugh. But, the time wasn't appropriate and the smile died aborning on his mouth.

Angela, not his lovely Sabrina, stood beside him. To enjoy this day in any way seemed obscene.

"Miss Angela, this is not the place to argue the meaning of the marriage ceremony." Reverend Wallner peered at her over his spectacles. "May I recommend you let your groom decide this issue?"

Ransom started to look around the drawing room for the groom, then realized he was the groom. He was the one targeted by the reverend to rule on the word "obey." To expedite a ceremony that was already distasteful to him, he made a fateful error in judgment.

"If she won't agree to it, you'd best leave it out."

The minister frowned, but his irritation failed to affect Angela, who pushed her veil back in place with an air of smug serenity. The Reverend Wallner studied his text for a moment, then resumed reading and skipped over the word "obey."

"You may now place the ring on Mrs. Champion's finger."

Ring? He shot Fletcher a panic-stricken gaze. He had no ring.

Fletcher pulled a small gold ring off his pinkie and handed it to Ransom.

"Marianne would want Angela to have it."

"Thank you." Ransom's fingers closed around the narrow gold band. He had never met Fletcher's wife, but he knew his friend valued the ring because it hadn't been melted down for a lost cause.

Angela's hands held the bouquet in a death grip. He pried her left hand loose, peeled off the threadbare glove and slid the ring over her knuckle. Her short uneven fingernails spoke of the hard work she now did. He turned over her hand to reveal a callused palm.

The small hand trembled in his, shafting him with an unexpected desire to erase the need for her to toil for her food. Slowly, he closed her fingers around the ring.

"Repeat after me. With this ring . . ."

Ransom recited his vows.

He didn't know where Angela got the simple gold band she placed on his hand.

Angela recited her vows.

All too quickly, the deed was done. They were husband and wife.

"You may kiss the bride." Reverend Wallner closed his Bible.

Ransom's heart slammed into his throat. He'd forgotten about this part of the marriage ceremony.

Angela stared at him as if he had sprouted a second head.

A roomful of people watched. He had no desire to humiliate her in front of her friends by not acting the happy bridegroom, but she didn't seem too eager to kiss him. He darted a glance toward her friends. A heartbeat later, she tilted her head upward.

To his surprise, his hands shook slightly when he lifted the veil. She presented an inviting picture of innocence with her ebony lashes fluttering closed over her smoky eyes. He leaned toward her. The siren song of her cologne lured him into memories of a night of passion. He squelched his reaction; he would place a chaste peck on his bride's cheek.

"Faith, now. Is it you, Miss Stapleton?"

Angela turned her head toward the imperious male voice. Ransom's lips missed her cheek and landed on her left earlobe. A jasmine-scented tendril of hair flirted with his nose. Lust jolted his body.

He wanted to lick the bare earlobe.

"Hellfire and damnation," Angela muttered.

His eyebrows edged toward his hairline. He had not wed his soft-spoken Sabrina.

"Now, then, what be the meaning of this?"

A Union captain strode up the makeshift aisle, stripping off a pair of riding gloves as he came. Ransom thought the ladies might find the man's dark

Irish looks handsome, his height imposing and his
athletic physique admirable, but he didn't like anything about this former enemy.

As if sensing his animosity, Angela stepped between
the two men. Ransom was not a man to hide behind
a woman's skirts; he rested his hand upon her shoulder and tugged her into place so they faced the
intruder together. Fletcher sidled toward the first row
of chairs.

The Union officer stopped inches from them. He
brought the scent of horse, leather, and bay rum into
the drawing room. The gloves slapped a restless tattoo against his muscular right thigh.

"Why, Captain O'Brion, what a surprise. We heard
you had been called to Nashville on military business."

Angela's low voice failed to display any of the tension Ransom felt in her shoulder.

The lust-hungry look in O'Brion's eyes annoyed
Ransom. How typically arrogant of a bluebelly to
think a Southern woman would have anything but
contempt for him. He dismissed the whisper of possessiveness that curled into his heart.

"You may be the first to congratulate Miss Stapleton," he said. "She is my wife."

Gratified by the appalled expression on the Yankee's face, he bent his head, hooked his finger under
Angela's chin, and kissed her. His bride, not this
damn Yankee's bride. The old rush of elation he always experienced when he bested a Yankee flowed
through his body, but when their lips met, the feeling
altered.

He meant to press a quick, hard kiss of possession
on her mouth, but her velvet warmth caught him by
surprise. The seductive scent of her perfume reminded him of their shared passion. He felt himself

softening the kiss, seeking her cooperation, needing her response.

The sound of clapping brought him to an awareness of where he was. Ransom raised his head, wondering if he looked as dazed as Angela. Enlarged pupils had almost eradicated the dark gray of her eyes. A rosy flush tinted her cheeks. The pouty fullness of her generous lips tempted him to kiss her again.

"Oh my." She blinked, as if to righten her world. Then her gaze slid past him and anxiety chased away confusion.

"Is it the truth he be saying?" The lilt of Ireland seemed incongruous on the captain's rigid lips.

"Major Champion speaks the truth." Angela stepped toward the captain, once again trying to put herself between the two men. "We're married."

The scowl on the captain's face gave new meaning to the term "black Irish." If he gripped his gloves any tighter, they would disintegrate. Ransom scanned the drawing room; Fletcher had disappeared.

"Well, now, I'm not believing you." The Yankee's eyes chilled to a cold blue. "It's an understanding we had—"

"Please forgive me, Captain O'Brion, if I gave you cause to believe we were more than friends."

Angela's shy smile and husky-honey apology surprised Ransom. If the little minx had used that smile and that tone when dealing with the captain, the man had every right to believe she had made some promises.

"I have known Major Champion most of my life," Angela said. "The affection between us is of long duration."

"Major?" The Irishman snorted his disbelief. "In an army torn asunder by the Union sword? It's a traitor he ought to be called! To think you'd be wedding this penniless Rebel rather than myself."

"Captain O'Brion, this is my wedding day." Angela interrupted the captain's tirade.

"If you had married me," O'Brion continued as if she had not spoken, "I'd have given you a wedding day as beautiful as a sunny morning. You'd be wearing pearls and a new gown, with shoes to match. And I'd," he added as he pulled himself even straighter, "now, then, I'd have worn a new uniform."

Ransom hated to see rose-tinted humiliation creep into Angela's cheeks. He hated that she had to wear Sabrina's old slippers. And he hated that a Yankee officer made him take a closer look at himself.

It had been a long time since he had worn a new uniform. Shabby would be the best description for today's garb, from his boots with their rundown heels, to the uneven hair which fell over the frayed collar of his frock coat. And the blue trousers he wore had been taken from an enemy supply wagon three years ago.

He reeked of defeat and it invaded their wedding.

He hadn't even let Angela wear a pretty gown.

The sleekly groomed, slightly dusty, but well fed Yankee wasn't finished. "It's an illegal marriage you have here."

This statement stilled the murmurs behind the captain. Ransom could see O'Brion wasn't one to ignore theatrics. His gloves now slapped into his waiting palm as he paused to ensure he had everyone's attention.

"Faith, and if he hasn't sworn the oath of allegiance he can't be marrying anyone. And, no minister of the church shall marry couples if he hasn't raised his hand and sworn the oath for all to hear."

"That is absurd, sir. We have spouted your oath of allegiance from day to dusk! I am an ordained minister. How dare you insinuate I performed an illegal . . ."

Reverend Wallner sputtered into silence when Ransom touched his arm.

The captain ignored Reverend Wallner to pin his angry gaze on Angela. Frustration ran through Ransom. If he knocked the arrogant Yankee unconscious—as he sorely wanted to do—he would end up in jail. He couldn't protect Angela locked up in a Yankee jail.

"Isn't it your sister engaged to a Major Champion?" Shrewd blue eyes raked Ransom. "And himself died during the war."

"I'm not dead and Angela Stapleton is now Mrs. Champion." Ransom swung Angela to the side and behind him. The bitter gall of defeat kept his voice calm. "The marriage is legally binding. We have all said your oath on repeated occasions. Now you may leave or I will personally escort you out."

His back ramrod straight, Ransom faced the junior officer. Defeat could not wash away his ability to command. He had ordered too many men to face death and had stood next to them when they did, to let this jackanapes cow him. His coat might be worn and frayed and his army defeated, but he had served honorably for four years.

For one moment Captain O'Brion hesitated, his years of military training responding to Ransom's voice. Then his lips tightened beneath his bushy mustache.

"See here, I won't be leaving until I complete me assignment." His gaze shifted to Angela. "It is sorry I am to do this, but I'm no longer regretting what I must do. It's off to jail with you, faithless woman."

"Jail!" Mrs. Kramer leaped to her feet, her hand clutching her throat. "Are you insane?"

O'Brion thrust his hand into his uniform breast pocket and pulled out a piece of paper.

The blood ran cold in Ransom's veins. He should have never submitted to Mrs. Kramer's entreaty for a marriage ceremony. He should have taken Angela away from Gallatin, but James had volunteered to find out the charges, whether arrest was imminent. He had not yet returned.

"Jail?"

Angela's bewildered question scored Ransom's heart. He wrapped an arm around her shoulder. "Don't worry, I'll protect you."

Captain O'Brion opened the warrant.

"You have no cause to arrest Mrs. Champion." Reverend Wallner's declaration silenced the buzzing of voices. "She has done nothing criminal."

"This warrant is saying the United States government has cause to arrest Miss Angela Stapleton."

"For what crime?" Mrs. Kramer demanded.

Captain O'Brion waited for the buzzing conversations to halt before he read, "Angela Anne Stapleton has been charged with the murder of Sabrina Stapleton."

Chapter 6

"Murder? Sabrina?" Angela whispered her question, unable to fix the charges in her mind. Her knees failed to hold her up. If Ransom hadn't slipped his arm around her waist, she would have crumpled to the ground.

"Surrender! Starvation! Smallpox! Haven't we paid enough? Must you now trump-up charges of murder?" Mr. Carmichael's voice filled the hushed drawing room.

"Not even a Yankee court could hold Angela responsible for her sister's death!"

Was that Mrs. Riverton? Angela's head refused to turn and look as her friends and neighbors rose to defend her.

"I demand to know who makes these false allegations against my niece."

The voices swirled around her in frenzied chaos. Seyler had chosen a diabolical way to seek his revenge against Fletcher. His trumped-up charge struck at the core of her being. For weeks she'd worried she could have done more to save Sabrina's life. She'd railed inwardly against her lack of medical training and a war that had prevented her from becoming a doctor. The murder charge, false as it was, renewed the crushing guilt she had tried to bury.

"Faint."

The murmured command wormed its way into the maelstrom of her thoughts.

"Pretend to faint."

Pretend? She had no need to pretend. The room spun around her. She was to be arrested for the murder of her sister. She could not grasp the concept and hang on to it, but she could faint.

Her knees buckled and she crumpled toward the ground, but Ransom swept her into the air. Her cheek rested on the rough fabric of his frock coat and his heart beat with a reassuring thud against her ear. She inhaled the scent that was uniquely his and felt a measure of comfort.

"Your outrageous charge has rendered my wife senseless. Out of my way, I must see to her well-being."

"If it's escape you're thinking to try," Captain O'Brion warned, "me men are posted outside. We'll not be leaving without Miss Stapleton."

"Her name is Mrs. Champion. Now excuse me while I try to repair the damage you have wrought."

Angela relaxed into Ransom's capable arms. She wanted to laugh hysterically at O'Brion's suggestion she might try to escape. How could one escape when one's limbs refused to move?

When they reached her bedchamber, Ransom dumped her on the bed. "Close and lock the door," he ordered whoever followed them.

Through lowered lashes, Angela watched her aunt enter the room, shut and lock the door. She had never seen Aunt Julia so distraught. Tears trickled down her face and she had twisted her handkerchief into a knot. She knelt beside the bed and grabbed Angela's left hand, rubbing it vigorously.

"Captain O'Brion made a horrible accusation."

Aunt Julia sniffed back her tears. "Look how it affected Angela. Why I've never known her to faint."

"Please don't cry." Angela opened her eyes and smiled. "Ransom told me to pretend to faint."

Surprise, then happiness lit her aunt's soft brown eyes. "How cunning!" She hugged Angela to her breast, rocking them both.

A final squeeze and Aunt Julia looked up at Ransom. "What are we going to do?" Anxiety threaded her question.

"Keep our voices down," Ransom said. "O'Brion probably put a guard outside the door."

"Don't worry." Angela comforted her aunt. "I'm sure it's a mistake. I'll go with Captain O'Brion and straighten everything out."

"It's not a mistake." Ransom's sharp words cut through her placating whisper. "The charges are false, but they put you in Seyler's control. Having you killed becomes much easier."

"My heavens! I'd forgotten about Mr. Seyler." Aunt Julia took Angela's hand. "You can't go with Captain O'Brion."

"Captain O'Brion would never let anyone kill me!"

"Why would Captain O'Brion be interested in whether you live or die?"

Aunt Julia rushed to Angela's defense. "Because the poor man is besotted with her."

In the silence that followed her aunt's disclosure, the guard in the hallway sneezed. Ransom leaned against the wall beside the window with his arms folded across his chest. His relaxed stance belied the leashed energy that radiated from his body.

Angela peeked at him over her aunt's shoulder.

"Does she return his affections?"

He asked the question of her aunt, but his cool aquamarine eyes pinned her. Angela refused to defend herself. How dare he look at her as if she'd slept with the enemy when it was his dearly beloved Sabrina who had bedded a Yankee.

"Mercy, no!" Her aunt's voice rang with horror. "The captain fancies himself in love with Angela. It's not her fault he tries to win her regard with gifts."

"Gifts?" Ransom's eyebrows shot toward his hairline. A scowl marred his handsome face.

"Food," Aunt Julia explained. "I made it quite clear to him she could not accept any other type of gift."

"Medical journals." The confession slipped out. He also gives me copies of the *American Journal of the Medical Sciences*."

Aunt Julia waved a dismissive hand. "How else could you prepare for medical school if you didn't keep abreast of the latest research?"

"How else indeed?"

Angela didn't like the sarcasm running through Ransom's observation.

Her aunt ignored it. "He's the local military commander, his friendship has proven useful what with all the new Yankee rules. Heaven knows, it's easy to break a military law when you have no idea what they are and they change daily." Aunt Julia paused to massage her furrowed brow. "In short, it made sense to stay on his good side."

Ransom's relentless glare never left Angela's face. "So you slept with him."

His accusation shocked her as much as the murder charge had. She leaped from the bed.

"How dare you accuse me of such a foul deed!"

"Angela! Your voice!" Aunt Julia pointed toward the door.

"You're my wife now." Ransom's tone was low and cold. "I have a right to know if you were a virgin when you came to my bed last night."

"Oh my heavens."

Angela ignored her aunt as she stalked across the room until she was toe to toe with Ransom. "I was a virgin until last night. If you searched the bed for proof, you found none. I lost my hymen when I was nine after my pony threw me."

She jabbed Ransom's chest with her index finger. "How do I know this? Because my father explained it to me." Fury permeated her low tone. "And if you think me so vile as to sleep with a man like Captain O'Brion, you had best run now and leave me to my fate with Archibald Seyler."

When he grabbed her finger, his touch jolted every indignant thought out of her head. They stood, bodies connected yet apart, with time suspended.

Someone tapped on the door.

Reality broke the spell. Ransom released her.

"Get back in the bed!"

Angela obeyed, shooting him an angry scowl before she threw herself on the bed and closed her eyes.

Aunt Julia's soft footsteps crossed the room. The door creaked as she opened it.

"Mr. Fletcher done sent me with a bowl of cool water for Miz Angela."

Angela relaxed at the sound of Tommy's voice.

"How thoughtful of him. Please, come in and set it on the dresser."

Angela peered through her eyelashes the tiniest bit. Behind Tommy's shoulder loomed an armed Yankee soldier. She scrunched her eyes shut.

Her aunt closed the bedchamber door in the soldier's face. Then, she locked it.

At the click of the lock, Angela opened her eyes. Tommy stood in front of her bow front dresser. Water sloshed out of the bowl when he set it down.

"I've come to save Miz Angela!" he whispered dramatically.

Hope shot Angela into a sitting position on the side of her bed. "How?"

"Do you have a plan?" Aunt Julia asked.

"Not me, Mr. Darring."

"Keep your voice low, Tommy," Ransom said. "And tell us Mr. Darring's plan."

Tommy's thin body swelled with importance. "I'm to change clothes with Miz Angela. Then she pretends to be me and I pretend to be her. Long enough fer her to get away."

Hope extinguished, Angela fell back down onto the familiar bed. She rubbed her temples, trying to erase the beginnings of a headache. Trust Fletcher to believe she could leave her bedchamber and waltz past the Yankee soldiers dressed as Tommy.

"Miz Angela?"

Angela peered through her spread fingers. Tommy hovered at the side of her bed.

"Mr. Darring done tole me I was to remind you he spent the war fooling the Yankees. He says if you play the part of a boy right, then they'll see a boy." He leaned closer, a sly grin on his young face. "And he says be sure and carry the chamber pot, when you leave. There ain't no soldier gonna look at you twice, iffen you're carrying a chamber pot."

Angela giggled. When she giggled yet again, she slapped her hand over her mouth. Trust Fletcher to figure out the perfect plan.

Tommy grinned. "It's a good plan, ain't it?"

"The best." She took Tommy's hand and pulled herself upright, again. "Did Fletcher have any other instructions?"

"Yes m'am, but I don't think you're gonna like this part."

His regretful tone chased away the last of her giggles. She sat up.

"What does he want her to do?" Ransom asked.

Angela saw relief in Tommy's eyes when he swung his gaze from her to Ransom. "Cut her hair so it looks like mine. It's about the same color."

Fletcher was right as usual, she didn't like this part of his plan. She sighed. She loved her hair. It might not be golden, it might not have any curl, but it was thick and long and she loved to brush it every night.

There was no time to discuss the merits of Fletcher's plan. He offered her a chance to escape. She had to choose. Either try and slip past the Yankees dressed as Tommy or accompany O'Brion to jail. And jail, she realized, would lead to a trial.

And a trial meant a lawyer who would try to prove her innocence. Questions would be asked, answers sought. And when it ended, Sabrina's secret would be revealed.

She'd promised to keep Sabrina's secret. Honor would keep her mouth closed, but what about the woman who had tried to abort Sabrina's baby? What if she came forward to protect Angela? What if someone else was involved?

No, she couldn't risk a trial.

She glanced at Ransom who had edged the curtain aside to peer into the yard. His return from the grave guaranteed she would never reveal Sabrina's secret. She had no desire to be imprisoned for a crime she didn't commit, but she refused to be the one to shatter his illusions about her sister.

Ransom stared out the window and wondered if vanity would ruin Fletcher's plan. From the frown on her face, Angela was not pleased at the idea of cutting her hair. Or did she worry Fletcher's plan would fail?

Medical journals! She'd allowed that arrogant Yankee into her home for medical journals. He didn't have time to figure that one out, not with that same Yankee determined to take Angela to jail. No, he had to concentrate on her escape.

He'd learned early in the war that a good commander figured out the objective, told his soldiers how to achieve it, and then led them. A good commander didn't give them time to think about failure. He hoped he was still a good commander.

"I see three horses and a dog cart to transport my wife." He glanced over his shoulder at Tommy. "Four soldiers?"

"Yes, sir. That's what Mr. Darring said to tell you."

"One is stationed outside this door. What about the other three?"

"Captain O'Brion wuz in the drawing room. One of 'em stayed on the front porch and the other one went out by the grapes. Mr. Darring says he'll signal when it's clear so Miz Angela, I mean Mrs. Champion, kin come out the back door."

One part of his brain cataloged Fletcher's plan; another part realized anew Angela was his wife. Guilt gnawed on his conscience. How could he put Sabrina aside this quickly?

He shoved away his guilt. "Anything else?"

"Yes, sir. Mr. Darring said for Miz Angela to go to the necessary. He says all the soldiers will go to the front door when we come out. Then, she can sneak away."

"Sneak away? To where? There's not a tree between here and Douglass Gap! I'll be in plain view on the road for miles."

"Mr. Darring's working on a way to fool the Yankees more."

From Tommy's shining eyes and wide grin, Ransom could tell the boy relished his part in the upcoming drama. Once again, Fletcher's smooth talk had won him another recruit.

"All I gotta do is fool the Yankees all the way into Gallatin. Then Mr. Darring's gonna have somebody report the Reece gang done attacked Mr. Barton's house."

"Which will put them racing out of town in the opposite direction." Ransom looked at Angela. "If you walk briskly, you should be able to reach my cousin's place before O'Brion realizes he's been tricked."

She frowned at him, hesitated a moment, but finally nodded in agreement.

"But she'll be alone!" Mrs. Kramer squeezed her hands together as if to keep them from clutching Angela. "With the woods full of bushwhackers and Freedmen. Why the newspapers report horrible murders and . . ."

Mrs. Kramer stumbled at saying the word "rape", but Ransom knew what worried her.

"She'll be dressed as Tommy," he said. "We'll have to hope that will protect her until either Fletcher or I reach her. We haven't much choice, Mrs. Kramer. Either she stays here and is tried for murder or she takes her chances on the road."

His assessment of Angela's choices didn't please Mrs. Kramer, but she accepted their truth with a nod.

"It sounds as if Fletcher has planned this well." He slid an assessing gaze over each one of the plan's participants. "If no one has any questions." He waited a heartbeat. When no one spoke, he dropped the curtain back into place. "We don't have much time. Let's get started."

To his relief, Mrs. Kramer put aside her distress and organized the exchange of clothing. She took Angela behind the dressing screen first. Within minutes Angela stepped from behind the screen wearing a dressing gown.

"You're next, Tommy."

"Mrs. Kramer is going to dress me!" Tommy backed away, shaking his head.

Ransom dropped his arm around the boy's narrow shoulders. "Believe me, Tommy. I would be more than happy to help you, but only another woman can get you into all those layers of clothing correctly."

With a disgruntled look, Tommy shuffled toward the dressing screen. "I wouldn't do this fer nobody but you, Miz Angela."

"And I appreciate it, Tommy."

Ransom watched Angela rifle through a sewing box. Once again, they were in a bedchamber. His blood thrummed through his veins with the realization it would not be the last time. If they escaped O'Brion's clutches, they faced a lifetime of being in a bedchamber together.

"Aunt Julia selected you to cut my hair." Angela offered him a pair of sewing scissors.

He took the scissors and watched her unpin the simple coronet she had coiled only an hour earlier. The loose braids tumbled to her waist. She picked up a hairbrush.

"My mother loved to brush my hair." Quiet sadness scented her voice.

Ransom plucked a silver hair brush from her dressing table. With his left hand, he scooped up a handful of her thick, black hair. Jasmine scented the air as he buried his fingers in the silk strands. When he lifted his hand, rivulets of black silk flowed through his fingers.

His hand recognized the texture of her hair.

"Do I gotta wear that!"

Tommy's low-pitched whine snapped Ransom out of his trance. He jerked his hand free of her hair. His jaw clenched. He tightened his grip on the brush and started brushing her hair. From the crown of her head, to her shoulders, down her back, to the curve of her buttocks.

Thoughts of them entwined on the bed crowded his brain. He squelched them. Focus on the task.

He gathered her hair into a fat ponytail, grabbed the scissors and began hacking. Each chop of the scissors shot a shaft of regret through him. The war had taken so much from this young woman, it seemed a sin to ask her to make yet another sacrifice.

"I cain't hardly breathe in this thing!"

Ransom wished he could smile at Tommy's indignant tone, but he couldn't.

With a final squeeze of the scissors, he separated twenty-four inches of shimmery black hair from Angela's head. She turned, her stricken gaze fastened on the hair he held.

"Oh my." One hand fingered her shorn head. "How odd." She shook her head as if to accustom herself to a new feeling. "I had no idea my hair weighed so much." She reached for the hair he held.

He swept it away, grabbed a pillow and stuffed the hair into the case.

Tommy emerged from behind the dressing screen.

"He'll have to wear his own shoes," Mrs. Kramer said as she followed him. "His feet are too large to fit into Angela's slippers."

"It'll be best for Angela to wear her own shoes." Ransom tossed the pillow back on the bed. "She'll need to move quickly. Do you have a sturdy pair of boots?"

"What?" Angela still fingered her new hair cut, as if searching for the lost hair.

"Boots?" Ransom repeated. She looked as confused as a freshly shorn sheep. And almost as ragged. He didn't make a good barber. "Do you have a pair of boots?"

"Yes." She clasped both her hands in front of her as if to keep them out of her hair.

"Doesn't Tommy make a fetching young lady?" Mrs. Kramer said.

"You can't be telling folks what I did, Mrs. Kramer." Tommy blushed. "I'm only doing it 'cause Mr. Darring said he done it all the time during the war. And he said a man's gotta do what a man's gotta do to accomplish his mission."

To Ransom's relief, Tommy's distress distracted Angela from her own misery.

"Don't let anyone tease you for being brave."

He watched his wife give Tommy a hug and a quick kiss. His wife. He rolled the phrase across his mind.

"Thank you for risking your life to save mine."

Tommy's blush darkened; he ducked his head. "It ain't near enough. You kept me and ma from starving."

"Come along, Angela," Mrs. Kramer interrupted briskly. "It's time to change you into Tommy."

Within moments, Angela came from behind the screen dressed in Tommy's shirt and trousers.

"How do I look?" She turned slowly around, arms akimbo.

Ransom swallowed. The small room was crowded with people and much too warm for the cool February day. He hoped Fletcher cleared the yard of soldiers, because he doubted any man would be fooled for long by Angela's disguise. One glimpse at the way the well washed, shabby fabric clung to her buttocks would set any man's blood to racing.

"Perfect." Mrs. Kramer plopped a slouch hat on the shaggy hair cut.

"Oh no, not his father's hat!" Angela said.

"It's all right, Miss Angela," Tommy said. "I'd be lying iffen I said pa's hat weren't important to me. But keeping you outa jail is more important. And I reckon he's watching from heaven and having a big laugh on accounta we're fooling them Yankees."

Someone rapped on the door and tried the door knob. Everyone stilled, their gazes flying to the rattling door knob.

"You in there, the Cap'n wants Mrs. Champion downstairs now."

"Soldier, tell Captain O'Brion my wife will be ready in five minutes." Ransom settled a large black bonnet on Tommy's head and tied a bow with the satin strings.

"Yes, sir. Five minutes or we'll have to break the door down. Cap'n's orders."

"Thank you for the warning, soldier." He dropped his voice a notch. "Between the rim of the bonnet and the veil, your face is well hidden." He gave the bow a final tug and pulled the veil into place.

"When we leave the room, lean on me as if you're too distraught to walk without support." He stepped back to survey his handiwork, liking what he saw. "You look convincing. When we reach the dogcart, remember to wait for me to hand you in."

"Yes, sir."

"I'll stay as close as possible." He knew O'Brion wouldn't let him drive the dogcart. "Remember, not a word to the soldier who'll be driving the dogcart. Do you have a handkerchief?"

"Here's one." Mrs. Kramer handed him a scrap of lacy, embroidered fabric.

"Keep the handkerchief near your mouth," Ransom shoved the handkerchief into Tommy's hand. "If anyone asks you anything, duck your head, sniffle, act upset. Whatever you do, don't speak."

He didn't say what was on all their minds. That the longer Tommy fooled the Yankees, the more time Angela had to escape. Nor did he discuss the consequences of the actions they were about to take. Sometimes, it was better to act than to debate.

"You're a fine young man, Tommy." He squeezed the boy's shoulder. "It would have been a privilege to have you in my brigade."

Angela's heart swelled with appreciation for Ransom, who had taken a moment to praise Tommy. The war had offered young men such as Tommy the opportunity for lawlessness, but he hadn't joined a band of bushwhackers. Instead, he'd shouldered responsibility for his mother when his older brothers joined the Confederate army. He was a good boy.

Tears threatened; she would miss him.

And her aunt, her friends, and her home.

The immensity of her loss staggered her soul. For one blinding moment, she wanted to curl up on her bed and close out the world. She had to leave her home unencumbered by any personal possessions. Her mother's hair brush, her father's medical bag, her favorite ribbons. There was so little left, but it meant so much.

Archibald Seyler's quest for revenge had brought her to this moment. Once she stepped outside that door, whether she escaped or not, her life changed forever.

"Angela. Listen to me, we haven't much time."

She blinked, unaware of how many precious moments had ticked past. Ransom stood in front of her, his hands gripping her shoulders.

Her brain focused on the present, pushing aside her fear of the future. "Give me my instructions, I'm listening."

Concern darkened the eyes that studied her. "You can do this."

She liked the warm feel of his hands on her shoulders. Reaching up, she patted his right hand. "It's not as if I haven't fooled Yankees before."

A fleeting smile touched his mouth. "Follow us to the hall." Ransom massaged her shoulders. She hadn't realized how tense they were.

"Let the soldier in the hall see you with the chamber pot. Fletcher's right, he's not going to pay any attention to you as soon as he decides you're a servant."

She leaned into the strength of his touch.

"He'll be watching Tommy and me." Ransom removed his hands from her shoulders. She felt cold and alone.

"I could stumble at the top of the stairs," Aunt Julia suggested.

Ransom nodded. "Good idea."

Angela squelched the desire to wrap her arms around him and bury her face in his chest. Instead, she concentrated on his instructions.

"When your aunt creates the diversion, slip down the servants' stairs and out the back door. Whatever you do, act normal." He paused, making sure he had her attention. "You'll have a chamber pot. It's normal to take it to the necessary and empty it."

Fear crept up her spine.

"Any questions?"

She wondered if his aquamarine eyes saw the fear in her soul.

"Where will you meet me?" She wiped her damp palms on Tommy's borrowed trousers.

"Have you been to Jordan's pond?" Ransom asked. "It's on the western edge of my cousin's land. Hide in the bushes and wait for me. I'll signal like this." He puckered his lips and quietly whistled the distinctive call of an Eastern meadowlark. "Two in a row. Understand?"

Angela nodded.

"It's been five minutes, sir." The brisk Northern accent sliced through the bedchamber door.

Aunt Julia hugged Angela. "We mustn't cry." She held Angela at arm's length. "But I will miss you. You're the dearest of friends as well as my niece."

Tears threatened Angela's composure. How she would miss Aunt Julia. Their close bond had strengthened during the years of enemy occupation. She had been fortunate to have had such a good friend beside her.

"Ladies?" Ransom's soft question parted them after one last hug.

"Do be careful, dear." Aunt Julia squeezed Angela's hands.

"And you be happy with Mr. Stillman."

Ransom took Tommy by the arm, Aunt Julia arranged herself a little behind and to the right of them, while Angela bent down and dragged the chamber pot from under the bed.

After one quick glance to ensure everyone was in their place, Ransom unlocked and opened the door.

When Angela saw the Yankee, her heart beat against her rib cage so loudly, she knew the soldier could hear it. Perspiration sheened her hands. The faint odor of urine wafted from the chamber pot, mixing with the rancid taste of fear tensing her stomach. She worried if she would drop the chamber pot, or need it when she lost this morning's pancakes.

Too soon she stood in the doorway, facing the first of the Yankee soldiers.

Chapter 7

Fletcher's plan worked.

Angela loitered in her bedchamber while Ransom helped Tommy down the stairs. Aunt Julia followed them, tripping on cue and winning the arm of the young soldier. When his attention was diverted, Angela slipped down the back stairs.

After donning the coat Tommy had left for her on a hook in the rear hall, she scanned the back yard. Nothing moved except the leaves on a baby hickory tree too young to fall victim to an ax.

"Corporal Mallis! Cap'n wants you front and center."

Angela shrank against the wall.

"Yes, sir." Boots thumped the ground near the remains of last summer's scuppernong vines.

A cacophony of voices floated down the hall from the drawing room. Ransom, Tommy and Aunt Julia must have reached the bottom of the stairs. She peeked out the back door.

Fletcher stepped into view near the barn and signaled her to go.

She elbowed open the back door, crossed the porch and headed for the necessary. Dead grass whispered beneath her boots and she wondered if anyone else heard the passing of her shattered dreams.

Fletcher gave her a quick grin of approval before he disappeared.

Voices floated over and around the house, carried by the warming breeze. Had they discovered Tommy's masquerade? Boots thumped on the front porch. Angela's legs froze. The delft chamber pot fell from her shaking hands, breaking the shepherdesses who had danced around its sides into jagged pieces.

She stared at the broken pottery at her feet.

"Sergeant Taylor, you be driving the dog cart." O'Brion's lilting command wafted around the house.

The disgruntled whinny of a horse unlocked her legs. She walked around the necessary, and slipped behind the storage room. Plastered against the wooden wall, she listened to the sounds of departure. Their house sat at the edge of Gallatin, but it wasn't that many blocks to the city jail. She had to put some distance between herself and the house before O'Brion uncovered the deception.

There was only one way to do it. She had to walk down the road in broad daylight for several miles. Fear pounded through her veins with each racing beat of her heart. Shorn of trees, the route to Douglass Gap beckoned. Sanctuary awaited in the tree line smudging the horizon.

Something scratched the storage shed door.

Her heart dropped to her toes. Had a Federal soldier been left behind? She heard a whine. Jackson?

She sighed in relief. Tommy had put Jackson in the storage room before the wedding. She crept to the door and opened it a few inches.

Soulful brown eyes, alight with happiness, greeted her.

She stuck her hand to the opening. Guilt flooded her. Intent on escaping O'Brion, she had forgotten about her best friend. And now, she didn't have much time to say farewell.

"I'd take you with me to Texas. Honest. But if anyone saw you with me, they'd know I wasn't Tommy." She didn't have the heart to tell him he was too old to accompany her. Had it been eight years since her father presented her with the puppy? White grizzled the nose that nuzzled her hand.

"Aunt Julia needs you." She scratched his soft floppy ears. "She'll take good care of you for me."

Jackson cocked his head and gazed toward the house. The hair along his back rose and a low growl rumbled in his throat.

"They're all gone for now." She stroked Jackson one last time, blinking away her tears as she pushed his head back into the storage room. "I have to go. Jackson, stay."

She closed the door. "Good boy."

His tail thumped the store room floor. She turned and walked away.

His sad, questioning whine followed her.

She kept the house between her and Gallatin until she reached a curve in the road. Although time meant the possibility of discovery, she stopped on the edge of Stapleton land. Behind her lay everything she cherished; before her lay an uncertain future.

One last quick glance to lock all she loved into her memory. Then, she stepped into the road, turned her back on Gallatin, and started west.

The trousers allowed her to walk briskly. Within a few hundred feet, she had fallen into the role of Tommy. Arms swinging, she strode down the road. The freedom of movement offered by a pair of trousers amazed her.

With fear of discovery nipping her heels, she didn't stop until she reached the scraggly tree line. By then, a painful stitch in her side hampered her breathing. She staggered off the road into the shelter of the woods. Although thinned of their leaves by winter, she welcomed what protection the trees offered her. Anything was better than the open road.

Propping herself against a tree about twenty yards from the road, she gulped air. Her loud, raspy breathing punctuated the forest stillness. Perspiration trickled between her breasts, while damp tendrils of hair stuck to her forehead. She shivered when the shaded forest breeze found the wet hair.

The rays of a weak winter sun filtered through the tree limbs above her. With the sun at the halfway point of its downward arc, the afternoon wouldn't last much longer. She figured she had another mile to Jordan's pond. As soon as she got her breathing under control, she needed to go. She didn't relish spending a night alone in the woods.

As her breathing eased, she could once again hear the rhythm of the forest. A squirrel searched the drying leaves for a tasty nut; insects droned, whirred, and chirruped; and, above them all, a crow cawed its displeasure from the sky. No human sounds interrupted nature's symphony.

The past week of freezing cold, snow, and then rain had left the forest dank and cool. It wasn't the perfect place to stop, but her legs screamed their rebellion at her fast pace. With a sigh, she slid down the tree trunk. One moment to rest. She lay her head back against the tree, closed her eyes and enjoyed the damp earthy smells. Underneath her exhaustion ran a heady feeling of triumphant. They had outwitted O'Brion.

Peace enveloped her. She felt safe, for the moment.

A twig snapped nearby. Leaves rustled as a squirrel scurried up a tree. He paused to angrily scold at whatever frightened him.

Angela's eyes flew open. Two men stood no more than five feet from her outstretched legs.

"Now what do we got here? A boy hiding from his Pa so he ain't gotta do his chores?"

Relief mixed with fear. From the look of their tattered clothing, they weren't Yankee soldiers. The thought didn't bring much consolation. Bushwhackers killed people, too.

She pushed herself to her feet, wincing at the stiffness of her leg muscles. How could she have dozed off?

"Cain't you talk, boy?"

Her interrogator had to be the hairiest man she had ever seen. Unruly black hair greased the collar of a dirty shirt whose top button remained undone, allowing a thick mat of black hair to protrude at the neck. Below his rolled up sleeves, thick hair grew on a pair of burly arms.

He stepped toward her.

Angela stepped back, but the tree trunk stymied any retreat. For once, her height was an advantage. Neither of the men topped her five foot seven inches.

"I ain't skipping chores." She deepened her voice, injecting a note of youthful defiance into her tone.

"Look at his boots, Foy."

Angela glanced toward Hairy's partner, who sported a nose that covered a third of his small, thin face. He stood several feet behind Hairy Foy, a scarred Enfield rifle held loosely in his right hand.

"Ain't nothing special about my boots," she said.

"Nothing special! Where you been, boy? You a Yankee or something? Those boots got shoe leather on the bottom." Hairy Foy laughed, revealing a set of teeth never touched by tooth powder. Laughter also made his close-set eyes creep closer together.

"I ain't no Yankee!" Angela wished she could pull out the knife she kept strapped above her right boot. One of her patients had given it to her and taught her the rudiments of knife throwing. She'd practiced diligently, but she knew a knife posed no challenge to the Enfield rifle the Nose now pointed at her chest.

"Ya know, Foy," the Nose said. "I bet them boots would fit me."

Since the only large part of the Nose's body was his nose, her boots probably would fit his small feet.

"Like I said, I ain't no Yankee. But there's Yankees chasin' me. And if the Yankees find you with me . . ."

Hairy Foy stopped mid-step to survey the woods around them.

Angela inched to the left.

The Nose rested the Enfield rifle butt on his shoulder. He sniffed the air. "I don't smell no Yankees. See any bluebellies, Foy?"

If every nerve had not been singing, Angela wouldn't have heard the stealthy rustle in the underbrush behind her. The hair on her neck lifted. She didn't know who or what was sneaking up behind her, but it was cutting off her escape path.

She kept her gaze focused on the two men in front of her. If help had arrived, she didn't want to give away the element of surprise.

When seventy pounds of brown and white dog launched itself at Hairy Foy's throat, Angela lost only one second to astonishment. Jackson?

"What the hell—?"

A grunting cry cut off the Nose's exclamation as Jackson landed on Hairy Foy, knocking the man off his feet.

Angela ran.

Hairy Foy's screams tore through the woods bracketed by Jackson's snarls.

When the rifle shot cracked the late afternoon air, Angela stumbled, slewing around as if the bullet had hit her. Her breath caught in her lungs. She wanted to go back, but without a gun, she couldn't help Jackson. And the war had taught her what horrors awaited an unprotected female at the hands of unscrupulous men.

Jackson had saved her life.

Tears streamed down her face, but she started running again. She needed to put a safe distance between herself and the men. She needed to prove Jackson had not sacrificed his life for nothing.

If she hadn't swiped at the tears blurring her vision, she would have run past the trail to Jordan's pond. She swerved and picked up the path, but kept looking back over her shoulder in the hopes of seeing a flash of brown fur behind her.

Her gaze swept to the front in the time to see the man who crouched beside the shadowy path.

Terrified, she skidded to a halt, but her left foot found no grip on the winter-slick leaves. Her feet slid out from under her. As she fought to maintain her balance, the man lunged for her.

His attack knocked her sideways, but she kicked and clawed as she fell. They rolled down a small incline, an intimate tangle of arms and legs. When they hit the bottom, she landed on her stomach, her face pressed into the decaying forest floor. With a thump, her attacker landed on her. His weight whooshed the air out of her.

Stunned into submission, she lay spread-eagle on the ground. Terrified that she'd suffocate, she twisted her head to the left and hungrily sucked fungus-tainted air into her lungs.

When she expanded her chest to breathe, she felt a hand clutching her right breast. A gasp stuck in her lungs. Judging from the man's weight, she figured Hairy Foy had caught her. Could he feel her breast through the thickness of the coat fabric? Fear of discovery ignited another frenzy of kicking.

"Sweet Jesu, Angela, stop kicking me!"

Ransom? Angela stilled. Her body relaxed; her panicked heartbeat slowed. For several moments she felt his body pressed along the length of her own. Then the weight was gone.

Gingerly, she pulled her nose out of the musty leaves. Twisting her head, she looked behind her.

Ransom was on his knees between her legs.

"Are you all right?" He brushed at the twigs and leaves that festooned her trousers.

The memory of what his hands had done to her naked body tumbled into her mind. She pushed it aside and flexed her legs. Pain rewarded her effort. From thigh to calf, every muscle in both legs burned—from running, not falling. "I- I think so."

Ransom stood and brushed leaves off his trousers, trying to brush away the lustful images plaguing his brain. The seconds he'd spent stretched over Angela with his nose buried in her hair had been heaven. She smelled of sun and forest and damp jasmine. He had grown hard with wanting her.

Somehow his right hand had gotten pinned between her breast and the ground. Her bulky coat hadn't dampened his imagination. Desire had rammed into his body along with the remembered weight and feel of her breast in his hand. He yearned to kiss his way along the lovely neck lying a hairbreadth from his mouth.

He wanted to take her right there in the leaves.

She rolled over. "Everything seems to work."

Her announcement jerked him back to reality. Guilt washed over him. Only twenty-four hours had passed since he learned of Sabrina's death, but a black-haired temptress kept interfering with memories of his fiancée.

"Good." He pulled her to her feet.

Sabrina was gone and in her stead stood a woman with dirt smudges on her face and twigs stuck in her hair. Angela, not Sabrina, had become his wife. He quelled the impulse to wet a fingertip and clean three tiny bloodstained scratches on her forehead.

"Thank God I found you!" She tottered a few steps, pulling him toward the trail. "Do you have a gun? We have to go back."

"Go back?" He grabbed her hat off the ground and jammed it on her head. "Are you forgetting O'Brion wants to put you in jail?"

"Not to the house! To Jackson. He's been shot."

"If they shot Jackson, Mrs. Kramer will take care of him. It's too dangerous for us to go back. We have to get out of Tennessee."

Angela tugged harder. "It was bushwhackers, not Yankees, who shot him."

"Wait a minute." Ransom dug in his heels. "Tell me what happened."

She swung around to face him. "I left Jackson in the storage room at the house. Somehow he got out and followed me. Then these two men found me." She tightened her trembling lips. "They wanted my boots . . . Jackson attacked them." She paused, took a shaky breath, and said, "I got away." She blinked back tears. "I heard . . . a shot."

A single tear escaped her left eye and rolled down her face. Without thinking, Ransom caught it with his fingertip. Experience told him the dog was dead. Experience also told him that without a weapon he couldn't fight the men if they were still there. But no experience had prepared him to deal with the feelings Angela created in him.

When she looked at him, her damp gray eyes held the hope he would set her world right. She believed he would take her to the dog.

Sweet Jesu.

Against all reason, he was going to take her to look for Jackson.

Ransom had seen enough death to know it hovered over Jackson when they found him. The two men had disappeared.

"Oh, Jackson." Angela dropped to her knees.

The dog whined softly.

"What a good boy."

Ransom watched Angela's hands move with quick efficiency over the dog's limp body.

"Will you please turn around?"

It took Ransom a moment to realize she spoke to him. He'd been scanning the area, looking for signs of the two men who had accosted Angela.

"I need something to make a bandage. Will you please turn around?"

From the expression on her face, telling her not to waste valuable clothing on a dog would be useless. He turned around. It didn't seem a good time to remind her they were married or that he had the right to look at her any time he wanted.

The rustle of her clothing evoked images better left unexplored for now. Good thing he had no buttons on his frock coat, because it had become unbearably warm for a February afternoon.

"You may look, now."

She sat on the ground with Jackson's head in her lap. One hand held a lace-edged pad of fabric against the bullet hole in the dog's chest.

"It won't be long, old friend." She stroked the wide brow with her free hand.

"I'll leave you with the dog," Ransom said. "I want to have a look around, make sure those men are gone."

When she nodded, a tear dripped onto Jackson's head.

He didn't know how to tell her they had no way to bury the dog.

A thorough search of the area led Ransom to a set of tracks that led away from signs of a scuffle. He followed them half a mile, but the men were gone. Relieved, he doubled back to Angela.

The sound of hoof beats sent him to the ground. Surrounded by winter-thin woods that offered little in the way of protection, he flattened himself behind a deadfall. The smell of decayed wood greeted him.

The horses trotted closer.

Ransom held his breath, trying not to sneeze at the forest debris tickling his nose.

The horses stopped.

Ransom tensed, waiting for the impact of a bullet.

"The gray part blends with the woods perfectly. But that pair of bluebelly pants. Those I saw a mile away."

Ransom lifted his head and peered over the log.

Fletcher grinned at him. His friend rode one horse and led two others whose saddlebags bulged. "I thought you'd prefer riding to walking."

"Should I ask where you got three U.S. government horses?" Ransom scrambled to his feet, swiping at the twigs, leaves, and dirt stuck to the front of his trousers.

"Let's just say, the Federal government owes me. I can always return one of them and get that sorry excuse for a horse you were riding yesterday."

"That's all right. I accept your gift." The entrenching tool attached to one of the saddlebags meant he could bury Jackson.

"If you want, you can give them back to the Yankees when you're finished with them." Fletcher looked around. "Where's Angela? I didn't see her at Jordan's pond."

"Do you have an extra gun by any chance?"

Fletcher's gaze swung back to him, his eyebrows cocked upward in question.

"Two bushwhackers threatened her. She got away because Jackson attacked them," Ransom said. "They shot him up pretty bad. I left her with the dog while I tracked the men. They're long gone."

"I have a Colt Navy pistol you can have." Fletcher pulled a gun out of his waistband. "I wouldn't let any Yankee soldiers see the gun. They might say you broke parole and toss you in jail."

"Sweet Jesu! It's been almost a year since the surrender. When are they going to do something about the bushwhackers? The Federal soldiers won't protect law-abiding citizens, but they say we can't carry guns to protect ourselves."

Fletcher leaned down and gave him the gun. "It's getting better. Some of them have quit taking our guns away, even allowed militia groups to reassemble."

Out of habit, Ransom checked the gun. Other than a few scratches, it appeared clean and well oiled.

"I don't think of these Yankees as soldiers." Fletcher fished in his saddlebag. "Ah, here it is." He pulled out some ammunition. "We fought soldiers who went home just like we did. The way I see it, those radical Republicans put together the meanest, orneriest bunch of men they could find and shipped them down here. The ones too yellow to fight in the war. They probably emptied the Yankee jails of murderers and thieves."

"You're probably right." Ransom stuck the gun in his waistband and took the ammunition from Fletcher. "Texas is a big state. I'm hoping it's big enough I won't have to see too many Yankees."

"I figure California holds the same promise for me." Fletcher tossed Ransom the reins of the two horses. "I brought you food and a little money."

"Money?" Ransom caught the reins. The two horses shied back. "Easy there, boys."

"Mrs. Kramer gave it to me. Said Angela's father had made sure they'd have a little after the war. My guess is he had funds in England. Anyway, she said it was for you and Angela."

Ransom held his hand out for the horses to sniff. After a thorough nuzzling, the larger one lowered his head so Ransom could scratch his ears.

"The minister's wife sent some cider cake," Fletcher said. "She was mighty upset you and Angela didn't have a wedding party." He leaned on the pommel of his saddle and watched Ransom check the cinches. "It isn't a lot of money, but if you're careful, it should get you to Texas."

"I'm taking Angela to Memphis, first." Ransom tightened the cinch on the horse he'd decided would be his. "It's been two years since I've seen my family."

"And they think you're dead."

He looked over the saddle at Fletcher. "I'll keep her safe."

"I know you will. I'll just feel better when she's out of Tennessee." His forehead creased with worry. "I wish I had someone like you to protect Angelica. I also wish I knew where the hell she was." His expression lightened. "But if I can't find her, I reckon Seyler can't either."

"How many women have you put in danger?"

"They were safer working for me during the war than freelancing." Fletcher's posture had gone military straight, his eyes flashed anger. "All I did was channel their talents. They were already eager to do something for the war effort."

Ransom doubted he could have used women as spies, but he always knew he belonged on the battlefield. His one attempt to play spy had put him at Fort Jefferson.

"There's no sense arguing, the past is the past." He mounted the horse, who danced a few steps while he adjusted to Ransom's weight. "My family had a steamboat line before the war. I'm hoping my father will have one or two boats back on the river by now. I promise we won't stay more than a few days in Memphis."

Fletcher nodded. "It should take Seyler a few days to figure out who you are and where you're going. Once he knows that, he'll come after her."

When Ransom saw Angela and Jackson, he thought of all the soldiers who would have preferred dying in her arms to dying their lonely deaths. He dismounted and pulled the entrenching tool from the saddlebag.

"Fletcher, why don't you stay with Angela while I take care of Jackson?"

Angela hugged the dog to her breast, bent her head and rubbed her cheek on his brow. Tears shimmered in her eyes. She pressed a soft kiss on his head. "He was a good dog."

"I know," Ransom said. The coppery smell of blood filled his nostrils as he stooped down.

He scooped the dog off her lap. Her hands followed the dog, trailing across his body one last time.

"Don't worry, I found a good place to bury him." When he reconnoitered the area earlier, he'd seen a peaceful glade that sheltered a small stream. It seemed a fitting place for Angela's best friend.

His life in the army had taught him to dig quickly and efficiently. By the time Angela walked into the glade, he was smoothing the top of the grave. Fletcher tagged behind her.

He shot an irritated glance at his friend, who shrugged his understanding. Yes, they needed to bury the dog and leave. And no, they didn't need female hysterics. But what man could stop a determined woman?

Angela stood next to the aging loblolly pine that marked the new grave site. Her forlorn stance begged for solace, from the too-large hat shading tear-shiny gray eyes, to the droop of the trouser cuffs over her scuffed boots. The sight tugged at a heart Ransom thought had grown calloused from too much grief. He wanted to take her into his arms and tell her he would make her world better.

Then she straightened her slumped shoulders. When she turned, there was no sign of tears in her eyes. When she spoke, her voice held only its familiar husky-honey tone.

"Thank you."

Without another word, she walked away. The men followed her to the horses. No one spoke for an awkward moment.

"I guess this is goodbye," Fletcher broke the silence.

"I'm sorry about the school in Pennsylvania, Angie darling."

"Isn't patience a virtue?" Her mouth tilted up briefly.

Not for the first time, Ransom wondered how she would deal with never going to medical school.

"I want you to know," she said to Fletcher, "I don't regret working for you."

"Thank you." Fletcher's quick smile vanished. "You've never dealt with Seyler, but this morning gave you an idea of how he operates." He took her hand and brought it to his mouth. His charismatic eyes caught and held her attention. "He has men everywhere and they'll be looking for you. Keep your eyes open, don't trust anyone."

"I understand."

Ransom steeled himself for the kiss he knew Fletcher would brush across her knuckles.

"There's a dress in the saddlebags. Your aunt packed a bonnet and hairpiece, too. Remember, all you have to do is look a little different, walk a little different, talk a little different—"

"Because people see what they want to see."

Fletcher grinned. "It feels good to know you listened to me." Then he kissed her hand. Releasing her, he turned to Ransom, hand outstretched.

"Oh my!" Angela grabbed Fletcher's arm. "I forgot all about Tommy. Is he all right?"

"My plan went perfectly." Fletcher patted her hand where it lay on his arm. "The Yankees went after Jonas and his men. When the sheriff discovered Tommy wasn't you, he released him."

"Thank goodness O'Brion didn't hurt him," Angela said.

"That reminds me, I never did get to kiss the bride."

Ransom didn't like the idea of watching another man kiss his wife. And he didn't like how easily she went into Fletcher's arms. But he didn't say anything.

"Take care of yourself." Fletcher kissed her cheek.

Her sad, sweet smile made Ransom wish he'd found the two men who killed Jackson.

He shook hands with Fletcher. "If you ever need a place to stay, you know you're welcome in Texas."

"I heard Texas was horses and beeves." Fletcher untied his horse. "I respect horses, but I don't like them enough to spend my life on one chasing wily four-legged animals with wicked looking horns. If you want to chase beeves across the state of Texas, go ahead. Just don't expect to ever see me doing it."

"That attitude probably explains your lack of interest in joining the cavalry and chasing wily Yanks," Ransom said.

"You're probably right." Fletcher mounted his horse. "As soon as I get Billie settled, I'm going to California. I have high hopes a man of my talents will find a way to make a living there." With a quick salute, Fletcher kicked his horse into a trot.

Ransom watched his friend ride away. Two men; two different dreams. Texas, horses, and beeves had called to him for five long years. Anticipation lightened his step as he walked toward his horse. Soon he would be living his dream.

Angela waved one last time at Fletcher, sighed, then turned toward her horse.

Ransom paused to look at her. No, he wouldn't be living his dream, because Sabrina would never share his life in Texas.

Chapter 8

"Is it this bad everywhere in the South?" Angela looked at the blackened ruins of the farm in front of them. The faint yet acrid smell of burned wood lingered in the air. "It's been too dangerous to travel beyond Gallatin for months. I thought the rumors exaggerated the destruction."

"Tennessee bore the brunt of their anger for three years," Ransom said. "I think it's worse here than anywhere else."

If she closed her eyes, she could remember acres of rich land filled with a prosperous people. Middle Tennessee had once been a breadbasket country. Now, everywhere she looked, the land lay fenceless and fallow. All their crops, dairy cattle, hogs, sheep, mules, and horses had been sacrificed on the altar of war. And so many of their sons, fathers, brothers.

"I think that's a well over there." Ransom's voice interrupted her sad thoughts.

"If the water's good, we'll spend the night here."

Her stomach growled with hunger.

"There's food in the saddlebags." He dismounted and took her horse's bridle. "I'll take care of the horses if you want to put together a meal. Keep it simple. It's safer not to have a fire."

Her search of the saddlebags yielded a packet of

that morning's pancakes, a loaf of bread, and a chunk of cheese. Mr. Carmichael had probably donated the cheese, because he had one of the few dairy cows in town. She also found her blouse and skirt rolled into one of the bags. A ruffle of lace peeked out of the skirt layers.

"What did you find?"

Angela crammed the skirt back into the saddlebag. "Pancakes, bread, and cheese."

Ransom squatted beside her. "Fletcher said Mrs. Wallner sent some cider cake. She felt we'd been cheated of a wedding party."

A wedding party wasn't all they had been cheated of, but Angela didn't want to think about what they had both sacrificed. She opened another saddlebag. The pungent odor of cinnamon filled her nostrils.

"Here's the cake." When she pulled the paper-wrapped packet from the saddlebag, a familiar leather pouch came with it.

"Is that the money?" Ransom didn't seemed surprised.

From its weight, Aunt Julia had stuffed it with all the money they had left. Angela frowned. What would her aunt live on? Most of her father's money remained in London. She had intended to transfer it to a northern bank when they reached Pennsylvania.

Ransom took the pouch from her, opened it and dumped some coins into his hand. "I haven't seen money in so long, I almost forgot what it looks like." He held a coin up, turning it to catch the dying light. "Why don't we head north and see if we can catch the L&N in Bowling Green? It's been a year, someone should have repaired the tracks to Memphis by now."

He flipped the coin into the air. Angela watched its shimmering arc. Her money was his, now. As a married woman everything she owned belonged to him.

Everything he knew about.

And she wasn't going to tell him about the money in England, because the farther they got from Gallatin, the safer she felt from Archibald Seyler. She'd spent the day convincing herself Seyler would lose interest once she left Tennessee. Thus, medical school wasn't an impossible dream.

All she had to do was convince Ransom to divorce her.

Guilt gnawed at her conscience, but she reminded herself they'd both be better off if they weren't married to each other.

He snatched the coin out of the air, dropped it back into the pouch and slid the money into his coat pocket. "Save your dress for now. We can travel faster with you playing the part of a boy."

Unsure how to broach the subject of divorce, Angela searched the last saddle bag. "Aunt Julia put my father's coat in here."

"My gray coat is not good enough?"

Angela pulled out the brown frock coat, her fingers caressing the fabric. If she closed her eyes, she could see her father greeting a patient at the door to his office. She smoothed the coat on her lap. Tomorrow morning, bright sunlight would show the darned patches on the elbows. How many times had she thrown the coat over her shoulders to ward off the evening chill?

"It'll be a little short in sleeve length." Then she realized what Ransom had said. "Gray will always hold a special place in our hearts, but the Yankees hate gray. Why there are restaurants and hotels that refuse to serve anyone wearing gray. If you plan to take the railroad to Memphis, you'd best wear father's coat."

"And Seyler's men will be looking for a man in a

gray uniform." Ransom shrugged out of his coat. "At least, it has buttons."

Angela ran her hand one more time over her father's coat, then handed it to Ransom. Do you think it's safe to go to Memphis?"

"My family thinks I'm dead. I'd like to convince them otherwise before I go to Texas."

"Good." She took his old gray frock coat, folded it neatly and stuffed it into the saddlebag. "Memphis is a large city and will suit my purpose well."

"And what purpose would that be?" Ransom wasn't having any luck buttoning the coat across his broad chest.

"Why, to lose Seyler's men. Then I'll go to Pennsylvania while you go to Texas." She knelt before a tree stump and smoothed a small lace-edged handkerchief she had found in the saddlebag across it. The faint scent of jasmine wafted from the scrap of cotton.

"You're my wife. You'll go to Texas with me."

Dusk brushed the sky, but enough light remained for her to see the scowl on his face. She didn't like the implacable note in his voice, but she knew men well enough to know they were more malleable with food in their stomachs.

Rather than get angry, she reached down, pushed up her trouser leg and pulled her knife out of its sheath. Setting the bread on the handkerchief, she sawed off several chunks. The yeasty scent made her stomach growl again. She positioned the dry cheese on the tree stump next.

Impatience got ahead of her dinner preparations.

"What if I wasn't your wife? What if we got a divorce?"

"Where did you get that knife?"

"Knife?" She pulled the blade from the cheese and

looked at it as if she had never seen it. His question interrupted the arguments she had marshaled during their ride.

"My wife keeps a knife hidden in a sheath attached to her ankle. I'm curious as to where she got it."

He took off his hat and tossed it onto the saddle bags. She wondered what had happened to the distinctive cavalryman's plume that once curled jauntily across its brim.

"A soldier gave me the knife after the battle of Pittsburg Landing," she said.

"You were at Pittsburg Landing?" Surprise laced his question.

She stared at the knife, fighting the vivid surge of memories, but they exploded into existence.

"I helped my father take care of the wounded." Her voice quivered on the last word.

She had arrived in Corinth, Mississippi, several days after the battle the Union called Shiloh. By then, Confederate and Union wounded had been crowded into every large building in town. Their bodies lay on the floor so close together it was almost impossible to walk without stepping on them.

She'd gone to work caring for the men immediately. It had been two days before she saw her father; two days before she slept. She thought she'd be prepared, because she had helped her father tend injured patients at home. Nothing could have prepared her for the mutilation of the human body caused by battle. Nothing could have prepared her for the foul air in the crowded rooms that made her ill to breathe it.

Ill, but alive. So many of the soldiers hadn't survived.

She slid the knife back into the cheese. "Sergeant Grancer Harrison gave me the knife. He also taught me how to use it." She wondered if Sergeant Harrison had survived the war. He'd been the thirty-eighth man to propose marriage to her. A little smile touched her mouth as she cut off another piece of cheese.

"Can you use it?"

She looked at the knife and then looked at a sapling twenty feet away. Vanity got the best of her. Without shifting her position, she threw the knife. It whirled through the air, shimmering dull silver in the fading light. With a thud, it hit the center of the tree. The handle vibrated gently from the impact.

"Yes, I can use it."

"I'll remember that." Ransom got up and retrieved her knife. Turning back to her, he ran his finger across the blade and then tested the knife's weight. "An excellent piece of craftsmanship."

"Sgt. Harrison's grandfather was a cutler. Knives are a family tradition."

Ransom handed her the knife.

"Do you have a handkerchief?" she asked. "We're a little short on plates."

"Champions don't get divorced." He pulled a large square of hemmed cotton from his pocket.

Recognition made her heart skip a beat. When he handed the handkerchief to her, her fingers caressed the silky initials she had embroidered in the corner. RLC. Ransom LaMarr Champion.

Dear Sabrina, Billie Stowe returned to camp yesterday and delivered your package. I appreciate the handkerchiefs you made for me.

Ransom's letters were hidden under a floorboard in her bedchamber. She had thought the letters to her sister were all she'd ever have of him. Never had she imagined she'd have this precious time with him as well.

Time in which to convince him they should divorce.

"Divorces are quite easy to obtain these days." She draped his dingy handkerchief across her left thigh. "Mrs. Foley told the Ladies Sewing Circle about this Ohio Yankee who went to Indiana, divorced his wife and married his mistress. The Yankee did all this without telling his first wife."

She wiped her knife on her trousers and slid it back into its sheath. It seemed barbaric to clean her knife on a pair of trousers and dine off handkerchiefs, but war had taught her to improvise.

"The first wife finds out she's been divorced when the newlyweds return home and kick her out of the house." She put some cheese and bread on his handkerchief.

"Mrs. Foley says it's easy to get a divorce in the Western states. And Texas is a newer state than Indiana. It shouldn't be difficult for you to get a divorce there." She handed Ransom his bread and cheese.

"I don't care what Mrs. Foley says. There'll be no divorce." Ransom bit into the makeshift sandwich.

She ignored him; she had one last important point to make. "There's no need to decide tonight. Just think about it." Tension knotted her stomach, chasing away hunger, but she had to make him understand. "A divorce is the only solution to our problem."

"I don't see our marriage as a problem."

"You don't see a problem?" Calm logic flew out of her brain. "Are you blind? Why every time you look at me, you'll feel guilty because you didn't marry Sabrina when you had the chance. It's not fair to you and it's not fair to me. I don't want to be married to a man who loves my sister."

Her outrage sputtered to a halt beneath Ransom's

intent gaze. He didn't speak until he finished his mouthful of food and took a sip of water.

"There's nothing you can do. We were married by a minister before witnesses."

"Have you taken the Oath of Allegiance?" She was searching for any way out of the marriage and she knew it.

"Dozen of times, so don't think the marriage can be nullified as your Captain O'Brion suggested." He ran his fingers through his shaggy hair. "I don't understand you, Angela. I thought all women wanted to be married and have children. Now I discover I married the only woman who doesn't. She'd rather be a doctor. And divorced."

He hadn't compared her to Sabrina aloud, but Angela knew what he was thinking: Sabrina would never want to pursue a medical profession. Marriage to Ransom had been the pinnacle of her sister's desires, but on her terms and not his.

As if I'm going to leave Tennessee! I'll stay at his father's plantation until he tires of this ridiculous notion of being a stock man in Texas.

"It's not that I want to be a divorced woman," she said. "But I see no other way out of our dilemma."

"We have no dilemma, and I don't care how many men have divorced their wives. I won't divorce you."

She tried another tack. "If you're worried there may be a child, I assure you one coupling doesn't necessarily produce a child. My father counseled several patients who couldn't conceive the first year they were married."

"I'm not worried there will be a child. I find myself wanting to father a child."

His announcement rocked her back onto her heels. A baby! He wanted a baby with her?

A baby didn't figure into the images her brain conjured up. *Making* the baby consumed her thoughts. Tension oozed out of her stomach, replaced by a different kind of hunger that food couldn't sate. Her skin tingled with the memory of his lips exploring her body.

Hellfire! She had avoided these treacherous thoughts to keep herself focused on persuading him they should divorce. Now she was giddy with imaginings no well-bred young woman should have.

Ransom watched Angela's mouth drop open and then slowly close. His disclosure surprised him, too. But her discussion of babies fueled an unexpected desire to mount her until she got pregnant. He wanted to take her to Texas and watch her grow large with his child. And then maybe, just maybe, the cold inner core of despair would melt.

Sick guilt stabbed his soul.

Sabrina. His love. The perfect wife. She would never seek a divorce any more than she would want to be a doctor.

Would he have to fight Angela's unnatural desire to be a doctor every day of their lives?

Yet she offered him a way to untangle himself from a marriage of convenience. Was he insane not to take it? Was it right to ask her to stay married to him when Sabrina's memory would always stand between them?

None of this mattered. They were married for reasons beyond their own feelings.

"There's more than the possibility of a child to consider," he said. "Have you forgotten Seyler? And O'Brion? I gave Fletcher my word I'd protect you from them. To protect you, we have to be together. To be together, we stay married and go to Texas."

Dusk had dimmed into shadows. Between the darkness and the brim of her hat, he couldn't see her expression. He disliked having to say what he had to say, but she harbored a dream Seyler had taken from her reach.

"You've been charged with Sabrina's death," he reminded her gently. "Pennsylvania is too close, too dangerous right now."

"What will stop Seyler from sending someone to Texas?"

"Nothing." He let her digest this truth. "But in Texas, you'll be with me."

"You can't possibly protect me every minute of the day."

"No, I can't. But you'll have a better chance at an isolated ranch surrounded by a dozen men. And well, Texas isn't Tennessee. Seyler won't find it easy to take you away."

"I didn't hurt Sabrina."

The evening chorus of insects droned into the silence following her softly spoken words.

The fading light bathed her high cheekbones. From the jut of her chin and the position of her head, he knew she looked at him, waiting for an answer. Her short black hair spiked out beneath the decrepit slouch hat.

"If everyone who cared for a sick person was charged with their death, the prisons would be overflowing," he said.

"I need you to believe I didn't do anything to cause Sabrina's death."

Words to absolve Angela lodged in his throat. His memory spun a wicked web of comparison between the sisters.

Sabrina had been lushly petite; Angela was slender height. Sabrina's hair had been a mass of golden curls; Angela's black, straight hair now feathered her collar. Sabrina had possessed eyes as blue as Texas bluebonnets; Angela observed the world through a pair of eyes the color of battlefield smoke. Sabrina's complexion resembled peaches and cream; Angela's retained a light tan in late winter.

"I'm sure you didn't do anything on purpose." It was all he could give her. Sabrina's death was too raw, his loss too keen, and O'Brion had planted seeds of doubt with his trumped-up charge. Had Angela contributed to Sabrina's death?

He didn't know.

"Finish eating. We need to get some sleep."

Chapter 9

Ransom walked a little faster as they neared the familiar entrance to Champion's Crest. Anticipation warred with apprehension. He hungered for the sight of his childhood home, but he worried about what awaited him.

Evidence of the war abounded in the shabby, unkempt fields, and the absence of slaves preparing the ground for spring. And no horses ran across fenced meadows to greet their arrival.

He paused by the wrought iron gates that guarded Champion land. They hung half-open, tilted in drunken surrender.

Angela stopped beside him. "It looks as if someone tried to tear them from their foundations."

"You've never seen Champion's Crest, have you?"

"I feel as if I have. Sabrina described it minutely when she returned from her visit."

"Those trees are as old as as my brother, Johnny. They were planted to commemorate the birth of the Champion heir."

Two rows of American elm trees lined the drive winding up to the house. Many of the trees remained, but there were frequent gaps in the line just as there were now gaps in so many families across the nation.

Angela slid her hand into his. Her unexpected gesture of support comforted him. His fingers closed around her hand, feeling the calluses that shouldn't be there. Something prompted him to bring her hand to his mouth. He placed a light kiss on her knuckle, marveling at how small and vulnerable her hand looked wrapped in his larger one.

He watched her watch him.

The pupils of her eyes widened infinitesimally while her lips parted. Her mouth might speak of divorce, but her body responded to his touch. He didn't remember the particulars of their one night together, but the hazy memory of her eager participation tugged at him.

He welcomed their physical attraction. Craved it. They were locked in a situation beyond their control, but that at least would make life bearable. If he'd drawn any lesson from the past few years, it would be life's unfairness.

And marriage to the sister of the only woman he ever loved had to be as unfair as it got.

But life had also taught him to work with what it gave him.

It had given him Angela as his wife. With any luck, they'd share a bed tonight for the first time since they were married.

Worry etched its way across Angela's forehead, dragging his wayward thoughts out of bed.

"Are you anxious about seeing my parents?" He wondered if she was embarrassed by the skirt and blouse she wore. Wrinkled from their sojourn in the saddlebag, her clothes also carried a layer of dust from their walk.

"A little," she admitted. "I hope their pleasure at seeing you will outweigh their displeasure at having me for a daughter-in-law."

Sabrina wouldn't be nervous about seeing his parents, she had won his family with her beauty, poise, and smile.

"Are you sure you don't want to take me to Memphis?" Angela urged. "Give me enough money to reach Pennsylvania?"

Her question chased Sabrina from his thoughts. Would Angela never abandon her dream of medical school?

"If you divorce me," she added, "they'll never know we were married."

He pulled her closer, not to kiss, but to reassure her. Less than an inch separated the toes of their boots. He rested his hand, which still held hers, over his heart. She let him pull her body close; he liked that.

"I've told you, I don't want a divorce. And if what I read in the *Daily Argus* is true, you're not going to Memphis under any circumstances. The city isn't safe for white Southerners, male or female. It's full of soldiers, freed slaves, and carpetbaggers."

"I think the newspapers sometimes exaggerate the situation."

"I'm sure they do. But there must be a grain of truth in what they write, or they wouldn't write it." He couldn't resist cradling her jaw with his left hand.

"We can't stay here more than a day or two," he said. "Once Seyler figures out who I am and where my family lives, he'll come after you." He squeezed the hand on his chest. "I promised to protect you. Don't ask me again to renege on my promise."

He wanted to kiss the lips that drew into a thoughtful pout. Silence stretched between them, but he knew the moment she accepted his ultimatum.

"I won't."

"Good. Shall we go tell my family we're married?"

* * *

Angela didn't get a good look at Champion's Crest until they rounded the last curve in the drive. From a distance, it retained the splendor of its antebellum days. But each step brought them closer, revealing the degradation of war. Peeling paint, overgrown shrubs, weedy flower beds, lopsided shutters all pointed to a large house no longer in the care of many hands.

But there was someone available to ring a large bell on the second floor verandah. Deep, bellowing tones signaled their arrival. By the time they reached the house, the front porch was filled with people. White and black.

An older white woman stood poised on the top step. One hand clutched the long skirt and petticoats she had caught upward in her hurry to reach the front porch, while the other hand rested below her throat.

"Ransom! Is that you? Is it really you? Thank the Lord, my son is alive!"

Mrs. Champion reached Ransom first, but he was soon surrounded by men and women who had to touch him to reassure themselves he was not an illusion.

"They told us you were dead!"

"Massa Ransom is alive!"

"Glory to Jesus, he done brought the Missus' son home."

Ransom swept his mother's stocky form into a whirling bear hug which elicited shocked squeals.

"Ransom LaMarr! Put me down this instant!"

He set her down, kissed her cheek and then picked up the thin black woman standing nearby, her eyes damp with happiness. "Zillah!"

"Lawdsy, Massa Ransom! You gonna squeeze the daylights outa me."

A joyous smile lit Ransom's face, making Angela realize how little he had smiled since his return. His face looked younger, more like the face in the locket. She rubbed her blouse, feeling the locket beneath and wondering if that more carefree man would ever exist again.

"Zillah, I can't believe you're here." He set her on her feet.

"And where did you think I wuz going?" The aging woman gave her skirts an indignant tug. "Didn't I help birth three generations of Champions? Ain't my Tobias in the graveyard yonder? When Missus says I's free to go where I want, I says, I'm there." She grinned. "And Missy Hannah's teaching me to read the Bible."

"Don't you have a hug for your sister?"

Angela recognized Ransom's younger sister from the long-ago engagement party, but Hannah was no longer a girl. During the war, she had matured into a young woman.

"Hannah!" Ransom seized her hand and twirled her around. "My little sister is all grown up."

Hannah's happy laughter gilded the unseasonably warm midafternoon. The deprivations of war had hammered away the childish plumpness Angela remembered, carving Hannah into a lissome young woman. A young woman with few young men left to court her.

"But Ransom, you have yet to introduce us to your companion." Hannah said when Ransom twirled her to a halt.

Draping an arm over her shoulders, he guided her to Angela.

"Don't you remember meeting Angela in Gallatin five years ago?"

"Sabrina's sister! Why, of course." Hannah bobbed a little curtsey.

"We were saddened by the news of Sabrina's death." Mrs. Champion joined her son and daughter. "Please accept our deepest condolences on your loss."

"Thank you, m'am." Angela curtseyed, grateful Aunt Julia had sent her a skirt and blouse. They had seen better days, but they weren't trousers. She had covered her short hair with the bonnet Aunt Julia sent.

"You have friends in Memphis you have come to visit?" Mrs. Champion smiled at Angela. "It was kind of my son to escort you here. There are so many dangers facing a traveler today."

Angela peeked up at Ransom, tilting her head to see around the bent brim of her bonnet. Its stay in the saddlebags had rendered it sadly crumpled.

Ransom pulled her into the sheltering embrace of his free arm. Together, they faced his mother.

"Angela's with me," he said. "We were married three days ago."

"And Sabrina barely cold in her grave!" Hannah clapped her hand to her mouth, her blue eyes wide with distress over her thoughtless comment.

Two men rounded the corner of the house and walked into the uncomfortable moment.

"Ransom? You're alive?" The younger one's pace quickened.

Ransom released Angela and Hannah. This time he was gripped in a bear hug and swept off his feet. The embrace quickly turned into back pounding as the two men became aware of their grinning audience.

Of all Ransom's relatives, Angela liked Johnny Champion the best, because he had not fallen head over heels in love with Sabrina as both his brothers had. Like Hannah, Johnny favored the maternal side of the family. He had a shorter, rounder figure than either Ransom or Teddy. She especially liked his eyes, a gentle blue that sparkled with intelligence and good nature from behind a pair of spectacles.

Those gentle eyes now looked at her.

"Angela Stapleton?"

She didn't get a chance to respond before the senior John Champion reached them.

"Welcome home, son." The patriarch extended his hand.

His subdued greeting wiped the smile from Ransom's face and straightened his posture.

"Good afternoon, sir." Ransom shook hands with his father.

Tears stung Angela's eyes. She wanted to stand beside Ransom while he faced a father incapable of showing happiness over having a son returned from the dead.

"May I present my wife to you? You met Angela when we visited Gallatin before the war."

Mr. Champion hid any surprise he might have felt at discovering he had the wrong Stapleton sister as a daughter-in-law.

"Welcome to our home, Angela." Ransom's father pressed a soft kiss on the back of her hand. The afternoon sun glinted on the head bowed over her hand, highlighting the gray-streaked ash blond hair. Some day Ransom's hair would also catch the light with more gray than blonde.

"Accept our condolences on the death of your lovely sister. I trust Mrs. Kramer is well?"

"She is to marry soon," Angela said.

"Why that's delightful news," Mrs. Champion said. "You must tell us all about it, and about your wedding to Ransom." She took Angela's arm. "I vow I'm surprised you were free to marry Ransom, dear. Exactly how many proposals did you refuse during the war?"

"Cousin Ellen said twenty-five men proposed to you."

Hannah's ringing announcement silenced the murmuring voices. Everyone looked at Angela. She didn't want to look at Ransom. She knew he already doubted her virginity. This war escapade would probably convince him she had lied about falling off her pony.

She plunged into her defense. "Your cousin misunderstood. It was a silly war time game. None of the men meant their proposals. Why some of them were already married."

From the shocked expression on her mother-in-law's face, her attempt to explain had worsened the situation.

She tried again. "Once the patients heard I had refused several offers of marriage, it became a game among them to ask me to marry them. Like a rite of good fortune. If you survived long enough to ask Miss Angela to marry you, then you would survive the war."

"Do tell, how many proposals did you receive?" Hannah begged with a pretty smile.

Angela waved off her question. "It was just a silly game."

"I'd like to know how many proposals my bride turned down before she accepted mine."

Angela looked at Ransom. Not only had his smile disappeared; his lips were drawn together in a taut line. With everyone watching them, she had little choice.

"Forty-one."

Ransom's mouth edged downward with displeasure.

"Make that forty-two," Johnny said. "Had I known you would grow into such a beauty, I would have proposed when we were in Gallatin." Johnny took her hand and brushed a kiss across her knuckles. "Welcome to Champion's Crest, sister."

Angela smiled. "I'm afraid it would have taken special eyesight to have spotted any beauty in the skinny girl you met five years ago." A lifetime spent in Sabrina's shadow had accustomed her to being unnoticed by men. Perhaps that's why she let her patients play their proposal game. It had been a novel experience to have so much male attention focused on her.

"That's enough of your foolishness, Johnny," Mrs. Champion said. "Can't you see Angela's tired. Poor child, did y'all walk from Gallatin?"

Ransom watched his mother cut Angela from his side as easily as he separated newborn calves from their mothers. His wife would be in good hands, because his mother was a warm, generous person. He often wondered how she had come to be matched up with his father. Although he needed to get to Texas, he regretted he couldn't spend more time with his mother. The war had taken its toll on her; she looked each of her fifty-five years.

"Your safe return calls for a celebratory drink," his father said.

He trailed his father into the spacious study that fronted the house. To his relief, Johnny followed them.

War had visited his father's study as clearly as it had visited Dr. Stapleton's office. Familiar furniture was gone, replaced by dented and scarred pieces once relegated to the attic.

Ransom tried not to notice how the sun's rays warmed the polished wood of the empty bookshelves lining the far wall.

His father poured three shots of whiskey. After handing them each a glass, he saluted his sons. "To your safe returns."

One of his sons had not returned.

Teddy. Youngest son; favorite son.

"To our safe return."

No one said Teddy's name aloud, but his memory flowed through the toast.

And if his father knew the truth surrounding Teddy's death, he wouldn't have welcomed his middle son home at all. Ransom downed the whiskey in one gulp, knowing alcohol would never erase the memory.

The whiskey burned its way into his stomach, reminding him he hadn't eaten since breakfast. He rolled the glass between his fingers, reluctant to end their moment of camaraderie. But he and Angela didn't have much time.

"Did you salvage any of the steamboats?"

"The federal government released *Champion's Belle* last month," Johnny said. "The repairs are almost completed, she'll be ready to leave dock in three days. We hope to retrieve the *Star* next month."

"What about the *Darling*?"

"The feds sank her two years ago."

His father thumped his small glass onto the top of the cherry desk his father had had built in New York and shipped to Tennessee more than forty years ago.

"I suppose it's too much to hope you'll stay in Tennessee."

Ransom set his glass beside his father's. "I have an opportunity to build something of my own in Texas."

His father scowled. "What kind of opportunity?"

"Uncle Richard asked me to be his partner."

His father's graying eyebrows almost reached into his hairline. "You'd rather live on that godforsaken ranch in Texas! What about your part of Champion's Crest?"

"Leave it to Johnny and Hannah."

His father roared his anger. "My God, the war takes one son and now my brother takes another!"

Ransom refused to be intimidated. "Uncle Richard left part of his leg in Virginia. He needs me to help run the ranch."

"Damn! You're still angry I didn't buy that new steamboat back in eighteen-sixty, aren't you?"

"No. What I didn't like was your threat to write me out of your will if I mentioned it again. Uncle Richard is my partner, not my father. He can't write me out of the partnership if he dislikes something I say or do."

Indignation stiffened his father's body. "I would never follow through on such a threat."

"I'd rather not test you." Ransom softened his words with a small smile. "I'm sorry, Father, but I like Texas. I like the ranch and I even like the beeves."

His father sighed. "Always the rebellious son. Fertile land in Tennessee holds no interest. My brother dangles a dusty Texas ranch in your face, and you're his."

Ransom figured that was as close to acceptance as his father would ever get. And he had more important matters to discuss. "Right now, I need your help in leaving Tennessee as soon as possible. Archibald Seyler wants Angela dead."

Quickly, he sketched out the events of the past few

days, glad to turn his father's thoughts away from
their argument.

"Fletcher and I doubt Seyler will worry with her
once she's out of Tennessee." He looked at Johnny.
"We'll need safe transportation south. Can we get a
ride on the *Champion's Belle?*"

"Ransom! I have never felt quite so decadent." Angela, seated on a stool in front of the fire, paused in
brushing her hair when he entered the bedroom.
"Imagine, a chamber for bathing!"

To have a half-clothed woman in his bedroom,
warmed him in a way the fire in the hearth could not.
The calico dressing gown she wore had seen better
days, but he liked the way the neckline gaped, giving
him an unobstructed view of one rounded breast.

"I'm glad you enjoyed it. Uncle Richard added one
to the ranch after I told him about it."

She peered up at him. "You look different."

He ran his hand along on his smooth cheek. "I
shaved."

"No."

He turned, to let her admire the blue velvet dressing gown his brother had lent him. She wasn't paying
any attention.

"It's your hair."

"Zillah cut it. She said I looked shaggy."

"And you're barefooted." She curled her own bare
feet back under the edge of her gown.

"That's not all that's bare."

She gasped. The sound sent a shimmer of desire
through him.

Crossing the room, he took the brush from her
hand. She made no protest when he turned her to-

ward the fire, but he could feel the tension radiating from her body.

He wanted to scoop her off the stool, carry her to the bed, and make love to her. Her rigid shoulders kept him from acting on his desire. To relax her, he brushed her hair.

He drew the brush slowly through her damp hair. Leaning closer, he inhaled the familiar scent of jasmine.

"It seems strange to have a man brush my hair," she murmured.

Her husky-honey voice grabbed his gut and wouldn't let go. Memories of their night together rushed into his imagination. His body ached with the need to make love to her. He had hoped the rhythm of brushing her hair would dampen his desire. It hadn't.

Had he lived twenty-six years without brushing a woman's hair? The idea seemed preposterous as he ran his fingers through the strands, relishing their softness. He dropped the brush.

Burying his hands in her collar-length hair, he spread his fingers wide and lifted his hands. The silken tresses flowed like an ebony river over, between, and through his fingers.

Jasmine mixed with feminine musk. His erection jutted against the velvet of his dressing gown. Her head lolled back to the left. Instinctively, he shifted, letting her rest on his thigh. Weaving his fingers through her hair, he grasped her shoulders, bent forward and kissed her exposed neck.

She moaned.

He smiled, his mouth arcing over her freshly washed skin.

Beneath his hands, her shoulders relaxed. His position gave him a wonderful view of her breasts and his hands wanted to go where his gaze rested. They slipped beneath the cotton fabric, across her shoulders, and down her arms.

He softly kissed her bare right shoulder while his hands escaped the confines of the dressing gown to cup the rounded fullness of her breasts.

"Sweet Jesu." He had died and gone to heaven. The ache become a raging need. His hands slid between fabric and flesh to scoop her off the stool. Without a body to give it shape, her dressing gown crumpled over the stool.

Her arms twined around his neck. He heard the soft gasp, muffled because her mouth pressed against his neck. As for her body, skin met skin only where his dressing gown had parted. He craved closer contact.

He lay her on the rug before the fire. Even in his adolescent fantasies, he had never dreamed he'd seduce a woman in his childhood bedroom. He wished the thick Persian rug that used to cover the floor remained rather than its thin, old replacement.

Kneeling beside her, Ransom shrugged out of his dressing gown. Once again, Angela's wide-eyed gaze fastened on his manhood. Memory burned into his consciousness. She had touched him there *that* night.

He needed to feel her touch again. Taking her hand in his, he guided her toward him. Once she realized what he wanted, she needed no help to cradle him. Her cool hand wrapped him in ecstasy.

His bones melted. He oozed onto the rug beside her, somehow maintaining contact with her hand.

"May I touch you elsewhere?"

Her husky-honey question twined its way into his gut, taking him to a new level of hard hunger.

"I'm here to please." He lay back on the rug, keeping his hands at his sides. A difficult task when she leaned over him. He wanted to take her by the arms and pull her body full length against him. He wanted to be in her. The need intensified when her hand trailed away from his manhood. A feeling of emptiness settled over him until her fingers feathered across his chest.

Not content to drive him insane by running her fingers through his chest hair, her inquisitive hands glissaded like gossamer across his shoulders, down his arms, back to his thighs and then his legs. Not even his feet escaped examination.

He willed her to return to where she started.

After excruciating moments, her hand resettled around his shaft. He knew what he wanted her to do next, but their marriage was too new. He didn't want to frighten her. Besides, he also didn't want to embarrass himself by climaxing the second her mouth touched the tip of his manhood.

"I have tended many men, but I have never studied the male body in such detail."

He felt as if the proverbial bucket of cold water had been poured over him. Steam should have billowed from his body. Propped on his elbows, he went nose-to-nose with her.

"Sweet Jesu! I should hope not." A wave of jealousy swept him at the thought of her touching another man as she had touched him. Its intensity startled him.

His snarl pushed her away.

He wanted to grab her hand and put it back where it had been. But then he wouldn't be able to talk coherently. "If you insist on being a doctor, you will restrict your doctoring to women."

He regretted his pompous words immediately.

Her pupils narrowed, losing the blurry-eyed passion of moments earlier. "May I remind you I didn't promise to obey you?" She cocked her head and waited for his assenting nod before she continued. "That said, I plan to care for women."

Relief skidded into jealousy, knuckling it out of the way.

"But a good doctor is acquainted with the physiology of both genders." She stared at him, daring him to argue.

He didn't want to argue; he wanted inside her.

"Let's make a bargain." He grabbed her hand and lay it back on his chest. "Why don't you use me to learn all about the male body?"

He liked the way her expression softened. He liked it even better when her hand uncurled into the hair on his chest.

"Hmmmmmm." A sweet smile curved her mouth. Her other hand joined the first. She spread out her fingers, each one sending its own promise of delight. "It does seem wrong to waste the chance to learn about the male body in such detail."

"Minx!" He couldn't take it another second. He rolled onto his side and pushed her flat on her back. "I don't want to be a doctor, but I want to learn your body."

He kissed the tops of her breasts. The dusky nipples, darker than her lightly bronzed skin, tightened in response.

"Oh, Ransom."

She licked her lips in an unconscious invitation. Hungry heat jarred his body, but he controlled it. He wanted to taste her puckered nipples.

Angela watched Ransom draw her breast into his mouth and suckle like a baby. Only she didn't think a baby would ignite these hot feelings that flowed from parts of her body she had not known existed. Her hands found his shoulders and she hung on.

He nibbled his way up her neck to her mouth. Hungry for something, not sure what, she opened her mouth to his nudging tongue. Nothing had prepared her for the plunging, thrusting invasion. Or for the fact that she liked it.

Her first foray into reciprocation elicited a deep groan from Ransom. Encouraged by his reaction, she thrust her tongue deeper into his mouth.

His lips, tongue, and hands created so many sensations, she couldn't experience them all. Her heart pounded and perspiration sheened her freshly washed skin. She writhed on the rug, decorum forgotten, wanting something but not knowing what.

Then she remembered.

That night he had touched her there.

Maybe if she touched him there now, he would touch her in return.

Her plan didn't work. When she wrapped her hand around him, he straddled her body, pinning her to the rug.

"Yes, little one. Show me where to put it."

She didn't get a chance to show him anything before his shaft nudged at the juncture between her legs. This wasn't what she wanted.

He plunged into her. To her surprise, she stretched to accommodate him and he slid easily into place. Having him sheathed inside her gave her an odd feeling of oneness with another human being. When he withdrew, her hips arched upward as if unwilling to release him. Poised over her, his breathing harsh and a thin film of perspiration gleaming on his brow, he stared into her eyes. She willed away the panic. Was he finished? Disappointment seeped into her soul.

"Are you all right?" he asked. "I don't want to hurt you."

"I'm fine." Relief washed over her, tipping her mouth into a smile. There must be more.

Then he plunged into her again, this time deeper and faster. Surprised by the intensity, she yielded to her body's innate knowledge of this strange ritual. Her hips rose to meet him. She felt her body striving for something, but it stayed out of her reach.

Again. Again. And again he surged into her. Then, he shuddered to a stop, his well-muscled arms taut with the tension of holding himself above her.

"Ah, Sabrina, my love." Eyes closed, he had a beatific expression of satisfied release on his face.

Once again his weight collapsed on her, but this time there was no feather mattress to cushion her back. Not that it mattered. Death by suffocation might be better than the path she faced. How it clawed at her heart to hear him call out Sabrina's name.

How it hurt to know he imagined her sister to be his lover. Yet, how could she protest? How could she tell him he loved an illusion without shattering the illusion?

He shifted positions, spooning them together and twining his legs around her with one arm wrapped across her breasts. Within moments, she heard the deep breathing of his sleep ruffling past her ear.

She couldn't relax into sleep with the rough hair of his legs rasping against her legs and his hand cupping a breast. If her naked body pressed to the naked body of a man weren't enough to keep her awake, a feeling of frustrated incompletion was.

A feeling that confused her. She had read enough in her father's medical texts to understand Ransom had had an orgasm. She also knew many learned male medical minds didn't believe women experienced this feeling.

But each time they coupled, she felt as if she stood on the edge of some wonderful precipice, that some earth-shattering feeling waited beyond her reach. No matter how hard she strained to capture this elusive feeling, she missed it. The glazed expression in his eyes, the explosive cry as he surged into her that final time, and the contented exhaustion when he collapsed on her, told her Ransom experienced something earth-shattering. And she wanted the experience, but for some reason it eluded her.

Perhaps the medical journals she had sneaked out of her father's office were correct. Perhaps a woman didn't have the capacity to experience this feeling.

That idea seemed unfair, since women were denied many things by either nature or society. She stared into the dying fire, feeling the coolness of the room settle on those parts of her body Ransom didn't touch.

Her own observations had led her to conclude her father and his learned male colleagues held opinions about women that were often false. At least, they were false if you used men as the measuring stick, which of course, men were wont to do.

They might be correct. Women might not have orgasms. Yet why did she ache with this feeling of incompletion?

Gently, she lifted Ransom's lean hand from her breast and rubbed it along her cheek, inhaling the masculine scent and the faint lemony fragrance of the soap. Each time they made love, he called to her sister. It made her doubt Aunt Julia's prophecy that he would come to care more for the living than the dead.

But she would keep her promise not to ask for divorce. They would go to Texas, but she knew he would soon tire of her because she wasn't Sabrina. Then he would set her free.

Chapter 10

Angela stopped on the landing. Yards of crimson taffeta billowed around her legs. From the skin out, everything she wore had been borrowed from her new in-laws. The Champion women had not emptied their wardrobes to make bandages. Not that satin, silk, taffeta or lace made good bandages.

The faint murmur of voices wafted into the foyer, but her feet remained glued to the winding staircase. She reached for the banister, curling her gloved fingers around the smooth wood finish. The French corset she wore precluded taking a deep breath. She scowled, unconvinced the fuller bosom and smaller waist were worth the discomfort.

"Sister-in-law! May I escort you to the parlor?"

She peered down at Johnny. The rhythmic ticking of the grandfather clock echoed in the foyer. She smiled at him, grateful to have someone's escort. Ransom had deserted her when his mother and a maid arrived with an armload of clothes. Gathering a handful of skirt in her left hand, she walked down the stairs.

"I envy Ransom such a beautiful wife." Johnny offered her his arm.

"A most delightful compliment, although untrue." She took his arm.

"Can it be? A woman unaware of her own beauty?" He looked at her intently. "Or a woman who grew up in the shadow of Sabrina Stapleton." His gaze gentled. "She was a beautiful woman, but your beauty surpasses hers."

Angela stopped, once again feeling the graceful sway of skirt, petticoats, and crinoline against her legs. "I think you've forgotten how beautiful my sister was."

Johnny shook his head. "I haven't. Your sister possessed physical beauty, but she didn't possess the qualities that make a good person." He patted her hand. "You, on the other hand, are beautiful inside and out."

Tears threatened Angela's eyes. Few men had seen past Sabrina's beauty to the unkind person beneath the blonde hair, blue eyes, and dimpled smile. To be fair, it wasn't Sabrina's fault she used people as she had. From childhood, everyone had doted on her. Sabrina had only to smile to get her every wish granted. Angela doubted her sister ever realized how carelessly she trampled the feelings of others.

"Now, now. No tears. I don't want my brother calling me out for making his new bride cry."

She knew Ransom would never care enough about her to challenge anyone to a duel, and the thought was enough to make her cry in earnest. Or laugh.

"How you do go on!" She swatted at Johnny with her fan, faking shock.

"That's better," he said.

Together they swept into the parlor. Their arrival quelled the murmur of voices momentarily.

"Oh, Angela, I was correct." Hannah approached them with outstretched hands. "That red suits your complexion much better than mine. You look beautiful."

* * *

Ransom had seen Angela in Sabrina's ill-fitting dress, in a worn nightgown, in a poorly dyed brown dress someone had rescued from the trash heap, in Tommy's breeches, and, he had even seen her nude. But he had never seen her dressed as a fashionable, gently bred young lady.

The sight stole his breath.

He wished his hands could cup her breasts the way the bodice did, or wrap around her small waist in place of the wide sash. Most of all, he wished he could taste the lips that trembled with nervousness, and caress the cheeks that were dusky rose with uncertainty.

He brushed aside his erotic thoughts, which were having a noticeable effect on his body, as brusquely as he brushed aside his grinning brother.

"You look enchanting, little one." He bowed, took Angela's hand, and raised it to his lips.

The light from the candles in the wall sconces beside the parlor door danced in the ebony of her hair, and shimmered off the crimson taffeta of her gown. He had an irresistible urge to push aside the low cut décolletage and find the birthmark he knew waited for him on her left breast. He smothered the urge. Kissing that particular spot would have to take place at a more appropriate time.

This was the woman who had received forty-some marriage proposals.

"Thank you, Ransom. You look, uh, handsome."

She stared at his waistcoat buttons. He realized she had yet to look him in the eye since their lovemaking on the rug. He found her discomfort enchanting.

"Handsome might be an overstatement." He grinned at her bowed head. "Less tattered, patched, and mended probably describes my clothes better."

He plucked at the loose fitting trousers. "Evita will see me as a challenge to her cooking skills. I'm sure it won't take her more than a few weeks to fatten me up."

"Evita?"

Her head snapped up.

Ah, she was glaring at him. Unfettered delight danced through his soul. Secure in her role as heart-breaker, Sabrina had never seemed concerned when another woman looked at him. He liked Angela's reaction.

"Ransom, stop teasing Angela." Hannah put an arm around Angela's waist. "Evita is Uncle Richard's cook. She and her husband have worked for Uncle Richard at least fifteen years."

"I'd rather not talk about Texas tonight." Mrs. Champion's announcement cut through Hannah's chatter. "I know we're going to lose you to your uncle in a few days." Her frown vanished into a smile. "Tonight I wish to enjoy having home the son I thought lost forever."

A servant appeared in the doorway. "Dinner is served."

When Ransom seated Angela at the dinner table, he let his hand trail across her bare shoulders. He liked the feel of her skin against his fingertips. They had made love only hours earlier, but he wanted her again.

She wanted him too. He could tell by her soft startled gasp and quick hot glance. Pride in his sexual prowess rippled through him. Then disappeared. Had he truly pleasured her? Or had he taken his pleasure of her?

Out of nowhere, snippets of late night campfire conversations about women teased his mind. Several married men had disputed society's claim women didn't experience coupling as intensely as men. He remembered their insistence that women responded wildly to the right touch. Had he touched her in the right way, in the right places?

Johnny cleared his throat. "Do you plan to stand while you eat, brother?"

From the amused gleam in Johnny's eyes, Ransom suspected his brother knew he wasn't thinking about food.

"Sorry. Guess I was just counting my blessings."

"You can do that while you're seated," his father said. "I don't relish eating a cold dinner."

His parents' table seemed strangely bare compared to dinners they had shared here before the war. There wasn't as much food, he'd never seen the mismatched chairs, and the yellowed tablecloth must have graced the table during his grandmother's reign.

From the looks of the chipped china, odd assortment of crystal, and dented silverware, the Yankees had helped themselves to the dinnerware as freely as they'd helped themselves to the furniture, paintings, and knickknacks that had once called Champion's Crest home. One small piece of crystal gleamed before him on the table. Complete with its tiny silver spoon, a swan-shaped salt cellar had survived the war.

He picked up the tiny spoon, dug it into the salt, and lifted it an inch above the swan's back. Tipping the spoon, he watched salt cascade back into the swan. His hand tightened until his knuckles were white. Sweet Jesu, had he called out Sabrina's name both times he coupled with Angela? An uncomfortable truth gnawed on his conscience: his body made love to Angela, but Sabrina ruled his mind.

He wondered if he'd made the worst mistake in his life.

"Ransom?"

His mother's voice broke into his whirling thoughts.

"If you're quite through with the salt cellar . . ."

For one fleeting second, her tone catapulted him back ten years. He looked up, to find everyone at the table staring at him. But he was ten years older. A war and prison wiser. And quite capable of hiding his wayward thoughts.

To his surprise, Angela rescued him.

"I'd have sold my soul for a bag of salt a year ago," she said. "Sometimes I think the small needs of everyday life defeated us."

That's when he knew he wanted Angela to experience what he experienced when they coupled. Tonight.

"Tish tosh." His mother waved away Angela's comment. "A lack of salt did not defeat the Confederacy."

"I agree with Angela." He dropped the spoon into the salt cellar with a gentle clink of silver against crystal. "The Confederacy couldn't meet the needs of its citizens or its soldiers."

His mother sniffed delicately, unconvinced.

"There are as many reasons for the failure of the Confederacy as stars in the sky." His father waggled a knife at the table in general. "It's a waste of time to worry about why we lost. We've better things to do with our time."

"Like enjoying a nice long visit with a brother I thought never to see again," Hannah said. "And a new sister." She leaned forward. "I'm sure Uncle Richard can do without you for a few more weeks, Ransom. And it'll be much nicer to travel in the spring when it's warmer."

Unwilling to frighten his sister or mother with the reason behind their short visit, Ransom smiled. "I'm sorry to disappoint you, but Uncle Richard needs me."

"Richard should have married and had his own sons instead of stealing one of mine!"

"Father, you know good and well, it wasn't Uncle Richard's fault his fiancée died of the fever before they married." Hannah's eyes got a dreamy look to them. "And I think it romantic that his love for her has survived all these years."

"Balderdash, daughter! My brother never married because he went to Texas to raise cows. Texas has cows and men. It has few women."

"Mr. Champion! You are using profanity at the dining table and you know how that distresses me."

Ransom grinned at Johnny. The familiar bickering of his parents eased the harsh war memories somewhat. It was good to be home.

Crimson shifted in his peripheral vision. His grin widened. It was even better to be home and have a woman in his bed.

By the time Angela and Ransom retired for the evening, every cell in her body hummed. From the fingers he trailed across her shoulders when he seated her at the dinner table, to the intermittent touch of his thigh against hers during the meal, Ransom had spent the evening seducing her.

Images of their entwined bodies had driven her to distraction. She couldn't dismiss the hope that if they did *it* again, she would reach the same pinnacle of satisfaction he reached.

She watched him close and lock the door. He turned and faced her. She licked her lips. Her heart had started beating faster as they climbed the staircase. She knew it wasn't from the stairs.

He walked toward her.

"I think the person who designed those hoops should be horsewhipped." His hands settled on her shoulders.

Warm skin against bare flesh. Her heart skipped into a higher tempo.

His hands slid under the ridiculous puffs of fabric that passed for sleeves, edging them slowly down her arms. She couldn't move; his mesmerizing gaze trapped her. Then he lowered his head and kissed the tops of her breasts where they rounded above the low décolletage.

Her breath hitched in her throat as she watched him scatter kisses on one breast and then the other.

He raised his head. "You have on too many clothes."

As limp as her childhood rag doll, she let him turn her around. His fingers fumbled with the row of tiny buttons that locked her into the gown.

"Should I ring for Ruby to help?" she offered.

"Sweet Jesu, no!"

His nervousness soothed the butterflies in her stomach.

Her dress, the finely embroidered white petticoat, the crinoline, the camisole—one by one the layers came off—until she was clad in her corset, drawers, and stockings.

"Trust my mother to save her silk stockings from the Yankees."

"She said she buried a box of them herself. She didn't even tell your father where they were located."

He pushed her onto the bed and knelt before her. "Can you imagine the face of some young boy, generations from now, digging for pirate treasure, but finding a box of ladies' stockings instead?"

The sweet thought that it might be their great-great-great grandson surprised her.

She pushed it aside, knowing from the intense look in his eyes he awaited some reaction. She giggled, as much from nerves as from his question.

His fingers feathered to the top of her left stocking. Heat pooled close to his fingers. Her insides quivered with anticipation and she thought she would melt into a puddle before he finished peeling the stocking and garter down her leg.

Especially when he paused and kissed her knee-cap.

"Oh my," she murmured.

Before she could collect her senses, he lifted her leg onto his shoulder and licked the back of her knee. So many delectable sensations swirled throughout her body, she couldn't pinpoint them all.

She dissolved onto the bed, too weak to sit upright.

He pulled the stocking off her foot, and to her, complete embarrassment, kissed the top of her big toe.

Hope escalated. How could she experience all these feelings and not reach satisfaction?

He gave her little chance for coherent thought. She felt his hands cup her calves and slide slowly up the length of her legs. Tiny kisses peppered the insides of her thighs. Dizzy with wanting him, she fought the urge to grab his head—and what?

She didn't know.

"Do you like that?" His warm breath dried the kiss marks.

She sighed her pleasure.

He pushed her all the way onto the bed. She opened eyes she didn't remember closing. His fingers grazed her breasts as he unfastened the corset hooks. Then she felt him hook the lacy edge of her corset and tug. Cool night air danced across her bare breasts, which rose and dropped in time with her quick, shallow breaths.

His gaze dipped to her breasts. She watched the pupils of his aquamarine eyes grow larger, making his eyes more blue than green.

He bent his head and kissed the birthmark that marred her skin.

"I've wanted to do that ever since Johnny brought you into the parlor tonight." He outlined the dusky mark. "South America."

"South America?" Had his caresses ruined her hearing?

"Your birthmark. It resembles the continent of South America." He captured a dusky-tipped nipple in his mouth.

The shock of pure, pulsating pleasure brought her two inches off the bed. She closed her eyes to savor the liquid heat spiraling through her veins. When it ebbed, she opened them to see him watching her as he teased the hardening tip with his tongue.

His hand at the curve of her waist nudged the lacy drawers down her hips. She offered no resistance. In fact, she pulled her legs towards her stomach so he could push her drawers over her feet.

Now his fingers tangled in the crisp curls between her thighs. With his mouth suckling on her breast and his hand caressing the juncture between her legs, she itched to touch him, but kept her hands at her sides. Her touch had driven him wild earlier. This time she wanted him to maintain control until he gave her what she needed.

He kissed a warm trail along her shoulder, then up the column of her neck, until his mouth touched her own.

When his tongue slid into her mouth, her body

acted on some indiscernible signal. Her legs opened. She pressed against his hand, searching for something to ease the fire his tongue, lips, and hands created. She lost any concept of who or where she was. All she knew was an overwhelming ache only he could ease. She continued to press against the hand that rubbed and probed, and rubbed and probed with sweet maddening patience until, to her complete surprise, shuddering waves of indescribable pleasure swept over her.

She spiraled up into mindless delight, rising to a pinnacle of pure sensation that drove all logical thought from her body. Then, she shivered into a quiet puddle of humanity. Whoever had been moaning, fell quiet. Reason seeped back into her brain. She still throbbed down there, against the gentle pressure of his hand. Out of nowhere, came the desire to rub herself up and down his body and purr like the happiest of cats.

"Did you like that?"

She dragged open her eyes. Speech eluded her, but she mustered a contented kitten smile.

He was smug male satisfaction. "We're not finished yet."

It took three heartbeats for his announcement to penetrate the fog around her brain. Her smile slipped.

"We're not finished?" Her voice sounded rusty. Could her body take more?

Ransom stripped off his clothes. Once again, she found herself mesmerized by his fully aroused manhood and his musky male scent.

When he mounted her, the silky touch of his shaft against her still sensitive skin shook off the lethargy that had stolen over her body. She raised her hips to meet his thrusts. Shock waves of pleasure reverberated through her again.

This time as he entered and withdrew, she felt every inch of the union. This time she savored each shuddering wave of pleasure. This time she knew why he collapsed in exhaustion to the bed, because this time she, too, was exhausted. Finally, she knew why Sabrina had let Nicholas impregnate her.

And she thanked God for not consigning women to some earthly hell.

And she was grateful for Ransom's rasping silence when he surged into her that last time. Better he say nothing, than that he call her out her sister's name.

When Ransom awoke, sunlight edged the striped drapes at the bedroom windows. He lifted his head from the cave he'd created with the pillow and his arms. How long had it been since he'd slept through a night without interruption? Although there was one interruption he would have welcomed if a lifetime of exhaustion hadn't claimed him.

He reached for Angela, but came up empty-handed. No soft, feminine body lay beside him. He shoved his pillow aside and scanned the room, disliking the tiny thread of desolation that skimmed his heart. The rustle of clothing alerted him to her presence behind the dressing screen.

Drowsy need leapt to life as he imagined her half-dressed. He wondered if he could interest his wife in a morning round of lovemaking. A smile eased across his mouth as he remembered her moans and shuddering sighs of the previous evening.

Softness. Femininity. Fragrance. Lace.

She represented everything the war had stolen.

When she tiptoed around the dressing screen in

her stockinged feet, perversity made him feign sleep. He willed her to approach the bed, envisioning her surprise when he dragged her down onto it. A grin threatened his mouth. He buried his face in the pillow, shrouding his grin in the faded scent of their lovemaking.

Blood rushed through his body. He angled his head so he could keep an eye on her.

As he hoped, his restless tossing and turning brought her to the bedside.

"Ransom? Are you awake?"

Her husky-honey voice spread over him with promises she could now keep. He hoped she wasn't too hungry for breakfast.

She leaned over the bed.

His heart raced with anticipation; his cock wanted to greet the morning.

She slid her hand beneath the pillow on her side and patted around as if searching for something. His eyelashes hazed his view, but her body appeared tense and her gaze stayed on him while she searched. He could tell when she found it. Her shoulders relaxed. She started to withdraw her hand.

His left hand snaked beneath the pillows. She gasped her surprise.

"Ransom! You frightened me. Let go, please." She jerked her hand, trying to pull it free.

He tumbled her down onto the bed, rolling her beneath him, their hands still clasped.

"Keeping secrets from your husband?" He smiled to let her know he was teasing.

No playful smile lightened her wary expression. Her beautiful pewter eyes watched him.

Oh, how he wanted her.

He looked at their clasped hands resting on the bed above her head. A thin gold chain spilled between her clenched fingers. He released his grip. "What have you got?"

With a sigh of defeat, she slowly opened her hand.

Sexual desire drained from every cell of his body. The past slammed into him. A small gold locket gleamed against her palm. He had given it to Sabrina before he went to war. It belonged in the grave with her, not on this bed of lust.

"What are you doing with Sabrina's locket?" He plucked it out of her nerveless fingers. His own fingers trembled and he cursed their awkwardness, but he opened the locket. The quiet click resounded in the tranquillity of the bed chamber.

Sweet Jesu, he'd almost forgotten what she looked like. Now Sabrina's golden beauty stared at him across a gulf of painful memories.

Guilt overwhelmed him.

He hadn't properly grieved her death because it'd been easier to put it aside until later. He had survived a war filled with death by not dwelling on it. Sabrina's death had caused the same reaction. He had mourned her briefly, as one did in war, and then convinced himself to get on with living.

By marrying her sister and putting her in Sabrina's place.

Shame blistered his soul. He owed Sabrina more than a few hours of grief and then forgetfulness in the arms of her sister. "You haven't told me why this locket isn't with Sabrina."

"It's mine. She gave it to me."

"And you hid it from me?" He tore his gaze from his beloved's miniature. "Didn't it occur to you that I have nothing of hers? None of her letters, not one pair of the socks she made, not even the sweater that didn't fit."

Disgusted with her, disgusted with himself, he rolled off the bed.

"But you said you loved the sweater!"

"As if I would write anything that would hurt Sabrina's feelings." He grabbed his drawers off the floor and pulled them on. "The sweater didn't go unappreciated, it kept our drummer boy warm."

"Did the socks fit?"

"No! Yes! What does it matter?"

Still sprawled on the bed, she shrank from his angry voice.

Good. He wanted to push her away. Push away what they had done. What she had done—trying to replace her sister in his heart.

In his guilt and shame, he did the unforgivable. "You're nothing like your sister. Sabrina would have never kept something as precious as this locket from a grieving fiancé."

Wide gray eyes watched him prowl the room. His clothes were flung everywhere, reminding him of their wanton night.

"Lust." He picked up his shirt and shook it at her. "We've experienced nothing but lust. You knew I'd been in prison for a year. Yet you came to my room in the middle of the night? A single lady alone with a single gentleman. Sabrina would never have behaved so improperly."

He thrust his arm into the sleeve of his shirt. "I know love. Believe me, this isn't love."

She watched him prowl, rant, and dress, but she didn't say anything. Why didn't she defend what they had done? Make it right. Ease the guilt that burned his gut.

"I didn't even observe a decent period of mourning. I defiled Sabrina's memory the first chance I got. Hours after learning of her death, I bed her sister."

Take A Trip Into A Timeless World of Passion and Adventure with Kensington Choice Historical Romances!
—Absolutely FREE!

Enjoy the passion and adventure of another time with Kensington Choice Historical Romances. They are the finest novels of their kind, written by today's best-selling romance authors. Each Kensington Choice Historical Romance transports you to distant lands in a bygone age. Experience the adventure and share the delight as proud men and spirited women discover the wonder and passion of true love.

4 BOOKS WORTH UP TO $24.96— Absolutely FREE!

Get 4 FREE Books!

We created our convenient Home Subscription Service so you'll be sure to have the hottest new romances delivered each month right to your doorstep—usually before they are available in book stores. Just to show you how convenient the Zebra Home Subscription Service is, we would like to send you 4 FREE Kensington Choice Historical Romances. The books are worth up to $24.96, but you only pay $1.99 for shipping and handling. There's no obligation to buy additional books—ever!

Save Up To 30% With Home Delivery!

Accept your FREE books and each month we'll deliver 4 brand new titles as soon as they are published. They'll be yours to examine FREE for 10 days. Then if you decide to keep the books, you'll pay the preferred subscriber's price (up to 30% off the cover price!), plus shipping and handling. Remember, you are under no obligation to buy any of these books at any time! If you are not delighted with them, simply return them and owe nothing. But if you enjoy Kensington Choice Historical Romances as much as we think you will, pay the special preferred subscriber rate and save over $8.00 off the cover price!

We have 4 FREE BOOKS for you as your
introduction to
KENSINGTON CHOICE!
To get your FREE BOOKS, worth up to $24.96, mail
the card below or call TOLL-FREE 1-800-770-1963.
Visit our website at www.kensingtonbooks.com.

Get 4 FREE Kensington Choice Historical Romances!

YES! Please send me my 4 FREE KENSINGTON CHOICE HISTORICAL ROMANCES (without obligation to purchase other books). I only pay $1.99 for shipping and handling. Unless you hear from me after I receive my 4 FREE BOOKS, you may send me 4 new novels—as soon as they are published—to preview each month FREE for 10 days. If I am not satisfied, I may return them and owe nothing. Otherwise, I will pay the money-saving preferred subscriber's price (over $8.00 off the cover price), plus shipping and handling. I may return any shipment within 10 days and owe nothing, and I may cancel any time I wish. In any case the 4 FREE books will be mine to keep.

KN04A

Name_____

Address_____Apt._____

City_____State_____Zip_____

Telephone (___)_____

Signature_____

(If under 18, parent or guardian must sign)

PLACE
STAMP
HERE

ll..l..lll....llll..ll..ll..ll..ll.llll..l

KENSINGTON CHOICE
Zebra Home Subscription Service, Inc.
P.O. Box 5214
Clifton NJ 07015-5214

He cursed the buttons on his shirt, then gave up trying to button them.

"I told you not to marry me," she murmured.

Her quiet statement spun him around, trousers in hand.

"Your advice came a little too late. Or do you forget you've been charged with your sister's murder?"

The heightened color drained from her cheeks. He watched her chin quiver.

A rap on the door stopped him from apologizing.

His brother stood on the other side. Excitement lit his eyes.

"Little Ned says there's a detachment of Yankees coming down the drive. We need to get you and Angela out of here."

The steady splashing of the huge paddle wheel pushing the *Champion's Belle* down the Mississippi River should have lulled Angela to sleep. Instead, she stared at the bottom of the narrow berth above her and listened to Ransom's soft snores.

Propping herself up on an elbow, she punched her pillow into a fluffier condition. Despair gnawed at her. Why hadn't she left the locket in Gallatin?

She collapsed onto her side. Had she needed a tangible reminder of her promise? She hoped not, since Ransom had claimed the locket as his own.

Forty-eight hours of hell. She sucked in a lungful of air tainted with the smell of new varnish, fresh paint, and Mississippi River. Then she expelled it on a long sigh.

She had known the marriage wouldn't work. She had known he'd despise her for being alive when Sabrina was dead. She had known this, yet she had married him. What a foolish woman she had become.

Here, in the darkness of night on a Mississippi River steamboat, she accepted the truth. She had created the woman he loved and that illusion stole any hope that he would ever love her.

Tied to her, he'd never have a chance to find happiness with another woman. The marriage condemned them both to a life of misery. She had to untangle them from this marriage.

Her future lay in Pennsylvania where she could attend medical school and forge a new life for herself. His future lay in Texas with beeves and horses. She'd promised not to ask him for divorce; she hadn't promised not to leave him.

When she was gone, he'd accept the idea of a divorce better. He'd probably institute legal action himself.

Her fingers twined a corner of the blanket. Lulled by the childhood ritual, her eyelids sank low. Her breathing slowed. Her mind relaxed into a better future.

Chapter 11

Angela hadn't expected to fall head over heels in love with Texas. The hills, the scorpions, the wild flowers, the tarantulas, the wily beeves, the dust, the awful-tasting water, even the rattlesnakes enchanted her.

Shorn of the gentling green of Tennessee, this land vibrated with raw, untamed power. She had quickly learned that March in the Texas hill country could mean warm days and cool nights, or a freezing cold that felt as if God had used a large broom to sweep the Arctic chill of faraway Russian America straight into Texas.

She stepped into the pool of warmth left on the front porch by the late afternoon sun.

"Afternoon, Mrs. Champion." Malachi Johnson waved at her from his seat on the corral rail. "Come to see the show?"

"Wouldn't miss it for the world." She settled into the rocking chair Evita kept on the porch.

Malachi jumped off the rail to open the gate for Ransom. Above them, a scissor-tailed flycatcher somersaulted in the air while a potential mate watched. Angela smiled as the aerobatic bird tried to convince his ladylove of his prowess.

When Ransom led a freshly broken mustang into

the corral, her smile faded. No man would ever perform stunning feats to capture her approval.

The mustang kicked and danced his way into the corral, as displeased about the saddle on his back today as he had been yesterday. Angela's grip tightened on the arms of the chair, and she waited for the horse to try to kill Ransom when he swung his long leg over the saddle.

As usual, Ransom won the battle of wills. Then he began to teach the horse how to cut beeves from a herd. The "beeves" were made of hay, but he worked the horse as if the hay bales were real Long Horns. Once the horse learned knee and hand commands, he would be introduced to Long Horns in the flesh.

"Easy boy, that's it."

Ransom's patience with the green horses had surprised her. The young bravado who courted Sabrina had matured. He no longer demanded the world pay heed. He didn't need to. Quiet self-confidence radiated from every pore of his body.

A movement on the horizon caught her attention. She shaded her eyes against the sun, hoping Seyler's Yankees had not followed her to Texas.

Four weeks ago Johnny had hustled them out of Champion's Crest before the Yankees arrived. He hid them five miles down river from Memphis, in the remains of a plantation that boasted an intact landing. *Champion's Belle* had picked them up the next night.

To Angela's Tennessee eye, Ransom had brought her to the middle of nowhere, although he claimed they were thirty miles northwest of Austin. Her ignorance of the surrounding countryside, the strange wildlife, and marauding Indians meant leaving Ransom wasn't a simple matter of walking away one night. The isolation of the ranch might make departure difficult, but its isolation helped protect her from Seyler.

"Is that Francisco's wagon?"

Malachi's question made her squint her eyes and study the wagon-shaped speck.

Ransom wheeled the horse in the direction she looked.

She should have pretended interest in the approaching wagon, but she stole a glance at Ransom. Beneath the rough work clothes, his body had been resculptured by food and rest into rippling strength. The broad shoulders now fought against the fabric that ensnared them.

"It looks like Francisco picked up a passenger," Ransom said.

His observation swung her gaze back to the wagon. Two people rode in the heavily laden wagon while three outriders guarded the cargo.

"Was your uncle expecting company?" Malachi asked.

"Not that I know of." Ransom dismounted and led the horse to the gate. "Probably someone who wants a job."

"He must count on being hired," Malachi said. "He'll have a hard time getting back to town without a horse."

Malachi fascinated Angela. An Indian father and a Negro mother gave his dusky skin a reddish hue. A handsome man with high cheekbones, he spoke excellent English as well as Spanish and his native Indian tongue. She longed to know more about him, but good manners forbid her from prying into his background.

"Angela, let everyone know Francisco is back."

She stared at Ransom blankly for a moment, then remembered the bell that hung on the far end of the wooden porch. She pulled the ringer three times, stopped for a moment and then pulled the ringer again.

By the time the wagon reached the farthest corral, half a dozen people waited in the yard. Something about the young man seated next to Francisco drew Angela off the porch.

The passenger took off his hat and waved it in the air. "Miz Angela! Miz Angela!"

"Tommy?" Angela ran to meet the wagon.

Tommy's feet scarcely touched the ground before she hugged him.

"How did you get here?" She held him at arm's length, then hugged him again. "How is everyone back home? Oh, Tommy, I can't believe my eyes!" A million questions pestered her brain, but most of all she wondered why Tommy had come to Texas.

"Good to see you, Tommy." Ransom peeled the blushing young man out of her grasp and shook his hand.

Tommy seemed to grow taller before her eyes. She needed to remember he was a young man now.

"Did you travel all the way to Texas by yourself?" Although Ransom's tone was cordial, Angela heard the hard edge beneath the question and knew he was worried, too.

"Yes, sir. Your father asked me if I'd like to come, after I done carried Mrs. Stillman's message to him. She weren't sure if you'd left Memphis, yet."

"Mrs. Stillman? Oh, Aunt Julia is married." Regret ran beneath Angela's happiness. She had missed her aunt's wedding.

"I brung you a trunk, Miz Angela. Full of yer clothes. Oh, and Mrs. Stillman said to tell ya she put your diary in there." Tommy reached inside his shirt and pulled out a crumpled envelope. "Here's a letter explaining everything."

Angela recognized her aunt's handwriting. Tears threatened her eyes, she hadn't realized how much she missed Aunt Julia until that moment. "Thank you. Thank you." She clasped the letter to her chest.

"And I got a message for the Major, too."

Angela didn't like the serious note in Tommy's voice. A message that could not be trusted to paper meant trouble.

"Why don't you tell me about it later?" Ransom suggested. "I bet you're hungry."

Only Uncle Richard knew about the threat hanging over her head. She recognized Ransom's desire to keep the situation in the family.

"Yes, sir." Tommy nodded his head. "I ain't had much to eat 'cause I used up all the money Mrs. Stillman gave me." He clutched a crumpled hat in his hands.

Angela smiled. He'd be happy when she returned his father's hat.

"But the storekeeper tole me Mr. Francisco was due any day. And then he let me work for food, but I sure was glad to meet Mr. Francisco."

"You poor dear!" She wanted to take the words back when she saw another blush flood Tommy's face. "I mean, how resourceful to have found work. And to have traveled from Tennessee to Texas by yourself. That shows maturity." She took Tommy by the arm, ignored the wink Ransom gave her, and headed for the house.

"You look positively skinny, but Evita will take care of that. She loves feeding hungry males. See how well she fattened up Ransom?"

Angela threw Evita a beseeching look over her shoulder. With a sigh, the plump woman deserted the treasures of the supply wagon to accompany them to the kitchen.

"Do you think the Major'll let me stay?" Tommy asked. "I promise to work hard."

"What about your mother? Doesn't she need your help on the farm?"

"Matthew said he kin take care of Ma. He said he don't wanna listen to me bellyache about missing the war no more. And he says Texas'd cure me of my itch. Whatever that is."

"Why don't you wash up?" Angela pointed to the wash stand in the corner of the kitchen. "We'll talk to Major Champion after you eat."

She asked Evita to serve Tommy's meal in the dining room. As she expected, Ransom and his uncle joined them before Tommy finished eating. The boy started to rise when the men entered the room.

Ransom's uncle waved him back to his seat. "Is that Washington Cake I smell, missy? Do you think Evita'll skin us alive if we eat some before dinner?"

"Since she left plates and forks, I think she planned on you having some." Angela picked up the knife beside the plate and slid it into the cake, unleashing the spicy smell of nutmeg and cinnamon. "I was so excited about seeing you, Tommy, I forgot to introduce Major Champion's uncle."

"Richard Champion." Ransom's uncle extended his hand. "Angela told me all about your part in her escape. Thank you for helping her."

"It weren't nothing, sir." Tommy ducked his head, yet another blush suffusing his smooth cheeks.

"It was something," Angela said. "You could have been sent to jail."

"We're embarrassing the young man," Richard said. "It might ruin his appetite."

"Then we shall talk of other things until he's finished eating." She smiled at Richard.

Although Richard hadn't inherited the lean elegance of his older brother, his shorter, stockier build exuded a type of earthy strength that appealed to Angela. Unlike John Champion, Richard liked to talk. Angela loved his stories. He'd come to Texas when it belonged to Mexico and fought to free her from Mexico. He'd driven wagons filled with Eastern trade goods deep into Mexico and battled Indians across the west.

More importantly, unlike his older brother, he'd been unabashedly happy to see his nephew alive. His hugs and damp eyes had secured him a place in Angela's heart forever.

"Colonel Champion served with Hood's Texas Brigade." She cut off another slice of cake. She didn't realize the tip of her tongue licked her upper lip until she looked up and caught Ransom staring at her mouth. The hot, hungry look in his eyes made her stomach sizzle.

"I got in the wrong line after the Second Battle of Manassas." Richard patted his left thigh. "I heard they were gonna issue everyone a new pair of boots. But some fool doctor whacked off my leg instead."

Tommy's face paled.

Angela dragged her gaze off Ransom and shoved a slice of cake at Richard. "Stop teasing Tommy. You're going to make him lose his meal."

"Sweet Angela." Richard grinned, deepening the lines and crinkles on his bearded face. "A crusty old man needs someone like you to remind him of his manners." He picked up his fork and looked at Tommy. "Welcome to Texas, young man. Let's eat."

Eager to defuse the tension she felt crackling between Ransom and herself, she diverted his attention back to Tommy. "Didn't you have a message for Ransom?"

Tommy looked at Ransom, as if seeking his approval.

Frustration nipped at Angela, but she kept silent. How quickly boys pushed aside women in their impatience to join the ranks of men.

"Whatever you have to say, you can say in front of all of us," Ransom said.

"I been bursting to tell you ever since I got here." Tommy's fork clattered onto his empty plate. He leaned forward and lowered his voice. "It's Captain O'Brion, sir."

His adolescent voice cracked on the "sir". Angela bit back a smile, but Tommy's excitement precluded embarrassment. "He done left the Army. He works for Mr. Seyler now."

Apprehension grazed Angela's spine.

Ransom nodded.

Angela didn't know how he controlled the temptation to pelt Tommy with questions, but she followed his lead and remained quiet. There had to be more, but rushing Tommy would likely garble the message. She forced herself to stab a piece of cake. It didn't look as appetizing as it had a few moments earlier.

"One of Mr. Darring's men came to see Mrs. Stillman," Tommy continued. "That's why Mrs. Stillman asked me to come to Texas. On accounta Mr. Seyler done paid Captain O'Brion to find Miz Angela and bring her back to Tennessee. That's the message, sir."

She'd never expected to see O'Brion again. Marrying Ransom, meeting his family, and traveling to Texas had pushed all thoughts of O'Brion out of her mind. Now Syler had hired him to find her and take her back to Tennessee.

She had spent months balancing O'Brion's annoying infatuation with her against the needs of the community. As the weeks passed, she had found it increasingly difficult to deal with his conviction they were going to marry. She realized his anger must run deep if he had resigned his commission to work for Seyler.

"You came a great distance to deliver an important message. We appreciate it." Ransom's compliment scattered her whirling thoughts.

"Well, sir. Major Champion, sir. I hafta tell you the truth, sir. I was awondering if maybe—"

"Do you want a job, son?"

"Yes, sir. Major Champion, sir. And I promise to work hard."

"I know you'll work hard, Tommy. And I could use another good man."

Tommy sat straighter in his chair, relief bringing a smile to his face. "You won't regret ahiring me, Major."

Although pleased Tommy had achieved his dream, Angela could think only of O'Brion. Deep in her bones ran the conviction he would find her. He had the tenacity of a bulldog.

"I had no idea Captain O'Brion would sink so low as to work for that horrible man." Her worry spilled into words.

"Are you thinking what I'm thinking?" Richard asked.

Relieved someone felt as she did about O'Brion's treachery, Angela looked up at Ransom's uncle. The dratted man was looking at his nephew.

Ransom nodded. "She'll be easier to protect."

"And more difficult to find," Richard said.

"Hellfire!" Angela said, frustrated at the way they ignored her. "Will you please tell me what you're talking about?"

At her outburst, both men looked at her.

"Angela, how am I going to learn better manners if you persist in saying cuss words?"

She glared at Richard. "What are you two planning?"

"You'll have to go on the trail drive," Ransom said.

She stared at him in horror. "But you said I'd be safe on the ranch. How can I be safe miles from nowhere with a herd of beeves?" And how could she leave him if he took her into more desolate country?

"I don't like it." Richard sighed. "But she's safer with you. It'll take a least a dozen men to get the beeves to Kansas. That means only one or two will remain here."

"I don't want to leave the ranch." She didn't like the way her voice quavered. She steadied it. "I feel safe here." To her surprise, she spoke the truth. Unlike Tennessee, she could see for miles in any direction. No Yankee could approach the ranch undetected.

"I'm sorry, missy." Richard reached over and took her hand. "We don't have the money to pay extra men to stay at the ranch to guard you. Most of the men will be with Ransom. It'll be safer for you to go with him."

"Money?" Angela's conscience kicked her. Her Eastern eyes, unaccustomed to the architecture of Texas, hadn't noticed the signs of neglect when she arrived. But after a few days, she'd come to see the ranch badly needed money.

"Short a little cash, that's all," Richard said. "It's nothing you need to worry about."

Angela wanted to laugh hysterically. Richard acted as if she hadn't spent the war worrying about money. She had money, but if she gave it to Ransom for the ranch, there'd be nothing left for medical school.

"It's a simple equation," Ransom said. "If we don't get the beeves to Kansas and sell them, we lose the ranch."

"Major Champion, sir. Kin I help, sir? You don't gotta pay me no wages. Just feed me."

Angela stared at Tommy. In her distress, she'd forgotten he was at the table.

"She could be your cook," Richard suggested. "Tommy could drive the wagon for her."

Cook!

"I don't know how to cook over an open fire," Angela protested.

"Drive a wagon! Cain't I hunt beeves? And have my own horse?"

"Enough!" Ransom's command cut through the duet of arguments. "Tommy, I need you to drive Mrs. Champion because I'm making you her personal bodyguard."

The scowl faded from Tommy's face. "Bodyguard?"

Ransom leaned toward the boy. "Only three of us know what Captain O'Brion looks like. You, me, and Mrs. Champion. It'd make me feel better to know you were with her on the wagon."

"Iffen you want me to guard Miz Angela, I best drive her wagon."

Ransom switched his attention to her. "You have five weeks to learn how to cook over an open fire for a dozen hungry men."

Two days later, Ransom walked out of the barn to see his wife wrapped in the arms of a stranger. The sight stopped him in the doorway. His hand eased down to caress the walnut grip of the Colt Navy revolver holstered on his hip.

The stranger held Angela at arm's length and

shook his head. "Miss Angela! I cain't believe my eyes, looking pretty as a picture! What are you doing in Texas?"

"Sergeant Grancer Harrison!"

"In the flesh, puny as it may be. But no longer a sergeant now the war's over."

"I never expected to see you again." She squeezed his upper arms as if to reassure herself of his existence.

"You're the one who had us all worried. Why the last time these eyes saw you—"

"I was white as a sheet and crumpled on the floor of the ward?"

"Scared us all to death to see you like that."

"It was my fault for not resting properly."

"I never knowed what happened to you. They sent me back to my regiment that afternoon."

Ransom didn't like watching the young man lift his wife off her feet again and twirl her around any more than he liked the affection shining in her gray eyes. His work-roughened fingers stole to his shirt pocket and Sabrina's locket. Absently, he rubbed the hard metal.

His decision to distance himself from Angela physically while he grieved for Sabrina wasn't working. Night shattered his resolution and the need to touch her conquered the guilt.

"Thank God, you survived."

He watched Angela grab the man's hand as soon as he set her down again. "You have to meet my husband."

A cocky grin lit the boyish face. "You did have a beau!"

Angela turned and saw him standing in the doorway. Ransom saw the happiness in her eyes dim.

"No," she said. "I had no beau during the war."

Ransom stepped into the midmorning sunlight, right hand extended.

Close up, the young man looked even younger, reminding Ransom they had sent boys to war. He looked into a pair of bright blue eyes, aged by having seen too much suffering. The young man shook hands with a strong and confident grip.

"Pleasure to meet Miss Angela's husband. She probably didn't tell you, but I was her thirty-eighth rejected proposal."

"No, my wife hasn't told me the names of all her suitors."

"May I introduce Sgt. Grancer Harrison? This is my husband, Major Ransom Champion."

Ransom almost smiled at the anxiety in Angela's voice. Did she think he was going to a punch her former suitor?

"Sgt. Harrison and I met in Corinth, Mississippi. After the battle of Pittsburg Landing."

"Met! You saved my life."

"You would have survived without my help."

"Now, that is where you're flat wrong, Miss Angela. I about bled to death before you came along." Harrison looked at Ransom. "Minié ball to the leg. I was lucky, it went clean through."

"And your ear," asked Angela. "Did it heal well?"

"Yes m'am, it did at that." Pulling off the hat he was wearing, the former Confederate pushed back a lock of longish, sandy colored hair.

Ransom expected Angela to faint at the sight of the mutilated shell which remained, but she examined it instead.

"Dr. Berkley did a fine job sewing it together, considering how it looked when you arrived. Can you hear with it?"

"Not at first, I couldn't. But it's working fine now."

"Excellent." Angela smiled as if she'd performed the surgery.

"May I ask a question?" Ransom winced inwardly at the sharp edge to his tone, but he had gotten their attention. "Could you explain to me why you asked my wife to marry you. If you knew she would turn you down?"

Harrison stared at him as if he'd been kicked in the head one too many times by a mule.

"Why, for good luck. Even Jethro asked Miss Angela to marry him, and he had five younguns and a wife. He said if getting Miss Angela to say 'no' meant he'd live out the war, he weren't gonna die for lack of asking."

Ransom hadn't heard of that particular ploy, but he understood the motivation.

"Oh, you should've seen her." Harrison grinned. "This little lady bullied us, but good. She were everywhere at onct. Why a man felt downright obligated to get better, just to please Miss Angela."

"Not everyone." Angela's tone held a wistful note.

"Nobody coulda saved Dozier, Miss Angela." Harrison patted Angela's shoulder. "Now don't you fret about him. He died thinking it were his wife holding him in her. arms, so he died happy."

Ransom's gut twisted at the tears sheening Angela's beautiful eyes. The battlefields had been terrifying, but the hospitals had held their own brand of horrors. He couldn't eradicate the past, but he could pull her back into the present.

"What brings you to Texas, Sgt. Harrison? I assume you weren't looking for my wife."

The idea startled the younger man. "Well, no, Major. Miss Angela's the last person I ever expected to see again."

"You serve with the Texas Brigade?"

"Oh, no, sir. Army of Tennessee, once it were put

together. Never planned to leave there, except the war done ruined everything. Didn't leave much for me and my brothers." He paused and pulled a battered hat off his head with an apologetic grin to Angela. "Seemed like a good idea to head west."

"You know anything about beeves?"

"No, sir. But a barkeep in Austin told me there was more beeves in Texas than men to find them. That I didn't need no experience, as long as I could stay in the saddle." Harrison nodded toward his horse. "Well, I kin stay in the saddle."

Ransom liked the young man's honesty. "You count yourself a friend to my wife, do you?"

The young man straightened into a military stance. "Why I'd die for Miss Angela."

Ransom smiled at Harrison's enthusiasm. "Good. That's just what I want to hear."

"Ransom! You can't mean to drag Grancer into this mess."

"He's exactly the man to drag into this mess. I need to know who I can count on."

Her lips tightened, but then she nodded.

"That's why I need you." Ransom quickly outlined the situation. "I can teach you to be a cow herder. But I can't teach you to defend my wife with your life." He stared hard into the younger man's eyes. "You have to want to do that."

He gave Harrison a chance to absorb the information. Then added, "You're welcome to take some time to think over my proposition. There's room in the annex for you to spend the night."

Harrison shook his head. "I don't need no time to think it over. Miss Angela was there when I needed her. I'd be lower than lice on a mouse if I were to refuse to help her."

Chapter 12

Angela propped her hip on the weathered wood railing that ran across the front porch of the main house. Milling confusion reigned in the yard before her. Horses bucked, beeves mooed, spurs jingled, and men cursed the morning, the beeves, and the horses.

Dust puffed around prancing hooves, snaking into the air Angela breathed.

"Did you have to pick the greenest horse in the corral?" Alex Thorne bellowed at John Shoehorn.

"He wouldn't have kicked yourn, if you knew how to control a horse."

"Are you sure you rode with General Morgan?"

"We didn't have to ride mustangs. We got to ride real horses bred in Kentuck."

The banter swirled through the dust, the unhappy whinnies, and the constant bawl of the beeves. With a command here, a gesture there, Ransom molded the chaos into order. Leadership came as natural as breathing to him and she could easily picture him leading a cavalry charge.

He had picked a beautiful cool morning to begin the cow hunt. Spring was not only in the air, but also beneath the impatient feet of the horses and men that trampled yellow clumps of squaw-weed.

Finally, the whinnies of the horses and the muffled

curses of the men quieted until only the jingle of the tin cups strung around one pony's neck was audible. One by one, the men filed through the ranch's wide gate and followed the parallel dirt tracks leading west.

Ransom stopped his horse a few feet from her.

"We'll need a medical box for the supply wagon. Would you put one together? Richard can tell you what types of injuries to expect."

She nodded. He must have seen something in her eyes. He leaned toward her.

"You'll be safe. You've got Harrison, Tommy, Francisco, and my uncle to watch over you." His right hand stroked his horse's neck. The same hand had slid down her back to cup her derriere and pull her against his arousal last night.

"The rest of the men will be finding beeves and herding them to the ranch."

His brisk tone severed her erotic memory.

"Don't worry," he reassured her. "This place will be crawling with herders."

She heard Richard's uneven step on the porch behind her.

"Don't worry about Angela," he said. "You know how ornery Long Horns can be. You worry about them, I'll worry about her."

She wished Ransom would kiss her goodbye, but she knew he wouldn't. The locket had changed their relationship. He seemed determined to keep her at arm's length during the day. But the nights, ah, the nights were a different story.

How she craved the evening hours. In bed, she could touch him, feel the strength of his muscles, and explore the wonders of his body. In bed, she could look at him all she wanted. Her blood ran warm with the memories he had created for her.

Ransom saluted his uncle. "Yes, sir." Then he wheeled his horse and rode away.

Knowing he wouldn't look back didn't keep Angela from wishing he would.

Richard draped his arm around her shoulder. She leaned into his solid strength.

"Do you think they'll find any beeves?" Lovesick fool that she was, she couldn't look away from Ransom's retreating figure.

"Why wouldn't they? There must be over a million head out there. Maybe two. All we have to do is catch some, brand them, and get them to a train."

"A million cows?" She looked at Richard. Her height put her almost level with his eyes. "Are you sure?"

He shrugged and removed his arm from her shoulder. "It's an educated guess. But too many cow herders and stockmen have reported seeing beeves all over the state. They can't all be seeing the same herd over and over again."

She scanned the horizon. "Where are they?"

"Drifting across Texas, Mexico. Up into Indian country and out to the New Mexico territory."

"I don't understand, don't they belong to anyone?"

"Some of them will be branded. Most of them were born during the war. Seems we Texans went off to fight and those ornery beeves took advantage of our absence to make more beeves."

She shot Richard an innocent look. "And none of them bothered to stop by a ranch and get branded?"

Richard grinned. "Not a one, missy."

"Which means there are a lot of Long Horns out there waiting for someone to catch."

"And get to market." Richard's eyes lit with excitement. "With the railroad in Kansas, we have an opportunity to make a profit and get this ranch back on its feet. All Ransom has to do is gather a herd and get them safely to the train at Baxter Springs. Once in Kansas, buyers from Chicago will buy whatever we provide."

When Angela heard the word "train", she realized she had been given an opportunity to leave. She would help Ransom get the herd to Kansas. Its sale would ensure the future of the ranch, and she could go to Pennsylvania with a clear conscience.

"You make it sound easy." She thought of the miles that separated Texas from Kansas. "Aren't Long Horns wild, unpredictable animals?"

"They are. And getting them to Kansas is only part of the battle. Getting them past the farmers may prove more difficult."

She made a shrewd guess. "The beeves trample their fields?"

"And carry Texas fever."

She'd heard Ransom and Richard discuss the fever.

"Can the farmers stop us from selling our beeves?"

"I guess we're going to find out."

In the distance, Ransom and his men stopped to divide a decoy herd between the three crews. The dust churned up by the horses' hooves had settled and she breathed in pure, sweet air. A tiny sigh escaped her as she watched her husband.

He had not turned around to wave.

Out of sight; out of mind.

"You love my nephew, don't you?"

Richard's quiet question jolted her into the truth. "My feelings are unimportant. He loves my sister. Or, his memory of her."

"Are you sure of that?"

"Every man who saw my sister fell in love with her." She stated a simple fact based on years of observation.

"There's a hunger in your eyes when you look at him and think no one is watching, missy."

The hills flowed across the distant landscape like huge, waterless waves. They were easier to look at than Richard. "I was fifteen years old the first time I met Ransom. It wasn't difficult to fall in love with him."

"But he didn't notice you?"

"Few males noticed me when I was fifteen." Her free hand went to the banister and her fingers curled around the smooth, warm wood. "They were too busy noticing Sabrina. Petite. Blue eyes. Golden hair. Beautiful. Men started to notice her when she was twelve. It was a long time before anyone noticed me. I was too tall, too skinny, too everything."

"Ah, the younger sibling," Richard said. "I found it to be a tedious role. And not one that I played well."

"Nor I." She refused to turn and see the pity in his eyes.

"Especially difficult when the older sister is beautiful."

"May I tell you a secret?" she asked. "One I would rather Ransom not know." The hills had swallowed the men, horses, and cows.

"I fear I know little about marriage, but is it wise to keep secrets from your husband?"

"When that secret would give him one more reason not to care? Then, yes. It's wise to keep a secret."

"I think you're wrong about his feelings, but you have my word."

Her hand tightened on the banister. Something compelled her to reveal her background to Ransom's uncle. She needed him to understand why she was unworthy of Ransom. Once she left, he could explain to Ransom how little he had lost.

"Sabrina is my stepsister. My mother was with child when she married Sabrina's father."

There was more, but the words stuck in her throat. Texas might have dulled the edges of Richard Champion's upbringing, but he belonged to a class of people who thought of themselves as the American aristocracy, inherently superior to the rest of their countrymen.

"That's not such a terrible secret." He squeezed her shoulder.

She turned, gazed into eyes so like the gentle blue of his oldest nephew's, and spilled her heart.

"My father was part Cherokee Indian."

Ransom watched a red-tailed hawk patrol the vast blue sky. It would make life a lot easier if he could hire that bird to look for O'Brion. He knew the former Federal officer would eventually find them, but his blood froze at the idea of taking Angela on a cow hunt. Long Horns were wild, unpredictable, and mean. Rounding them up on the open prairie offered them too many chances to attack herders. He'd seen a Long Horn gut a herder; it'd taken the brutality of the war to blur the memory. God knows, a gut wound led to the most hideous kind of death. Better to shoot yourself and be done with it.

Or ask your brother to shoot you.

Teddy's last moments barreled into his memory.

That was the trouble with the past. It always waited in a man's thoughts, ready to jump into the present when he least expected it. Logic told him he wouldn't have been able to keep Teddy out of the military. What Confederate regiment would turn him down? He was seventeen, healthy, and eager to fight.

Logic also told him no man could keep another safe during the hell of war. But raw experience shattered logic. His younger brother had died while under his command. Plain and simple, Ransom had failed his brother.

Would he fail Angela? Wasn't it arrogant to believe he could he protect her every moment of every day? Uncertainty gnawed at him. He didn't like leaving her at the ranch while he went on the cow hunt any more than he liked the idea of taking her on a trail drive.

If he killed O'Brion, would Seyler send another man? And another? Seyler could send all the men he wanted, but as long as he drew a breath, he'd stand between anyone Seyler sent and Angela.

Angela. Her image glided into his mind. She had taken lonely nights and woven jasmine-laced pleasure into them. She came to bed each night dressed in the threadbare nightgown she had worn in Tennessee. It had to be the most erotic piece of clothing he had ever seen. Countless washings had softened the fabric until it was a transparent gauze that molded to her body in gentle curves.

Her early hesitancy exploring his body had grown bold, although her touch remained delicate and often drove him to the brink of climax with its meandering explorations. She seemed as enthralled with his maleness as he was with her femaleness.

And when those small, cool hands closed around his shaft, he felt invincible.

At night, he found himself wanting to give her the moon.

Last night, he thought perhaps he came close.

They had been making love when he shifted their bodies, settling her on top of him. To his dismay, he nearly exploded inside her at the look of surprised wonder on her face. Her pupils widened until he thought they were going to eclipse the gray of her irises.

"Oh my."

Her husky-honey voice pushed him closer to climax.

She wiggled to fit more comfortably against him.

"That's not a good idea," he said.

"It feels like a good idea." She wiggled again.

"Sweet Jesu!" He lost it.

A few seconds later, he pulled her down against his chest. "I told you not to do that."

"I couldn't help it, it felt good."

He buried his nose in the sweet smell of her hair. "Next time, we'll go a little slower."

She snuggled into his chest. He liked the soft feel of her pressed against his body. He also liked the idea of pleasuring her.

His wayward thoughts, coupled with the gentle rock of the horse beneath his thighs, gave the memory of riding his wife a tangible life of its own. He could feel his body readying itself for the act. Thankfully, his horse stumbled and broke the erotic daydream that had grabbed his mind.

"Damn!" Only he heard the curse above the horses' thumping hooves. Only he felt the tendrils of cool morning air caress the sheen of perspiration that coated his face and neck.

If this was any indication of how he lusted after his wife, he faced a grueling six weeks with her on the trail. She would be part of his crew, but he couldn't touch her once they left the ranch. It wouldn't be fair to his men.

But it would force him to grieve Sabrina's death. Perhaps then he could put his guilt behind him and think about a future as Angela's husband.

"Bueno, Señora Champion."

"Gracias, Francisco." Angela savored the musical

cadence of the new language on her tongue. Evita and Francisco had assured her she was an apt pupil.

"Mañana, una vaca, sí?"

"Sí, una vaca mañana." A beeve instead of a fence post! Francisco must believe her skill at throwing a lariat from horseback had progressed.

"Miz Angela! Miz Angela!"

Her horse's ears flattened. Angela tightened her grip on the reins. "Easy, girl," she soothed the horse.

Tommy skidded to a halt at the corner of the ranch house. "Sorry Miz Angela." He tapped the book he held in his hand. "I done finished. Can I go practice yoking the oxen? Evita said we won't eat for another hour."

"Did you enjoy the *Iliad*?"

Tommy shrugged. "I reckon. It had lots of battles and stuff. And lots of hard names."

"Very well. We'll discuss the last chapter tomorrow morning. Will you return the book to Mr. Champion's office?"

"Yes, m'am. I gotta get my hat."

She had returned his father's hat to him the day after he arrived at the ranch. Although he tried to maintain a nonchalant attitude, his joyous expression told her how much he'd given her that day in Tennessee.

The front door banged shut behind him. Her horse shied backward three steps.

From the sounds of Tommy's happy whistle, he'd rather yoke oxen than read.

"You'd better supervise him, Francisco. I'd rather not have to write his mother and explain an ox stepped on her son."

"Sí, Señora."

Angela dismounted and led her horse into the stable. The rugged little mare danced into her stall, her feet stirring up the pungent odor of manure-tainted straw.

"You think you should be rewarded for standing around while I toss a lariat over a fence post? Why, you probably think you're well trained." She dumped a pail of oats into the trough. "Well, Francisco assures me you have a long way to go."

Humming, she began to brush the dark mahogany flanks. She had missed the routine of caring for a horse since Stockings died two years ago. Her experience with the aftermath of battle made her glad Stockings had been too old to interest either Confederate or Union soldiers.

The faint jingle of spurs silenced her humming. She turned to see a man silhouetted in the doorway. The familiar cavalry hat shadowed his face, but the late morning sun played across shoulders clad in a shirt she had sewn on Evita's treadle machine.

Giddy delight washed over her. It'd been two weeks since she'd seen Ransom. The currycomb thumped into the straw at her feet, startling her horse into an anxious whinny.

Ransom stepped deeper into the barn, close enough for her to see the hot look in his eyes. Her heart hammered blood into every cell of her body, tingling her nerves with a heightened sense of awareness. For a split second, she wondered if she were dreaming, if her hunger for him was playing tricks with her mind.

"Ransom?"

His name hung in the air between them while his long-legged stride brought him across the barn to scoop her off her feet. If it was a dream, his strong arms felt solid beneath her back and legs.

Two weeks of beard shrouded his face, reminding her of how he had looked that morning in February.

This time she knew the beard would be soft. This time his face wasn't gaunt and his eyes were less haunted.

She licked her lips.

He groaned.

The sound kicked up the heat burning in her belly.

How she had missed the taste of him. And the scent that was purely Ransom, tinged today with mesquite, horse, and perspiration.

"We don't have much time."

His words burned into her conscience. No, they didn't have much time left together. His soft breath lifted the hair beneath her left ear. Anticipation shivered along her spine while a liquid warmth pooled in her lower abdomen. She would indulge this weakness again because soon she would be alone in a future that didn't include Ransom Champion.

He set her feet on the bottom rung of the ladder leading to the loft. "Are you averse to hay lofts, madam?"

Her knees were weak with wanting him, and she wondered if they would carry her up the ladder rungs. Somehow, she turned her head and gave him a jaunty smile. "I love hay lofts, Major."

Ransom watched her climb. His hands wanted to cup the sweet derriere that rose above him as she stepped up the rungs. It was easy to picture her naked and between his thighs while he buried himself in the wonder of her warm femininity. She was lucky he hadn't taken her on the barn floor.

He followed her to the loft and pulled the ladder up after them. Satisfied they wouldn't be discovered, he turned to her.

"I need a bath, and shave, and a good meal. A gentleman should clean up before doing what I want to do."

"And a lady would probably insist."

His heart sank to his toes. He'd thought about this moment for the past two weeks.

"But you're a cow herder and I'm a trail cook. We don't need to follow the rules."

She squeaked when he dived across the few feet that separated them. He pulled her down into sweet smelling hay, taking the brunt of the fall with his body, then rolled her beneath him. She tasted of honey and biscuits.

Every inch of his body ached for her. Beneath him, Angela inhaled, the action pushing her breasts against the damp fabric of her white blouse. With a quick jerk, he untied her blouse and then lowered his head to taste the salty dew that glistened on the skin exposed by the vee of her shirt.

While his tongue licked her skin, he slid his hand beneath her skirt. Fabric barred him. He pulled back to look and realized her skirt was really two loose pants legs sewn together. If he hadn't been so entranced with her derriere when she went up the ladder, he probably would've noticed.

"What in blue blazes are you wearing?"

"Hmmmmmm?" Dazed gray eyes stared at him.

He grabbed a handful of fabric. "This!"

"My skirt?" She blinked. A degree of clarity returned to her eyes.

"I've never seen a skirt like this." But he'd heard about women who rejected female attire. "Are you one of those bloomer women who want to wear men's clothing?" Suspicion edged out passion for the moment. What did he know about the woman he had married for life?

"Men's clothing? Isn't that against the law?"

He scowled. "Only in some towns."

"Evita and I weren't making men's clothes. We sewed two narrow skirts together."

A thankful sigh echoed in his brain. Her desire to attend medical school didn't make her eager to wear men's clothes. Then he realized he had yet to discover the reason for the odd skirt. "Why?"

"Richard has no sidesaddles. How else could I ride a horse?"

"That makes sense." He dropped the handful of cotton calico. His questions answered, desire flared back to life. "Forget about the skirt, how do I get to what I want?"

She took his hand and placed it on her waist. "There's a button, here."

He growled and unbuttoned the waistband, pulling her skirt and pantaloons down to her knees.

Her fingers busied themselves with the buttons on his shirt.

He could tell there wasn't going to be anything slow about this coupling. They were both too hungry. He pushed the loosened neck of her blouse off her shoulders and freed her breasts. Nuzzling, sucking, nibbling and coaxing, he soon had one nipple erect. Satisfied, he kissed his way into the valley toward the other breast.

He felt Angela tugging on his trousers. "In a hurry?" he murmured against her breast.

Her hand fondled his shaft. "And you're not?"

He closed his eyes, praying he wouldn't embarrass himself. To his great relief, she guided him into the warm opening. Their coupling was quick, sweaty, powerfully passionate.

And somehow in her clutching and twisting of his shirt, Sabrina's locket fell out of his pocket. He watched its spiraling, glittery tumble through the air.

It hit Angela's left nipple and slid to rest in the valley between her breasts.

Soul-wrenching guilt seared him.

"Ah, Sabrina." He begged forgiveness as he shoved himself one last time deep inside Angela.

She flinched at her sister's name. If he hadn't been staring at her, he would've missed it. He wanted to bite his tongue off, because he'd promised himself not to say Sabrina's name aloud while he made love to her sister.

He couldn't change the past.

Sabrina was dead.

Angela was his wife.

And a man couldn't touch a memory.

It was an hour before he got his bath, shave, and a good meal.

His uncle joined him in the kitchen while he ate.

"Another man showed up. He's been helping Francisco with the horses. Says he served with you in the war. Name of Creighton, Sawyer Creighton."

Of all the men Ransom had invited to join him in Texas after the war, Sawyer Creighton was the last one he expected to see. Sawyer had bored his fellow soldiers with rapturous descriptions of the small plantation he had carved out of the wilds of Mississippi. What was he doing in Texas?

Ransom found the lean ex-soldier in the annex. "Sawyer! Welcome to Texas."

"If you ain't a sight for sore eyes! We heard you were dead."

"I guess I'm a hard man to kill even for the Yankees." His grin made his mouth ache. He grabbed Sawyer's hand, shook it and then pulled him into a quick hug.

The two years since he'd seen Sawyer had taken a toll on the older man, deepening the creases in his face. Although he grinned his pleasure at seeing Ransom, sadness lingered in his eyes.

"Damn, Major!" Sawyer slapped Ransom on the back. "You're alive."

"No more rank, Sawyer. We're civilians now. Tell me, how's that family of yours?"

His question dimmed the other man's eyes. "They didn't make it through the winter, sir. They were wore down by hunger. A fever took 'em, one by one."

Fresh, unhealed pain lanced Sawyer's voice. Ransom was well-acquainted with that side of war. Little or poor food led to death off the battlefield as easily as a minié ball did on the battlefield.

"The place had gone to ruin while I was gone. What with taxes I couldn't pay, no field hands to help, and Margaret and the younguns gone." Sawyer shrugged.

"I know words don't mean much right now," Ransom said. "But I'm sorry."

Sawyer swallowed, then nodded his thanks.

Ransom decided a change of subject might help his friend. "So tell me, what brings you to Texas?"

A small smile touched Sawyer's mouth. "Where else would a man go? I remembered all your talk about Texas needing good men after the war. I hoped your uncle would have a soft spot for a worn-out cavalry-man who served with his nephew. Didn't once think you'd be here in the flesh."

"You know you have a job if you want one, Sawyer. I never rode with a finer man."

"Well, don't be making your promises too fast. I don't know one fool thing about beeves, I grew cotton. But I learned to ride about the time I learned to walk. And I got to thinking that chasing after cows probably wasn't much different than chasing after Yankees."

Ransom laughed, glad to have his friend beside him again. Not only would he have another cow herder, he'd also have a dependable man to help him protect Angela. "I'll let you in on a little secret. Chasing beeves is easier. They aren't as ornery! Now, let's go up to the house and get a cup of coffee. We got two years to catch up on."

Chapter 13

Angela hung onto the rain-slicked branches of a juniper tree as she vomited. In between heaves, she inhaled the pungent odor of the wet juniper, a smell she had come to despise. At last, the spasms stopped and she rinsed her mouth with water from the canteen.

Her free hand crept to her stomach. She could neither see nor feel the baby who caused her morning nausea.

After recapping the canteen, she wiped her mouth. Off to her right the Long Horns grazed their way north, oblivious to the drizzling rain. She couldn't believe she had tied her future to such flighty creatures. At first, the stampedes had frightened her, but the herd spooked at everything and the thundering roar of their departure became as much a part of the trail drive as the constant need to feed the men.

She massaged her aching back. Thirty miserable days on the trail preparing a monotonous menu of black coffee, sourdough biscuits, beans, meat and gravy. Day after day, she cooked breakfast in the dark, woke the men, fed them, cleaned up after they left, loaded the wagon, traveled a few miles, unloaded the wagon, and then prepared another meal. A repetitious process of pure drudgery with no end in sight.

And she seldom saw Ransom. If he wasn't scouting the trail ahead for good grazing, river crossings or Indians, he was rounding up stray beeves or checking on the men and horses. When he did stop by the wagon to eat or sleep, he didn't linger.

She trudged back to the camp site.

To her great relief, Tommy had broken camp.

"Feelin' better?" He peered at her over the broad back of the harnessed oxen.

"I'll survive." She wondered if he'd figured out the real reason she threw up every morning.

"Walking or riding?"

"Walking, for now."

With a nod, he climbed into the driver's seat. He flicked the whip, snapping the thin leather strip over the lead ox's ears. With a grunt, the two large beasts moved forward.

Angela fell into step beside the right front wheel. The discomfort of the hard wooden wagon seat held as much attraction as stomping through mud. Fatigue would send her onto the wagon seat later, but now she preferred to walk. Silently, she blessed Francisco who'd insisted they bring several pairs of comfortable, thick-soled moccasins on the drive.

"I wuz wondering, do you think if I asked the Major he might let me ride herd one day?"

Angela swallowed her frustration. Tommy asked her the same question a dozen times a day; her answer had yet to vary.

"You'll have to ask him."

"I reckon I'd even ride drag without complaining."

Her frustration softened.

"Drag" was the dirtiest position on the drive. The herder who rode it followed the herd and had to contend with stragglers as well as the dust kicked up by the herd. Harrison's inexperience had landed him one of the drag rider positions, but Angela doubted Ransom would let Grancer drive the wagon while Tommy played cow herder.

"Ask him. All he can do is say no." She shaded her eyes to better see the rider headed toward them. A momentary flare of hope evaporated; it .was Sergio.

"Buenos días, señora." Sergio eased his horse into a walk, beside her.

"Buenos días, señor.¿Cómo está usted?" She had asked Sergio to continue her Spanish lessons.

"Bien, gracias. Hoy, llegaremos un rio, el Rio Rojo. ¿Comprende?"

"Sí, el Rio Rojo." Angela chose a question from her small, but growing Spanish vocabulary. "¿Cuánto tiempo?"

Sergio shrugged his shoulders, "Esta tarde."

This afternoon. They wouldn't try to cross today.

"Gracias, Sergio. Hasta luego."

Sergio touched the brim of his sombrero before turning his horse and riding back to the herd.

"We'll reach the Red River this afternoon," she said.

"Too late to cross?" Tommy asked.

"If we're lucky, the Major will hold the herd a few miles from the river and cross tomorrow morning."

"Do you reckon it'll be as bad as the Brazos?"

"Good Lord, I hope not." She shuddered at the memory. The river crossing had cost them several days because the wagon flooded on its way across. The search for soggy food supplies and utensils had taken the herders most of the afternoon.

Within an hour of putting the wagon back together, the beeves stampeded. It had taken the weary cow herders a night and a day to get them back on the trail.

No, they didn't need another Brazos crossing. Her

right hand strayed to lightly rub her stomach. With a babe in her womb, she wanted to reach Baxter Springs as soon as possible.

As she predicted, Ransom halted everyone several miles south of the river. Angela and Tommy were up before dawn the next morning, coaxing the dormant embers of the fire back to life for warmth and cooking.

Malachi brought the remuda close to the wagon before the sun crested the horizon.

"Horses. Horses." His gravely, singsong voice coupled with the stamping hooves of the horses and oxen brought the men from their makeshift beds. The temperature had dropped during the night and dawn brought a cold morning kissed by a freshening breeze that promised more wind as the day grew older.

As Tommy helped Malachi stretch the ropes of the corral, lariats whistled through the air in search of a particular horse.

"Hey Judd, you gonna trust your carcass in the river on that crock head?"

"He may be dumb, but he's the best swimmer I got."

"That ain't saying much considering none of your string likes water."

Lariats sang alongside good humored banter while the frisky horses played keep away. Tossing their heads, they let the strengthening breeze ruffle their manes, but they couldn't dodge the ropes forever. One by one each man captured his swimmer. When all the herders had a horse, Malachi led the remaining horses back towards the main herd.

"If this is June in Texas, I may have to rethink the idea of making Texas my home," Sawyer said as he poured himself a cup of coffee. The former cavalryman had wrapped himself in a worn greatcoat that might have once been gray.

"Wait'll December." Alex Thorne claimed to be a native Texan. "And a blue Norther. Now that's cold."

"Cold is Tennessee in November and no campfire." John Shoehorn shot a stream of tobacco juice at the ground. "The Major didn't want to give away our position to the feds. That was the coldest I ever been."

"Well, you ain't been in the Red River on a windy June day."

Shoehorn shoved his hat on his head before answering Thorne. "I ain't planning to, either. I had my fill of jumping off my horse when we crossed the Brazos."

Men chuckled as they drifted toward the fire. With the prospect of a wet, cold day facing them, they were reluctant to leave the fire's warmth.

While Angela awaited instructions as to where to cross, she and Tommy secured everything in the wagon. She kept the coffee pot on the fire and left several battered tin cups on the side of the wagon.

It was midmorning before Ransom and Sergio returned to camp. Angela met them with cups of coffee.

"Did you find a good crossing?" Ransom asked Sergio. He accepted a cup with the barest nod of gratitude. A perpetual frown seemed to have lodged itself on his face whenever he was around her.

"Maybe, about ten miles down el rio. But the water, Señor Major. She is high everywhere."

"My feelings, exactly. I found a possible crossing about three miles up the river. They can start the herd that way, but we better take another look at it." He sipped his coffee. When he realized it wasn't too hot, he gulped down half the cup.

Finally, he looked at her. She kept her expression serene, hiding any hint of her joy at being near him.

"Angela, take the wagon north, stay above the herd and fill the water kegs as soon as you can. I'll send some men to help you reload them." The fire sputtered as Ransom tossed the half a cup of coffee into it. "Let's ride, Sergio. I want to get this herd across today."

Ransom didn't get his wish.

Everything went well in the beginning. More than twelve hundred cattle followed the two lead horses and four oxen into the river, but the last one hundred head balked at the river's edge and refused to swim.

Twenty-four hours later, he and Sergio sat on their horses at the edge of the river. Four attempts to cross the remaining recalcitrant Long Horns had failed.

"Do you have any tricks left in that bag of yours, Sergio? Or do we leave these beeves in Texas?"

"¿Por los indios?" His question was followed by a wide grin that crinkled a face as weathered by the elements as the rocks beside the river.

Ransom grinned back at the Mexican. "The Indians would like that, wouldn't they?"

The two men gazed at the beeves who remained on the wrong side of the river.

"I have one more trick, Señor Major. I do not like to cross the beeves this way, but . . ." his shrug told the story. They were running out of options.

"What do you suggest?"

"To pen each beeve between two riders and cross el rio."

"An escort. Slow but effective." Ransom thought

about the five foot tip to tip span of the beeves' horns. "And dangerous."

He weighed his options. Every beeve he got to Baxter Springs meant money. And money meant keeping the ranch. "Let's try it."

As Ransom forced the first reluctant Long Horn into the river, he wondered what made him place his future on the back of such a contrary creature. With a disgruntled bawl, the beeve went into the water swinging pointed horns that could gore the life out of a man.

He dove off his horse three times that morning. Like a fool, he removed his wet shirt for several hours and got a painful sunburn.

By the time he returned to camp for something to eat, every move reminded him of his stupidity. Angela must have seen him wince when he dismounted. She met him at the edge of the campfire.

"I have a salve for sunburn that Evita gave me. Shall I rub some on your back?"

"No!" His shirt scratched across his back like a thousand stinging nettles, but her hesitant offer brought a scorching image to his mind.

His harsh refusal knocked her backward a step. Her tentative smile crumpled as if he'd hit her.

Her reactions clawed at his soul. He wished he could answer again, but it was too late to erase the injured look on her lovely face.

But he had to try. "I meant, thank you for the offer."

Her gray eyes darkened to black in the twilight. He wanted to lean closer and inhale the scent of her. Brush his lips across her brow.

"You're welcome." Her banal words hung in the air between them.

His horse shook his head. The jingling bridle sent her gaze skittering toward the ground.

"I'll be fine," he said. "Nothing a little sleep and food won't cure."

The image of her fingers sliding over his hot skin caused him more problems than the sunburn. He'd rather chase Long Horns all night than submit to her healing touch. Because if she were to touch him, he might explode with need.

That's when he realized his well-conceived plan had failed.

The trail drive offered no furlough from desire. Enforced chastity hadn't cleansed his soul of guilt over his lust for Angela. Rather than come to terms with Sabrina's death and put her in the past, he'd spent his days craving Angela while his guilt escalated.

No. He couldn't afford to let Angela touch him.

With slow care, he gingerly stretched his sunburned body on the ground near the fire. Food could wait, he thought as he let exhaustion claim him.

Ransom joined Sawyer the next evening to watch the sun set. It wasn't as spectacular as usual; the dimming rays had trouble penetrating the clouds mounded in the sky.

With the Red River behind them, they had entered Indian country with a herd of unpredictable Long Horns, exhausted men and tired horses. There were also two other droves of cattle within a few miles. The potential for disaster hummed in the air along with the promise of rain. If Ransom could feel it, he knew the beeves could.

"It's going to be a long night." His gaze shifted from the sky to the restless herd grazing before them.

Sawyer expelled a stream of tobacco. It hit the dry ground with a wallop. "A long night of singing or swearing."

"Probably a little of both. Here's hoping it's mostly singing." Ransom tapped the brim of his hat as he urged his horse forward.

He spent the evening hours crooning every song he knew to the jumpy beeves. Around midnight, strong winds and lightning ushered a hard storm across the prairie. More than a thousand head milled in a bawling mass illuminated by distant lightning. Then a jagged bolt snaked to the ground a mile away.

The beeves stampeded.

"Double damn your worthless hides!" Ransom kicked his horse into a run alongside the dark, roiling mass. Loosening his hold on the reins, he let his horse have his head. There was an element of sheer madness in their race to the front of the herd, but turning the lead beeves was the only way to stop the stampede.

The ground rumbled beneath the pounding hooves. The odor of mass panic billowed off the beeves while the friction of so many bodies rubbing together singed the air. Weird blue flashes quivered at the tips of their long horns, burnt into insignificance when nearby lightning flashed.

Rain lashed Ransom's face, streamed off his hat and found every possible crevice in his oilskin coat. Fear rode beside him, filling the darkness with the specter of death. He clung to the mustang, his survival tied to the agility of an animal who ran on instinct in the midnight ink, as blinded as his rider by sudden flashes of lightning. One false step, one unexpected prairie dog hole, one washed out gully and they would fall, probably never to rise again, trampled by thousands of pounds of Texas beeve.

But if they didn't follow the beeves, he could lose the whole herd.

He broke free of the herd. Pulling his Navy Colt from its holster, he shot at the raindrops.

"Turn, you mangy sons of bitches!" He shouted into the wind. "Turn!"

It took three attempts to turn the main herd. By then, the storm had moved through the area. When the sun rose, it lit a bright, clear morning.

Ransom counted half the herd with six herders. Now they had to round up the missing beeves and account for all the men.

As they trailed back the way they had run, the herd gained numbers, but many of the beeves and men who joined them belonged to the two other droves that had been camped nearby.

The sun had reached its zenith by the time they drifted the beeves back to where the stampede started. Tired, hungry and thirsty, Ransom was glad to see the supply wagon. Angela met him with a plateful of stew and a tin cup full of strong black coffee.

His stomach growled at the enticing smells.

When she handed him the plate, their fingers brushed. In that split-second, he wanted to grab her, hug her close, and feel the life thrumming through their bodies. Strange, how he felt more in tune with life after each encounter with death.

"Everyone except Grancer, Sergio and Alex is accounted for." Her calm assessment bridled his maudlin thoughts. "Malachi and the other wranglers found the horses, but the remudas are all mixed up. They're sorting them out now. Tommy brought a dozen horses back with him. They're tired, but not as tired as the ones you rode all night."

Ransom swallowed a mouthful of stew. "Pack me some jerky and biscuits. And fill several extra canteens. When we find the men, they'll be hungry and thirsty."

She offered him the cup of coffee. He took a swig and looked around the camp for Sawyer.

"Sawyer? You ready to ride?"

"Just like the old days, Major. Except we got a mighty fine cook this time." Sawyer grinned at Angela. "I saw my gray and your black in that group Tommy brought in. I'll saddle 'em."

Ransom scraped his plate clean and handed it to Angela. "Be sure the men I send back for fresh mounts get food and extra water."

The sun rode low in the afternoon sky by the time Ransom and Sawyer saw the trailing dust of the last group of strays. As they rode closer, the smell of beeves, dung and dust rode a freshening breeze that heralded the arrival of evening. Human voices, urging the beeves back the way they'd run, mingled with the low bawls of tired beeves.

Sergio saw the rescuers first. Spurring his horse into a canter, he pulled his sombrero off his head and waved it in the air.

"I knew you would find us, Señor Major." His smile flashed white in his dark face.

"It looks like you picked up a little help along the way." Ransom nodded toward the two Indians who rode on the far side of the herd.

"Sí, los indios found us this morning. They offered to guide us to camp. I promised them una vaca."

"They would have gotten one or two, anyway," Ransom said.

"What tribe are they?" Sawyer asked.

Ransom studied the flat, circular hats the Indians wore. "Seminole?" he guessed, glancing toward Sergio.

The Mexican nodded. "Sí, Seminole."

"Might as well make them work for the beeve." Ransom dug into his saddlebag. "I expect y'all are hungry."

Sergio grinned and patted his flat abdomen. "My stomach, Señor Major, it rubs my backbone."

"Then you won't complain because all I have is jerky and and some day-old biscuits."

"Ah, but they are Señora Champion's day-old biscuits."

Sergio was right. Even stale, Angela's biscuits were better than any Ransom had eaten during the war. They were all fortunate to have Angela as their cook.

Ransom handed Sergio a packet of food and a canteen of water. "Sawyer, will you take some food to those other men? And don't forget to offer some to the Indians; I'd prefer to keep them friendly."

Sawyer tapped his hat and rode toward the herd. Ransom watched him, trying to ignore the fatigue seeping into every cell of his body. Beside him, Sergio devoured the biscuits and jerky. Twenty years separated the two men, but mutual respect bridged the age gap. Everything Ransom knew about beeves, Sergio had taught him.

While Sergio ate, Ransom brought the older man up to date.

"They should have most of the beeves and horses sorted by the time we return. If those strays we picked up near the south Canadian are still with our herd, we can give one of those to the Indians."

Dusk had deepened to dark when they saw the light of the campfire. Sawyer rode ahead and returned with several herders. The herd was bedded down a mile to the north, and Ransom let fresher men take this last group of runaways to the main herd. The Indians, promising to return in the morning for their beeve, disappeared into the night.

Ransom watched them go and wondered if he should have insisted they stay the night. At the camp, he could keep an eye on them. Now he had to worry if they'd return tomorrow with a larger party and demand more beeves. Or, worse, start a stampede, help round up lost beeves, and expect a reward.

Chapter 14

Angela opened her eyes to the damp scent of an early dawn, John Shoehorn's snores, and two Indians sitting cross-legged next to the embers of last night's fire. Excitement mingled with apprehension. She had never met a full-blooded Indian.

Sabrina's taunting tales kept her in her bedroll for a few indecisive moments. The two men didn't appear ready to scalp her. She squinted her eyes, searching their attire for a tomahawk. Although both Indians sported knives sheathed at their waist, and the younger one had a rifle lying at his feet, neither seemed to have a tomahawk.

A little sigh of relief whooshed out.

The sound caused the older Indian to look at her. Eyes set in a face contoured by wind, sun, and age studied her. High cheekbones bracketed a proud nose. Straight black hair with the shiny gloss of a crow's wing suffered the indignity of graying streaks.

She wondered if her father's face had held some of these characteristics. Her fingers slipped up to touch her own straight black hair. A gift from her father's Indian heritage.

"Buenos dias, señorita." The gravely voice gave a different lilt to the Spanish.

"You speak Spanish? I mean, ¿habla español?"

"I have memory of the español, sí. And some English."

She scrambled out of her bedroll. "Excuse me for a moment?" For some reason, she didn't want to formally meet her first Indian before performing her morning ablutions.

The Indian nodded.

Ten minutes later, face freshly washed, hair brushed and clipped back, she returned to the campsite. Unsure of how to greet an Indian, she smiled at the guests.

The older Indian pointed to himself. "Ho-ko-lin-shee." Then he pointed at the younger man seated beside him. "E-cho-ho-low-chee."

Angela nodded. She tapped her chest. "Señora Champion. Would you like some breakfast?" She pantomimed scooping up food, putting it in her mouth and chewing it.

With a regal nod, Ho-ko-lin-shee accepted her offer.

He didn't speak again until she had rolled out a tray full of biscuits. She liked the way the pungent smell of sourdough wove its way through the damp morning air.

"Es india."

Her hands stilled in their task. Sabrina may have harped on Angela's Indian blood, but she never told anyone because she feared rejection from local society.

Angela looked at the mounds of sleeping men, their snores punctuated by the distant "yip yip" of Malachi's singsong call to the horses. No one appeared awake. She didn't want anyone else to hear her whispered admission.

"Esta roja." She sliced her flour-bedecked hand across the lower portion of her body. Then she motioned upward across the greater part of her body, stopping to touch her heart. "Esta blanca."

"Ah. La corazón."

She saw sadness and understanding in the molasses-dark eyes. Shame gnawed at her conscience. She had spent her life denying her father's heritage. Despite Sabrina's lurid tales about Indian cruelty, Angela found herself drawn to Ho-ko-lin-shee. For a fleeting moment, she wished she wasn't on a trail drive and could spend time with a man who could introduce her to her father's culture.

"Horses. Horses." Malachi's gravely voice heralded his arrival with the remuda. Men stirred, yawning and grumbling themselves into wakefulness.

To Angela's relief, the herders captured Ho-ko-lin-shee's attention. She busied herself with breakfast preparations, eager to get the men fed and on their horses. As she hoped, the herders motioned for the Indians to join them when they finished eating.

When Ho-ko-lin-shee stood and looked at her, Angela's mouth went dry. Would he refer to her Indian blood, again?

"Gracias." He motioned toward the food. "Es muy bueno."

Angela couldn't stop the sweet smile of relief. As the Indians rode away, someone came to stand beside her and watch them.

From the tingle of awareness that caressed her neck, Angela knew it was Ransom. "That went well."

He grunted.

"I've heard so many stories about Indians." She wiped her hands on her apron and wondered if her voice sounded as giddy to Ransom as it did to her. Striving for a conversational tone, she continued. "I didn't know what to expect, but I'm glad breakfast and a beeve mollified them."

"It didn't."

"What do you mean?" She seized handfuls of cotton apron, hoping Ransom didn't hear the panic in her voice.

"We'll see them again." He watched the Indians guide their beeve away from the herd. "They'll haunt the edge of the herd, ready to help us round them up after the next stampede. Then we'll reward their work with another beeve."

"How long will it take us to cross Indian country?"

"Depends." His blue-green gaze settled on her.

"On what?" Fear he would discover her Indian blood evaporated beneath the hot and hungry look in his eyes. Memories of his body entwined with hers flared to life. She wanted to press her face into his chest and bury her nose in the familiar scent of leather, sun and Ransom. The bawl of the beeves, whinnies of the horses, and Tommy's whistling faded into silence as she stared into his eyes.

"Beeves, rivers, weather, and now, Indians."

He lifted his hand and brushed at her cheek. She closed her eyes and leaned toward him, savoring the butterfly touch on her skin. Then it was gone.

"Got any coffee left?"

"Ask Tommy." She heard the jangle of his spurs as he walked away.

Beeves. Rivers. Weather. Indians.

For the next two weeks, it seemed as if these forces contrived to ensure the trail drive failed. Frequent thunderstorms stampeded the beeves while the accompanying rains made the fordable creeks too deep for anything but swimming the beeves across a river.

Angela hated swimming as much as the reluctant beeves whose feet often got trapped in the treacherous bottoms of the deceptively smooth flowing rivers. To free a beeve's hooves, the herder had to scoop out the sand around the Long Horn's legs and tie them together so an ox or horse could drag the protesting animal from the river.

The process meant flailing horns, panicked beeves, and fickle currents. It also meant frequent injuries. When Angela heard the word "swimming," she put her diary on the wagon seat alongside her medical box. The diary contained the only paper she had on which to record the injuries, her choice of treatment, and the results. It would go with her to medical college.

"How does a bath sound?" Ransom leaned his arm on the saddle horn and looked down at Angela. With the Arkansas River running too high to cross, they'd been stranded for a few days.

His horse's ears swiveled forward as if he were as anxious for Angela's answer as his rider. The smaller horse he led shook its head.

She stood before a makeshift table lined with five apple pies. Four of them were ready to be cooked, the fifth awaited its top crust. Only a woman would think to bring cinnamon along on a trail drive. He wondered how many miles the smell of apple pie traveled and how many herders it would lure to their campsite.

"Like heaven," she said. "But I can't." Regret colored her answer. She shoved moist tendrils of hair out of her eyes with the back of her floured hand. Flour now dusted her damp forehead. A fly landed on the apple pie filling she had not yet covered with a crust. She shooed it away.

"Tommy made an oven he claims will cook pies," she smiled at Tommy who tended a box-like contraption near the campfire. "And Ho-ko-lin-shee traded me the apples for some coffee beans. So, we're baking pies."

Slowly, she peeled and folded a top crust off the table top. The horse he brought for her to ride swished its tail.

"You've become friendly with that Indian."

The crust split. "Hellfire!" She swore softly, dabbing her finger in a cup of water before mending the dough.

He wondered if she was going to answer his implied question.

"There," she said, patting the mended dough. She lifted the folded crust up and settled it onto the apple filling. "He's a healer among his people." She smoothed the crust over the filling and pinched the edges together. "And he's teaching me about local herbs."

Ransom didn't like Indians because they usually meant trouble for a stock man, but he didn't want to argue right now. "I found a quiet place near the river where you can wash clothes and bathe."

"I'd love to have a bath and the chance to wash some clothes, but . . ." An underlying tension hummed through her tone as if she worried about something other than apple pies.

Ransom took the decision out of her hands. "Tommy, can you handle the pie baking?"

"Yes, sir. Major."

"Then I see no reason for you to forgo your bath, madam."

Angela lingered. "Are you sure you won't mind if I leave? You remember how to test them for doneness?"

"Miz Angela, I can handle the pies."

"Of course, you can," Angela agreed. "Pie baking isn't difficult for someone who built an oven."

Tommy grinned at her compliment.

Ransom grinned, too. Apple pies, beeves, stampedes, high rivers, and Indians evaporated as he watched Angela untie her apron and hurry around the wagon. Within moments she returned with a bundle of clothes.

"Tommy, will you string a line for me between the wagon and that tree?" She tied the bundle to her saddle with a leather tie. "I'll need somewhere to dry these clothes when we return."

Ransom snuggled his hat onto his head, using the brim to shadow his face and hide his anticipation, although he doubted Tommy was old enough to realize why a smile tweaked at his mouth.

They were about a mile from the secluded natural pool he'd discovered while scouting for a crossing. Spurring his horse into a canter, he led her to it.

She followed him to the pool's edge, nudging her horse until they were standing side by side. Oak, willow, and maple trees shaded the cool, beckoning silver of a small pool while the warm, sweet smell of early summer perfumed the air.

"It looks as if a giant hand reached down and scooped the pool right out of the hill."

Her husky voice, tinged with awe, slid over him like a dollop of thick honey. He hadn't let her voice reach out and grab his gut for weeks, but for the next few hours he wasn't going to ignore his wife's sexuality.

She looked at him, a smile on her lips and happiness shining in her ebony-lashed eyes. Those eyes crowded out sanity, leaving only the desire to bed her. He wanted to lean over and kiss her, but the pool had given him other, satisfying plans for the afternoon. Plans that didn't include the distraction of laundry or fretful horses.

"Why don't you get your clothes washed while I see to the horses?"

"What I want to do is jump in the water."

He started to agree, but the blush tinging her cheeks kept him silent. Tension hummed in the air along with the drone of insects. He figured her thoughts now traveled the same path as his.

She patted the bundle tied to her saddle. "I should wash our clothes first."

The moment evaporated, but he knew it would return. Soon.

She slid off her horse.

He dismounted and led the horses to the water's edge for a drink. With the bundle of clothes clutched to her chest, Angela explored the large boulders that jutted above one end of the pool.

"This is perfect," she said.

Almost perfect, he thought. You lying on the shore nude would be perfect.

He led the horses into some grassy shade, loosened their cinches, removed their bridles and hobbled them. One final pat on their necks, and he left them to enjoy an afternoon of rest.

Angela knelt beside the pool, soiled clothes puddled at her side while she looked at the water.

"Forget the soap?" he asked as he joined her.

"No." She held up a bar. "But I wonder if I should bathe first and then do the clothes. They're dusty enough to turn the pool muddy."

He pushed away the image of her bathing. Washing the clothes took priority. They needed to return to camp with a bundle of wet clothes unless he wanted to depress the men's morale lower than stampedes, swimmings, and Indians had already done.

"Don't worry, you can wash the clothes, first. The pool appears to be fed by an underwater spring." He pointed beyond the boulder. "If you look over there, you can see where the overflow runs out. It goes into the creek which feeds into the river. If you wash here, the dirty water will flow into the creek, not the pool."

"Then, I'll wash first." She plunged one of his shirts into the water and rubbed it with a bar of soap she had taken from the wagon. The familiar scent of jasmine filled Ransom's nostrils. He wondered how much would remain on the shirt after it was rinsed and dried in the sun. The men might tease him, but he wouldn't mind carrying her scent with him while he trailed beeves.

"It's not deep on this side." He squatted next to her and plucked a blade of grass. "You should be able to sit as if you're in a large bath tub."

He pulled the blade through his callused fingers. The brim of her hat hid her downcast eyes, but he could see the tension in her hands that scrubbed his poor shirt so energetically it would soon be shredded. Good, her thoughts were headed in the same direction as his. He decided to back off and let her wash the clothes.

"Mind if I take a nap?"

Did her eyes hold disappointment when she glanced at him? "Sounds like a good idea." She plunged his shirt into the water and sloshed it around.

Ransom sprawled on a sun-warmed rock overlooking her washing area, settled his hat almost to the bridge of his nose, and pretended to nod off. But the hat was not so low on his brow as to interfere with a view of Angela, who peeked his way as she wrung out his shirt and draped it over a boulder.

His heart smiled, but he didn't let it reach his mouth.

* * *

Perspiration seeped between Angela's breasts. She wrung out Ransom's trousers, her fingers aching from the afternoon's work. Her whole body ached from bending over the water's edge and washing clothes. Standing, she stretched her muscles, rubbed her back, and stared at the pool. It was her turn in the water.

The sweet cry of a meadowlark pierced the summer afternoon. Behind her, she could hear the even rhythm of Ransom's sleep. She turned to look at him; knowing it was better he nap while she bathed, but wanting him with an intensity that surprised her. With Baxter Springs only days away, there would be no other opportunity to make love.

Her fingers trembled as she took off her hat, knife sheath, and knee-high moccasins. She undressed as quietly as possible, but awareness tingled up her back. She had the uncanny impression that Ransom, for all his relaxed hat-over-his-eyes sprawl, watched her. Fear of discovery warred with desire.

And how would she explain leaving this veritable Garden of Eden without taking a bath?

Sucking in her breath, she unfastened the button to her skirt and eased it down. Now she stood by the pool clad in the serviceable white cotton camisole and drawers she had sewn on Evita's wonderful Singer sewing machine.

She slid the camisole over her head and then stepped out of her drawers. A tiny afternoon breeze fondled her body while the sun warmed her. She felt sinfully wanton standing nude beside a pool in the mid-afternoon sun. Ransom wasn't snoring anymore. She wasn't sure he was breathing.

With a grin, she grabbed the soap and waded into the pool. A reckless mood seized her. She wanted

Ransom to wake up. She wanted him to join her in the pool. She wanted this one last memory.

Cool liquid flowed over her legs. She didn't look behind her, but imagined a trail of muddy water followed as layers of dust and sweat washed off her body. A few feet from the bank, she sat down and closed her eyes to better enjoy the caress of each water droplet. Never had she expected to experience such sensual ecstasy over a bath.

She took a breath of sun-scented air, leaned backward and dunked her head. It wasn't until she lathered her hair that she realized she couldn't set the soap down without losing it. Eyes scrunched closed to keep the suds out of them, she pondered the situation. It was her last bar of jasmine soap.

"I can either wash your hair or hold the soap."

A delicious, startled thrill ran up her spine. "I thought you were sleeping." *But hoped you were awake.*

"I was."

"I'll hold the soap," she said and leaned toward his voice. A moment's hesitation and then he touched her head. His fingers threaded into her soapy hair and she sank into their strength.

It felt so good, she wanted to purr. Too soon he was finished and his hands were gone.

"Shall I hold the soap while you rinse?"

She relinquished the soap, then dunked her head to rinse her hair. If anyone from Gallatin could see her, they would be scandalized beyond belief. *She* should be scandalized beyond belief.

But she wasn't. She liked sitting naked in a pool with cool water streaming off her hair and shoulders and flowing in a dozen tiny rivulets down her body. She liked knowing Ransom sat in the water behind her. Nude.

Another delightful shiver ran across her spine and settled in her abdomen.

"You look like a water goddess."

His words mingled with the water running off her hair. She smiled, pushed the hair off her forehead, and opened her eyes.

She looked over her shoulder at her husband. The hungry look in his eyes melted her bones. Proof of his desire waited for her, visible below the surface of the water.

"I've decided I'd rather be a wash cloth than a soap holder." He grabbed her wrist and pulled her to him, sliding her slick, wet body over his.

Weeks of enforced separation evaporated. Every cell in her body responded to the feel of him, remembering, wanting his touch. His mouth tasted faintly of coffee as it swooped down to capture hers. She wove her fingers through shaggy hair that curled above broad shoulders tanned by hours in the Texas sun.

The trail drive had shaved off some of the weight Evita's cooking had added, but he looked better than the day he had kissed her in the cemetery. A beard once again skirted his lower jaw, but she welcomed its softness. His mouth made her weak with need and she melted into a puddle softer than the ooze of the flooded river beds.

When his hands cupped her breasts, a tiny alarm bell went off in her head.

He broke off the kiss, his hands feeling her breasts. "Trail food must agree with you, you're gaining weight."

Her heart skipped a beat in panic. She plucked the soap out of his hand and waved it under his nose. "Weren't you going to wash me?" To ensure she distracted him, she wiggled closer, pressing his erection into her stomach.

Ransom sucked in a deep breath. Her curly hair tickled his groin. Sane thought disappeared. He grabbed her hips and drove himself inside her. Surprise lit her gray eyes as he used the water's buoyancy to slide her up and down until he shuddered to a climax deep inside her.

He leaned his head against her wet forehead. His ragged breathing startled him into a wry smile. "God, I've missed you."

If possible, she melted closer to him. Few creatures stirred in the heat of the June afternoon. The horses had tired of eating and dozed in the shade.

The rapid beat of his heart slowed.

"I need a few minutes," he feathered a kiss on her eyelid. "And then we'll do it again, take more time." He pulled back to look in her face. "If you want to."

With a sultry smile, she offered him the soap. He took it along with her hand and led her into shallow water.

The soap, softened by its sojourn in the water, lathered easily in callused hands more used to lassoing ornery beeves than washing a fragile neck. He curved his hand over her slender shoulders, rubbing and sliding his way down her arms.

When their fingers collided, he caught her right hand in his and lifted it from the water. His eyes locked on hers and he brought her hand to his lips. Regret shimmered through him when he saw the calluses, reminding him anew of how her life had changed because of war. He kissed each finger before washing her hand.

He'd never realized washing a woman's hands could be so erotic.

Next, he washed up her arms to her shoulders. To

his surprise, she arched backward, thrusting her breasts into the sweet summer air. Droplets of water beaded on the taut skin. He couldn't resist the temptation and leaned forward to lick a drop of water off one breast. She moaned.

He smiled and suckled the nipple into hardness before he released her long enough to wash her breasts. Pulling her against him, he reveled in her soap-slick breasts sliding through the hair on his chest while he scrubbed her back and rubbed himself slowly between her legs.

"Oh." The small word held worlds of surrender as she sank lower in the water.

"Stay with me, little one. I'm not finished yet." He turned her so her buttocks snuggled into his rigid shaft.

"I don't know how much more I can take."

"You're a strong woman." His soapy finger slid down her abdomen and into her. "You can take it."

Her breath came in shallow gasps at odds with the gentle lapping of water as it ran over rocks into the river. He eased himself into her, all the while stroking her. When she climaxed it was quick and strong.

"Ah, Angela love." He had paced himself to her. One last stroke and he followed her into heaven.

Chapter 15

Angela lay sprawled in shallow water, her head resting on Ransom's stomach. Eyes closed, she let the peace of the afternoon seep into her body. A cicada sang, leaves rippled and water lapped softly against her legs. The sounds soothed her toward sleep until warm water dribbled on her left breast.

"You're not going to let me sleep, are you?" She pretended to be grumpy, but her heart wasn't in it.

"We didn't come here to sleep."

"We didn't?" She felt him lean toward her breast and blow a gentle gust of air. Her nipple hardened. A sweet yearning unfurled in her stomach. She wanted to turn over, bury her nose in his chest and breathe in the damp, sun-kissed scent of him.

He dribbled water on her other breast. "You make me glad I'm alive."

The yearning stilled. She waited, eyes closed, every fiber of her body tuned to his voice.

"You know I'll always love Sabrina."

Did regret color his matter-of-fact words?

"But I've had time to think about her death. God knows, trailing beeves gives a man plenty of time to ponder life."

"I've had a lot of time to think, too." She had the

insane desire to tell him she had decided to leave him at Baxter Springs, but her courage deserted her.

If he heard her comment, he ignored it.

"I've had to accept she's dead . . . and we're not. That I'm married to you . . . not Sabrina."

She kept her eyes closed, unwilling to let him see the misery in her eyes. Did he realize how much it hurt every time he said that?

"It's not your fault Sabrina died. And I'll never know why I let O'Brion poison my mind against you."

"A grieving person doesn't always think straight." She ached to take him in her arms.

"That's no excuse for the way I acted, the things I said." He was quiet for a moment. "The way I see it, you weren't my choice for a wife."

Her eyes popped open. Pride shoved her into a sitting position. The need to console him evaporated.

"And you weren't my choice for a husband." The bar of soap that had been cradled on her chest plopped into the water. She fished it out, keeping her back to him. Damp jasmine scented the air.

"I know."

The gentleness of his agreement pushed her to the edge of tears. He touched her slumped shoulder. "I'm saying this all wrong. We both know circumstances forced us into marriage. But it hasn't been all bad, has it?"

"No," she admitted reluctantly.

"I can't imagine Sabrina going on a trail drive no matter what the provocation. And I know she'd never agree to cook."

Neither could she. Habit kept her from telling him Sabrina couldn't cook. The memory of her sister's disastrous attempts to cook created a tiny smile in her heart.

"I don't wish to speak ill of the dead, but she lacked

your fortitude. Your ability to believe everything will work out for the best." His hand curved to the shape of her shoulder, massaging it. "You've endured days of stampedes, hard rain, and injured herders."

The earnest quality to his voice made her turn to look at him. Intense blue-green eyes met her gaze.

"And then, I watch you cooking our meals, mending our wounds, smiling your smile. You give me hope." His hand slid down her arm and pulled her left hand from her thigh.

Her heart thudded against her rib cage.

"When I look at you, I believe everything will work out for the best." Then he kissed her callused palm, closed her hand around the kiss and said, "Thank you."

Joy expanded in her soul, drowning her doubts. Perhaps Aunt Julia had been correct. Perhaps his present and future would be hers. She squeezed the shrinking bar of soap in her right hand, wanting hope to become truth.

He pulled her against his chest. The sun-bleached hairs tickled her spine. He nuzzled the skin beneath her ear and whispered, "Isn't it my turn to be washed?"

The smile stole from her heart to touch her lips.

His right hand shaped the curve of her stomach, massaging skin only inches from his child.

"I find myself wanting to father a child."

Her smile faded. Guilt hovered over her. Was this a good time to tell him about the babe?

"Of course, if you use that soap, the beeves'll probably stampede when they smell me."

His teasing chased away the moment. Uncertainty won. She believed his feelings toward her were changing, but had they changed enough? Would he come to love her? And could she trust him to love their child?

For now she would ignore Sabrina lurking in his heart. For now she would forget she planned to leave him as soon as they reached Baxter Springs. For now she would enjoy this moment and accept his compliments, but she would not reveal the pregnancy. Not yet.

"The beeves'll have to run," she said, forcing a cheerful note into her voice. She lathered her hands with soap. "I have nothing else."

She wiggled her derriere, feeling his arousal.

"Sweet Jesu, woman."

She dropped the soap and watched it land in his groin. Assuming an innocent look, she raised her hands. "Where shall I start?"

He threw back his head and laughed. The rusty sound rounded into full-fledged merriment, igniting laughter in her.

"It's been a long time since I've heard you laugh," she said.

"God, that felt good." He grinned at her. "You're bound and determined to drag me back into the land of the living, aren't you?"

"I've missed your laugh."

For an evanescent moment, the past shimmered between them as ethereal as soap bubbles, tying them together rather than driving them apart. They both remembered a time when he'd laughed and enjoyed life.

"I was younger then." Sadness tinged his voice.

"And freer."

"Because I was young. War steals your youth. Gives you responsibilities. And changes your life forever."

"I'm sure time in a Yankee prison didn't help any."

"Now, that . . . " he looked past her, seeing something she had never seen and hoped to never see. "That steals your joy."

Pain shadowed his beautiful aquamarine eyes. Wanting to erase it, she waved her soapy hands in the air. "You never did say where you wanted me to wash first."

Amusement chased the pain from his eyes. His mouth twitched. "You may wash me anywhere you want."

And she did.

"You make me glad I'm alive."

"What'd you say, Miz Angela?"

Elbow deep in biscuit dough, Angela looked at Tommy blankly. Hellfire, she'd spoken aloud, but she couldn't seem to get Ransom's words out of her mind. Did he believe he could come to love her? Should she forfeit her future as a doctor for that possibility?

"Nothing much," she lied to Tommy and tamped down her swirling thoughts. "Just making sure I added all the ingredients." She wiped her damp brow on her sleeve, looking for a way to divert Tommy's attention. "How are the blackberries doing?"

John Shoehorn had stumbled across a patch of blackberries the previous day. After several hours of picking berries, she planned to have blackberry pies for dessert.

"They're about ready for the crusts."

She slapped the biscuit dough onto the work table and started rolling it out. Five miles of prairie and a flighty bunch of beeves separated her from Baxter Springs. Sometimes she wondered if the herd would stampede itself back to Texas if given the chance.

"I reckon we'll see another stampede," Tommy

pointed a berry-stained ladle heavenward. "Look at that sky."

She did, and the beauty above them stole her breath. To the west, the sun set in a sky filled with billowing, dark clouds herded toward them by flashes of lightning. To the east, a rainbow of pink, gold, and purple lit an aerial stage that spread for miles across the firmament.

Nature promised quite a show for that night.

Tommy sniffed the air. "I smell stampede."

"Lean this way, you'll smell the blackberries."

"Ah, Miz Angela. You know what I mean."

She did. Energy zinged through the air, raising the hair on her bare forearms. The beeves weren't going to sleep tonight, they would run. It was just a matter of when.

"We're in for a long night," she said. "We'll keep the fire going and the food warm. If they get a chance, the men need to eat."

As the shadows lengthened and night approached, the herders stayed with the beeves and crooned soft songs to soothe their fears. Men drifted in to eat when they could. Angela spent most of the night keeping the fire going, the coffee hot, and food warm.

The sky continued its lightning show, a distant promise with no wet substance.

Fatigue lulled Angela to sleep in the wee hours of the morning.

"Stampede! Wake up, boys!"

The cry brought Angela scrambling from her bed roll, moccasins in hand.

"Step lively, men! They're headed this way!"

Dark lumps resolved themselves into herders who had tried to snatch an hour's sleep by the dying campfire. Backlit by periodic flashes of lightning, they shoved stockinged feet into boots, crammed guns into their waistbands, grabbed spurs from the pile by the fire, and ran to their saddled night horses. Within moments, they rode off into the darkness.

Lightning flashed, thunder rumbled. The very ground beneath Angela's stockinged feet shook. Something made her turn around. She froze, her moccasins clutched to her chest. A wall of panicked beeves raced toward her.

"Miz Angela, get in the wagon!"

She heard Tommy's shout, but her body refused to comply. Several thousand hooves pounded the prairie. Aimed straight for her.

Tommy grabbed her hand and dragged her toward the wagon. Mesmerized by the swirling mass of beeves, she saw blue flashes quivering at the tips of their long horns.

Then the lightning flashed again and she saw the eyes of the lead beeves. Fear goaded her brain into action. Now she was pulling Tommy.

"The horses?" She screamed to be heard above the thundering hooves.

"Spooked!"

The hooves of the lead beeves tore across her bed roll.

Her outstretched hand slammed into the wagon. Hauling herself upward, she felt Tommy pick her up and shove. She went over and into the wagon bed.

Mingled with the pounding hooves, she now heard horns clash against horns as the tightly packed herd rampaged nearer.

Heat billowed from the beeves and she could smell their terrified breath. Scrambling to turn around, she grabbed at Tommy's hand.

* * *

"You are the ugliest creatures alive." Angela watched the six turkey buzzards rock gently from side to side as they circled high in the sky above her. She doubted if they heard her croak, but she couldn't do any better. The hot sun had baked all the moisture out of her mouth.

Pain kept distracting her from feeling thirsty. It also ruined her enjoyment of the lovely rain washed summer day. As if pain and thirst weren't enough, she was pinned beneath the remnants of the supply wagon.

And she couldn't find Tommy. She tried calling his name, knowing in her heart he would have to be quite near to hear her faint cry. He didn't answer. And if she slid her eyes to the right, she saw his crumpled hat beside the flattened coffee can.

A turkey buzzard wheeled lazily lower.

"I'm alive you miserable excuse for a bird." Did turkey buzzards wait until their prey was dead? If help didn't arrive soon, she'd find out.

Another vulture floated into view. She hoped what was left of the wagon fell on them when they swooped down to dine on her. Frustrated, she wanted to kick, thrash, pull, shove—anything to get herself free. But when she'd tried to wiggle out earlier, excruciating pain rewarded her effort.

Her efforts had jostled the wagon and now the water barrel hung suspended above her head. A trickle of water ran down the barrel, seeped through the shattered remains of the wagon to splash onto her stomach. It may as well have been a river in China. With her arms pinned, she couldn't cup her hands and capture any of the precious liquid. She was going to die of thirst with water only inches away.

Above her, the swirling circle of turkey buzzards edged ever downward. Her right leg throbbed. Water trickled onto her stomach, while she had no moisture to lick her dry, split lips.

She didn't want to die.

Having vultures size her up for a meal made her realize how much she wanted to live. She had things left to do. She had to

tell Ransom she loved him.

attend medical school.

clear her name of a murder charge.

have a baby.

This was not a good time to die.

"Señora Champion?"

A melodic voice twined its way into Angela's dream. She opened her eyes, relieved to discover her eyelids hadn't been pecked off by vultures. Little had changed in her limited world, although the splintered wagon now shaded her from the afternoon sun. Vultures still wove patient patterns in the sky above her. She squinted, trying to figure out if there were more.

The water barrel was gone.

"Señora Champion?"

"Ho-ko-lin-shee?" Her brain said his name more clearly than her mouth. Relief made her try to smile. She wouldn't die alone on the vast prairie.

"Sí Señora." His face hovered over hers. He smiled. Several of his teeth were missing. "Water?"

If eyes could speak, hers said "please."

Strong, weathered hands raised her head and slipped something under it. A metal cup pressed against her lips. Cool water trickled over cracked lips, swollen tongue, and down her dry throat. If she hadn't been so dehydrated, she would have cried with happiness.

He patted her face with a damp rag.

"Can you help me? Ayuda?"

"No, Señora. Dos, tres hombres." He pantomimed lifting the wagon.

She nodded.

Another drink of water and he was gone, the hoof-beats of his unshod pony fading quickly into silence.

Three turkey buzzards perched on the scattered remains of their campsite.

"Sweet Jesu!" Ransom reined in his exhausted horse. The Seminole Indian's broken English hadn't prepared him for the sight of Angela pinned beneath the shattered remnants of their supply wagon.

For one dazed moment, his tired brain couldn't grasp the enormity of what his eyes told him. Then a buzzard flapped a wing. With a hoarse cry, Ransom pulled his pistol and emptied its contents. Only one turkey buzzard made it back into the sky.

Ransom didn't care. All he saw was the oddly twisted, ebony-haired figure tangled in the wreckage of the wagon. A cold knot of fear clenched his gut along with a wave of raw anger. The depth of his feelings startled him, but this wasn't the time to wonder when it had happened.

Right now, he had to see if she lived.

Sliding off his horse, he fell to his knees beside her. "Angela?"

"Hellfire . . . Ransom." Pain underscored her weak husky-honey protest. "You scared . . . the daylights . . . out of me."

"I think that old Indian exaggerated." He hid his concern beneath a teasing tone. "You sound too feisty to be at death's door." He pushed a strand of hair from her sun-darkened face.

"I'll feel more . . . feisty when you get this . . . wagon off me."

He uncapped his canteen and eased it against her cracked lips. "Your wish is my command." The ground grumbled with the approach of the men Harrison had gathered to help.

He pulled the canteen from her mouth. She licked her lips. "Ho-ko-lin-shee?"

"He and a half a dozen men are right behind me."

"Let him . . . take care of me."

"Are you sure? He's an Indian. They have peculiar ways."

"Trust him."

Ransom wasn't eager to ask an Indian to care for Angela, but she knew more about doctoring people than any of them. "All right. Ho-ko-lin-shee it is."

He added a smile to soften his brusque agreement, but she didn't see it. She had fainted.

It took all the men to free her.

Ho-ko-lin-shee examined her while the men pretended to clean up the camp. Ransom paced back and forth, not pretending to do anything but wait for Ho-ko-lin-shee to finish. While he paced, his brain wrestled with the possibility of her death. The thought of a world without Angela twisted his soul into a knot.

In those agonizing moments of uncertainty, he realized the depth of his feelings. His love for Angela had snuck up on him while he was busy telling himself he had lost the perfect love. If he admitted the truth, he and Sabrina had shared little time together.

Hours, days, weeks, months constituted the time he and Angela had spent together.

His selfish behavior beat at his conscience. What he felt for Angela surpassed the feelings he'd harbored for Sabrina all these years.

"Sorry to bother you, Major. But we found Tommy."

Ransom looked at Sawyer. "Tommy?" He tore his mind from its painful spiral into despair. Sweet Jesu, he'd forgotten about the boy. "Is he all right?"

"He's dead, sir. Trampled."

Ransom massaged his forehead. How was he going to tell Angela? "Find a good spot to bury him. I'll say a few words."

Ho-ko-lin-shee rose, brushing the dust from his buckskin leggings.

"Get Sergio for me. I need a translator."

Ten minutes later, Ransom knew the extent of Angela's injuries. No broken bones. Several deep cuts, superficial lacerations and a badly bruised leg. She wouldn't be able to walk or ride. The old Indian worried more about the time she spent unprotected from the rain and sun.

Ransom had seen enough on the battlefield to know why Ho-ko-lin-shee worried. By nightfall, Angela burned with fever. Her restless discomfort threatened to undo Ho-ko-lin-shee's stitches.

When the Indian left to find more herbs to ease Angela's fever and pain, Ransom took over nursing her.

The campfire had burned down to a red glow when Angela shoved away the cool cloth Ransom held to her forehead.

"I wish you'd stop telling me it's unseemly to help Father at the hospital, Sabrina."

"Hush, little one. You need to rest."

"Those poor soldiers need me. I'll rest later. Now, let me get back to work."

"You need to concentrate on getting better." He ran the damp cloth down her arms as Ho-ko-lin-shee had shown him.

She raised her head and looked at the sky. "God, why are all these men dying?" Her voice held a petulant tone he'd never heard. "I work as hard as I can to help them, the least you can do is heal them."

"Lie back down for me, Angela."

She stared at him, but he knew she didn't see him. "Yes, Dozier, I'm here. Of course, I'll tell Mary you love her. Here, hold my hand, I won't leave you alone."

Her muttering ceased as abruptly as it started. From the limpness of her body, he couldn't tell if she slept or was unconscious. He felt her forehead; the dry heat scorched his hand.

Night faded to dawn, but he remained at her side. Over and over again, he sponged her arms, her neck, her face, waiting for her to recognize him. Exhausted from two days without sleep, his head drooped down to rest on her stomach. Just a few moments' rest and he would resume cooling her fever.

"Not my legs, stop cutting off my legs, damn you!"

His eyes snapped open. Sweet Jesu! What the hell was going on?

"Butchers, you're all butchers. Shoot me! Bayonet me! But leave my damn legs alone!"

Before he could raise his head, she shoved him off her stomach. A fist hit his shoulder. He dodged her foot. Damn! If he didn't stop her, she would break open her stitches.

"Sons of bitches, all of you!" Her right fist swung wildly. He ducked.

"Let my legs rot off! For God's sake, man, let me die with my legs attached."

Harrison appeared out of the gray dawn to help him restrain her. Within moments, her thrashing ceased and she slept.

"Poor Miss Angela," Harrison said, "she done saw

terrible things. But she were always such a brave little thing." His troubled gaze swung from Angela to Ransom. "She'll be all right, won't she?"

Ransom dipped the bandanna into the pan of water, wrung it out, and placed it on her forehead.

"I don't know."

Chapter 16

"I can give you money after I sell the herd, Mrs. Oates. Or I can leave a steer here today. If you wish the steer, we'll slaughter it for you."

Ransom disliked leaving Angela, but Ho-ko-lin-shee advised a week of rest. Then Harrison found a farmer's wife who agreed to take care of Angela while they drove the herd to Baxter Springs. What seemed a good idea yesterday lost its appeal when he stood in the farmyard.

"A beeve'll do nicely, but you have to kill it right now." Mrs. Oates waved her work-gloved hand toward the Long Horn they had cut from the herd. "I heard your cattle carry Texas fever. I won't have sickness tainting my dairy cow."

"I understand, Mrs. Oates. Sergio, will you see to the slaughter of the cow?"

"Sí, Señor Major."

Mrs. Oates' thin upper lip curled slightly. "Major?"

"An unfortunate slip of the tongue, madam. My military days are over."

"Confederate, no doubt." Now her thin lips drew together in a tight line. "And bringing beeves from Texas."

Ransom tipped his head slightly in agreement.

"Well, you won't find a warm welcome in Baxter Springs."

"The war's over, Mrs. Oates."

"It's not only because you're an ex-Confederate. They're also frightened of the Texas fever your beeves carry."

"Thank you, ma'am, for the warning." The problem of how the Kansas farmers would deal with the threat of Texas fever had gnawed his subconscious for weeks. He wondered how they were going to react to the thousands of beeves on the trail headed to the railroad depot in Baxter Springs.

He pushed the worry aside, more concerned about Angela than potential problems in Baxter Springs. He disliked leaving her at a farm that held an air of general neglect. Nor did he care much for Mrs. Oates, whose brown eyes were as sun-bleached as the ribbons on her faded poke bonnet.

"A bag of flour'd be nice," Mrs. Oates said. "If you have any. Your wife will want some biscuits, won't she? And it'll cheer Mr. Oates when he and the young'uns get back from town if he finds hot biscuits waiting."

"I think there's some flour." Ransom gestured toward a pack horse. With Baxter Springs only a few miles away, Sawyer had suggested they give the farm woman as much food as they could to make sure she treated Angela well. The woman's gaunt frame made him wonder if she had any food.

"I'm afraid the stampede that hurt my wife also tore up our supply wagon," Ransom said. "We salvaged what we could. It's all on that horse. If you'll show Mr. Creighton where to put it."

Mrs. Oates nodded. "This way, Mr. Creighton. You can unload the horse over here."

He knelt beside the travois Ho-ko-lin-chee had fashioned for Angela's trip to the farm. Cocooned in the contraption, she slept. He disliked waking her, but he couldn't leave without saying goodbye.

Trailing a finger along her jaw line, he squelched the urge to kiss each yellowing bruise on her body. He had so many things he wanted to tell her, but this was not the time or place.

He would never forget the horror of watching a panicked herd of beeves stampede toward his wife. On the far side of the herd when the stampede started, he could no more stop them than he could cut across their path and scoop her out of harm's way. All he could do was cling to his horse and pray he would live long enough to tell his wife he loved her.

He also prayed Angela would live to hear the words.

Somewhere in that catastrophic night, he lay Sabrina to rest.

He cupped his hand behind Angela's ear and slid his fingers into the hair he had cut so many weeks ago.

"Another four or five years. It'll be long again." Large gray eyes flickered open. A wan smile touched her mouth.

"I won't be gone any longer than it takes to sell the beeves. You'll be safe here." He disliked reminding her of Seyler as much as he disliked leaving her at this rundown farm. "There's no reason for O'Brion to find you here, if he is following us."

"Don't worry about me, I'll be fine. Ho-ko-lin-chee said I was more bruised than anything else. A little rest and I'll be good as new."

"If we didn't need the money to keep the ranch going, I'd . . ."

She shushed him with her hand. "Go to Baxter Springs for Richard and Evita and Sergio and Francisco and . . ."

When she hesitated in her list, he kissed the fingers trailing across his lips. "And you and me."

She opened her mouth as if to say something, then closed it.

He smoothed the hair from her forehead. "Baxter Springs is not more than a day's ride. Once I sell the beeves, I'll come back. A week, maybe less. Then, we'll go home."

"Not all of us." Her bottom lip trembled. "Tommy's dead, isn't he?"

"Yes."

Tears leaked from her eyes. "Before we go home, I'd like to visit his grave." She swallowed. "I'll have to write his mother."

"Sergio carved a nice cross." He thumbed away her tears. "I think you'll like the spot. Ho-ko-lin-shee chose it."

He carried her into the crowded, one-room cabin and placed her on a small bed in the corner.

"We didn't salvage much of your clothing. Do you think Mrs. Oates will lend you a dress?" A vision of Mrs. Oates in her shapeless, faded cotton dress flashed into his mind. "I'll buy you a dress as soon as I sell the beeves. Something pretty."

He realized he'd never bought his wife anything. Nor had she ever asked. Sabrina would have wanted gifts in every town between Gallatin and Austin. The locket had been a gift instigated by a pretty pout. He reached into his shirt pocket and pulled it out.

"This belongs to you. I shouldn't have gotten angry because Sabrina gave it to you." He lay it on her palm and closed her fingers around it. Then he kissed each knuckle.

"I have to go."

"Don't worry," she said. "I'll be fine until you return."

He bent over and sealed her pledge with a kiss. "I'll be back soon."

Outside the cabin, Ransom took the reins to the horse Harrison offered him. He touched the animal's sides with his spurs and gave the pony its head, stamping down the urge to stay with Angela and let the trail herd take care of itself until she recuperated.

But responsibility for others locked him onto a path he couldn't leave. Once again, circumstances forced him to make a decision that served the group, not the one. And once again, he heard his brother's pleas.

"Ransom, for God's sake, finish me off. Don't leave me here for the Yankees. You saw what they did to Dodd."

Wanton mutilation had no place in war. A man had the right to die with honor, not in horror as parts of his body were hacked off piece by piece. Torturing another human being held nothing but shame to whoever did it.

There was no time.

"Better my brother, who loves me," said Teddy, "than my enemy who hates me." His bloodstained hands clutched at his stomach, but neither they nor the cravat Ransom had wrapped around his brother's abdomen could stanch the blood.

Gut shot. A horrible enough way to die without the threat of a renegade group of Tennessee Unionist militia hounding them.

"Major, the Union men are at the river ford."

"Thank you, Lieutenant." Ransom had no choice. They were deep in Union-held territory where they had come in the perennial search for fresh horse-flesh. They had to ride. Now. He couldn't risk his command for one man, even if that one man was his brother. "Take the men, Lieutenant. I'll rejoin you at Ridley Cross Roads."

"Yes, sir." One last moment for five men to clasp Teddy's shoulder, murmur words of farewell, and the brothers were alone.

Ransom knelt beside Teddy, smelling the blood, the gunpowder and the scent of death.

Raising his uninjured arm, Teddy grasped the barrel of Ransom's Colt Navy pistol and placed it against his temple. "Pull the trigger, big brother." A weak smile curved his mouth. "And promise me one thing. Don't tell anyone how I died."

Teddy never heard Ransom's promise.

Ransom joined his men at Ridley Cross Roads two hours later.

Alone.

Responsibility. A cold, thankless bed mate.

"Mary Ann. Becky. Be quiet while your father says the blessing."

A brisk Yankee accent jarred Angela awake. The clipped cadence of the voice reminded her of the way Nicholas Stevens, Sabrina's Yankee fiancé, had spoken. But Nicholas came from New York and Angela didn't know anyone else from New York.

Disorientation gripped her. She didn't even recognize the quilt hanging over the footboard a few inches from her feet.

"Becky, share that fresh baked biscuit with your sister."

The crisp words chased away the cobwebs of sleep. She remembered where she was—in a bed in a cabin on a Kansas farm. Her stomach grumbled.

She inhaled a deep breath, expecting to fill her nostrils with the fragrance of freshly cooked biscuits.

The faint aroma of human perspiration mixed with wood smoke and the ever present prairie rewarded her effort.

She wrinkled her nose and sniffed harder. Not a whiff of food. Baked, fried, boiled or even raw. She propped herself up on an elbow and looked toward the kitchen area. Mrs. Oates sat alone at the rough deal table that filled most of the small cabin.

"It's your turn to wash the dishes tonight, Mary Ann."

Mrs. Oates spoke to an empty chair.

"You need to take a look at the cow, Edward." Mrs. Oates looked at the head of the table. "She's favoring her left front foot." Mrs. Oates cocked her head to the side as if listening to someone. Then she shook her head. "No, I didn't forget. I made apple pie this morning."

The hairs on the back of Angela's neck stood on end. She saw no one in the cabin except her and Mrs. Oates. There wasn't any food on the plates or in the serving bowls Mrs. Oates had set on the table. The woman talked to a nonexistent family who ate a nonexistent meal.

Afraid to say anything, Angela remained in the narrow bed while the invisible Mary Ann washed the dishes and the invisible Becky played with her doll. Then Mrs. Oates put the invisible children to bed. Angela may as well have been the invisible one.

"Now you girls behave and go to sleep."

Unsure of what to do, Angela pretended she wasn't there while Mrs. Oates stood by the bed.

"Your Pa and I need to check on the milk cow." Mrs. Oates smiled down, then raised an admonishing finger. "I don't want to hear you two giggling."

Little light from the oil lamp on the deal table reached the corner of the room, but what did illuminated a careworn face softened by love. The light brown eyes saw two young children where none existed, but the depth of her affection brought tears to Angela's eyes.

What had happened to Mrs. Oates' family?

Angela remained awake long after Mrs. Oates went to bed. Although she pitied Mrs. Oates, anxiety skimmed across her mind. She was alone at the edge of Indian country in the company of a crazy woman.

Somewhere outside the cabin, a pack of coyotes howled her loneliness. Their chorus was caught by the evening wind and flowed around the cabin walls seeking a way through the cracks and crevices. She shivered, afraid to look right or left, in case she saw Becky or Mary Ann.

"Mrs. Champion. Wake up, Mrs. Champion."

Angela fought the heavy bonds of sleep it had taken her hours to find last night. When she opened her eyes, Mrs. Oates stood by the bed. The older woman gave Angela no time to gather her sleep scattered thoughts.

"Here's your breakfast, Mrs. Champion. I'm working the south field today. Until my family return from town."

"Family?" Memories of the previous evening prodded Angela into wakefulness. She studied Mrs. Oates, worried her disbelief might activate the woman's madness.

"Mr. Oates and our two daughters." Mrs. Oates put a bowl of corn mush where Angela could reach it. "They left before dawn."

"I'm sorry I missed them." Angela kept her tone casual.

"They're always home by nightfall." Mrs. Oates'

voice faltered on the last word. Then she straightened as if in response to some inner belief. "You can meet them at dinner."

Did she know they'd never return, but couldn't accept it?

"I'm sure they'll be home by nightfall." What misguided sense of sympathy led her to reassure Mrs. Oates?

"Why wouldn't they?" The older woman went to the deal table and put a few biscuits in a small cloth bag. "If you need anything, bang a pan bottom loud enough I can hear it."

Between her injuries from the stampede and lack of sleep the previous night, Angela spent the day tending to her personal needs and sleeping. Late that afternoon, she awoke to observe Mrs. Oates dining alone, speaking to people who didn't exist and eating food that wasn't there.

This time Angela didn't go hungry, because she'd scrounged herself another bowl of corn mush before Mrs. Oates returned from the field. Tomorrow she planned to raid the hen house she'd seen near the barn.

The next morning repeated the first. Angela had no idea when Mrs. Oates' family had left or where they'd gone, but she knew with deep certainty they were not returning, except in Mrs. Oates' imagination.

By the second day, Angela recognized the pattern. Mrs. Oates acted sane each morning before she went to the field, but when she returned from a day's work, her imaginary family awaited her.

Baxter Springs might as well have been Paris, thought Ransom as he, Sawyer and Harrison watched a contingent of Kansas farmers approach. It was that far out of his reach.

Above them, a warm July sun headed toward the horizon through clouds that promised rain. Ransom pulled the large white handkerchief Sabrina had embroidered for him from around his neck. He wiped at the dust streaking his damp face, his nose unconsciously seeking the faint scent of jasmine soap.

"Well, lookee here," Harrison said. "A welcoming committee. But I don't see no cake."

"Mostly rifles and revolvers." Sawyer's hand rested on the butt of his Remington revolver.

Ransom looped the handkerchief back around his neck, tying it in a loose knot.

Five riders halted their horses a few feet away from them. A large man, riding a horse more accustomed to the plow than a rider, urged his mount another foot closer.

"Are these your beeves?" He addressed his question to all three men, but looked at Ransom.

Tipping his hat up, Ransom nodded at the designated spokesman. Nervous at the closeness of too many strange horses, Ransom's horse pawed the ground and sidled sideways.

"We're here to tell you Cherokee county is under quarantine. We ain't allowing Texas beeves in."

The other four men glared their support.

"You're blocking the route to the railroad." Frustration simmered beneath each word. He wanted to knock the farmers off their horses.

"We're keeping Texas fever out of our livestock."

"Do you realize how far we've come?" Ransom bit out the question, thinking of all the hardship Angela, his men, his horses, and the beeves had endured to reach Kansas.

"We didn't ask you to bring your beeves here."

The implacable truth hit Ransom: he was going to lose the ranch. "And if we try to reach the railroad?"

"We'll shoot your beeves." As if to reinforce the promise, each farmer rested his hand on his rifle or revolver.

"That's not very neighborly of y'all." Harrison expectorated a stream of tobacco juice that landed in the prairie grass between the two groups.

Ransom wanted to shoot the messengers. After miles of hardship, the beeves grazed within spitting distance of the railroad and a sale. These men stood between him and success.

A year ago, civil war placed them on opposite sides. Today, fear of Texas fever put them on opposite sides again.

"That's all we came to tell you."

Ransom watched the Kansans ride away. If he couldn't sell the herd, it meant more than losing the ranch. It also meant he couldn't pay the men. How could everyone get back to Texas without money?

"Looks like we have a problem," Sawyer said.

"I'm open to suggestions," Ransom replied.

"Damn Yankees." Harrison settled his hat more firmly on his head. "It's not enough they won the war, they gotta starve us, too."

"That's the difference between winning and losing. The winner gets the upper hand." Ransom saw a large puff of dust resolve itself into three riders. "Is that another welcoming committee?"

Sawyer studied the approaching men. "Nah, those men know how to ride."

Ransom agreed. These men had an easy grace that spoke of hours in the saddle.

The larger of the three men rode a buckskin Ransom would have liked to own. The stranger brought his horse to a dancing halt.

"Good evening." He touched the brow of his hat with his finger. "Name's Chancellor. Our herd's about three miles west of here. Was your welcoming committee any warmer than ours?"

Ransom grinned, glad to hear the man's lazy Southern drawl. "Nope. Seems the good people of Baxter Springs have quarantined their county in order to keep our beeves out." He introduced himself and his men.

"I've got a little plan to get my beeves to market," Chancellor said. "Would you like to hear it?"

"Why don't you and your men join us for supper?" Ransom said. "Not that it'll taste too good, our trail cook was injured in a stampede the other day."

Sergio had volunteered to cook the evening meal. The beans were a little chewy and the biscuits burned on the bottom, but none of the herders complained. Neither did their guests.

No one said much during the meal. If they did, Ransom didn't pay attention. His thoughts chased themselves in circles as he tried to find a solution. He wondered how much the horses, oxen and saddles would bring him. The stampede had demolished the supply wagon.

"I say get all the herds together and run them through Baxter Springs."

John Shoehorn's suggestion shattered Ransom's swirling thoughts. From the disgruntled muttering, he realized the men were as frustrated as he.

"What's this plan you have?" he asked Chancellor, hoping to divert attention away from Shoehorn's suggestion.

"We've been here two days." Chancellor used the bottom half of a biscuit to sop up the gravy in his tin plate. "The way I see it, it's going to be nigh on impossible to sell a herd in these parts. Too many irate farmers lie between us and the railroad." He paused to smile a most devious smile. "But I think I've got a way to outwit them."

Ransom felt the old elation he always experienced when he was working on a plan to get the upper hand with Yankees.

"I have to admit," Chancellor set aside his plate and pulled a map out of his pocket. "The Union army did a damn fine job of mapping this area." He smoothed open the map and laid it on the ground.

His finger traced the familiar rectangle that was Kansas until he stopped at its southeastern border. "We're here and there are farmers to the west of us, but they're not as densely situated as the farmers in this county. The way I see it, we'll have to dip back down into Indian country then swing west to get around these farmers. About here," his finger tapped the map, "we should be able to go north to Nebraska, cross the the Missouri River into Iowa."

"Iowa!" Ransom thought of Angela. "Why Iowa?"

"According to a man named George Duffield, Iowans are hungry for our cattle and they'll pay top dollar. He should know, he's from Iowa. And he went all the way to Texas and put together a herd for the sole purpose of driving them home."

The possibility of trailing the herd to Iowa intrigued Ransom. He had over a thousand head of cattle to sell, but he also had an injured wife he couldn't leave in Kansas. "How long do you think it'll take us to get there?"

"I'm counting on two or three more months," Chancellor said. "We're going west and it'll be dry, but if we drive them slow there should be enough for them to eat. We'll be in Indian country, but if we run several herds together, Indians won't be a problem. Or outlaws."

"It's a good idea, Major."

"You're right, Sawyer." Ransom stared at the map.

"Be a shame to let them Yanks win this skirmish," Harrison said. "But you got Miss Angela to worry about."

At Chancellor's quizzical expression, Ransom explained. "My wife was hurt in a stampede. We had to leave her at a farm not far from here."

Could she endure another two or three months of driving beeves? He hated knowing he had to ask her.

"Major, I got me an idea that might appeal to you."

Ransom looked at the man who claimed Angela had saved his life. "I'm listening, Harrison."

Chapter 17

"I'm going to shoot that damn mule one day, see if I don't."

Startled to see Mrs. Oates home in the middle of the day, Angela dropped the wet skirt beside the wash tub. Hellfire! Now she'd have to wash it again. She swallowed her frustration.

"What's the matter with Old Mule?" She wiped the perspiration off her brow, bringing the clean smell of suds and water to her face.

In the five days since Ransom left her, she had rested to the point of senselessness. With her lacerations healing nicely and her bruises fading into the purple-yellow-green stage, only her right leg still bothered her. It had taken the brunt of the weight of the wagon.

She had decided clothes washing would fend off boredom. It also eased Mrs. Oates' chores.

"He's gone, that's what," Mrs. Oates said. "Damn fool mule, he ran off to the Schecklers' cabin. See if I unharness him for a little midday rest again."

"How do you know where he went?"

"He has an unnatural, Lord help us, liking for the Schecklers' she-goat. Whenever he gets loose, he runs over to see that goat."

Mrs. Oates stomped toward the front of the house.

Angela awkwardly bent over and scooped the skirt off the damp ground. Mud streaked it. With a sigh, she brushed off what she could and dropped it back into the washtub. As she reached for the dolly, Mrs. Oates reappeared, jamming a dilapidated bonnet on her head.

"I'll be back before dark." She tied the sun-bleached ribbons under her square chin. "If Mr. Oates returns before I do, tell him where I went. He'll worry because he wasn't here to go, but I can't change that. One of us has to get that damn mule."

Then she was gone.

Angela rammed the dolly into the washtub and swished the skirt vigorously. Mrs. Oates switched back and forth from reality to fantasy, dragging Angela with her from world to world. If Ransom didn't return soon, she might be unable to separate the two worlds.

Midsummer hung heavily over Kansas and the stifling heat of the cabin kept Angela from going back inside. After she finished washing clothes, she followed the small creek that ran behind the cabin, searching for a cool retreat.

About a hundred yards from the house, she found the graves. The sweet smell of summer vied with the damp scent of creek life. A black willow tree shaded the graves, its lance-shaped leaves stirring in the desultory breeze.

Three names had been whittled into the wide hickory crosses: Edward William Oates, beloved husband of Charity Amelia Oates. Mary Ann Oates. Rebecca Jane Oates. A husband and two children who would never return from town.

* * *

Angela met Mrs. Oates in front of the cabin when she returned with Old Mule.

"Why don't I take care of him?" Afternoon had turned to dusk, hiding the pity Angela knew was in her eyes. The promise of rain scented the sun-baked air.

"Have Mr. Oates and the children eaten?"

"They're inside." Angela took Old Mule by the halter. "Waiting for you."

Mrs. Oates looked into Angela's eyes. "You're a good person, Mrs. Champion." Then her gaze slid over Angela's shoulder to the small cemetery hidden by the trees near the creek. "Knowing my family comes home for dinner each night makes it easier to get up in the morning."

Tears pooled in Angela's eyes and sadness tugged at her mouth. She watched Mrs. Oates straighten her shoulders and walk toward the cabin, untying her bonnet as she went. She disappeared into the cabin, the murmur of her cheerful voice seeping through the cracks of the roughhewn walls.

Angela rubbed her face against Old Mule's soft cheek, inhaling the pungent mix of mule, leather and sweat. "I hear you have a goat girlfriend."

Old Mule stared at her with his big brown eyes.

"I bet you worked up an appetite running off to visit her." The mule followed her without protest as she led him into the small barn.

While Old Mule munched his dinner, Angela brushed him. His skin quivered with pleasure when she drew the brush across his flanks.

"Feels good, doesn't it?" Her thoughts strayed to the time Ransom had brushed her hair. She longed for him to do it again.

Old Mule swished his tail in frustration. Startled, Angela realized she'd stopped brushing the mule.

"Sorry, I was daydreaming." She ran the brush over his rump, unable to stop her thoughts from returning to Ransom. She hadn't had a chance to tell him she loved him before he left for Baxter Springs. And she still hadn't told him about the baby. Her left hand drifted to her stomach and she splayed her fingers across the gentle swelling.

The stampede had changed everything.

Ransom's actions after the accident made her believe he cared for her. She decided she would tell him she loved him. Then she would wait a few days and tell him about the baby.

They would have plenty of time to talk during the trip home. She would explain they needed to return to Tennessee and clear her name of that ridiculous murder charge. He couldn't expect her to spend her life worried someone might come and drag her back to Tennessee.

Medical school posed yet another problem, but no problem seemed insurmountable. She was just too happy.

Bending over, she picked up Old Mule's left rear hoof and started cleaning it.

"Miss Stapleton. How it breaks me heart to see yourself dressed in rags and cleaning a mule's hoof."

The sound of O'Brion's lilt shattered all Angela's plans. Old Mule's foot slid through her lax grip, hitting the straw covered dirt floor with a dull thump. Unbending like an old woman, she turned and faced O'Brion. Fear clamped her heart but she forced her voice into its normal pattern of Southern courtesy.

"Why, Captain O'Brion. La, you frightened me. What brings you to Kansas?" She wiped her damp left palm on the aging cotton skirt Mrs. Oates had given her to wear. She hid her right hand and the hoof pick in the folds of her skirt.

"Faith and I've missed the sound of your sweet voice. It runs through a man like honey on a warm summer's day. Is it yourself doesn't know what your voice does to a man?"

When he glanced downward, she did, too.

"Oh, my!" She jerked her gaze back to his face.

His sensuous lips parted into a knowing smile. "What a hurricane of rage ran through me heart when yourself escaped. Now, to be sure, didn't I tell yourself not to marry Rebel scum." He stepped toward her.

"Major Ransom Champion is not Rebel scum." She stood her ground beside the mule, although every fiber of her body screamed "run!" Another two steps and he would block the stall door. Her brain churned with escape plans. She tightened her grip on the hoof pick and tried not to think about the bulge in his trousers.

The broad brim of his hat shadowed his face, making it impossible to read his expression. But his harsh tone, so at odds with the musical lilt of his Irish accent, told her he had nursed his anger about her marriage over many miles.

"Hasn't yourself led me on a merry chase across half a dozen states?" He took another step, his large frame filling the stall door.

Old Mule shifted restlessly, snorting his displeasure.

The dim light from the lamp hung in the center of the barn caressed the gleaming black metal of a gun pointed at her. Angela pressed her back against Old Mule.

"Are you going to kill me?" Her question rushed out in a breathy squeak.

"Isn't it Mr. Seyler as paid me to kill yourself?"

"I don't understand." She tried to lick her dry lips,

but there was no moisture in her mouth. "What about a trial?"

"Well, now, Mr. Seyler decided not to buy a judge and jury. It is me he sent."

"He can send a Union officer after me?"

"Didn't Mr. Seyler make it worth me while to resign me commission?"

And then he slid the gun into his waistband and was in the stall with her. He pulled her into his arms, cradling his erection between her legs. Horrified at the intimate contact, she tried to pull free. His grasp tightened, locking her between himself and Old Mule, who was pressed against the wall.

"I'm not after killing yourself," O'Brion whispered into her hair. "Faith and its destiny. We belong together." His left hand crept between them to cup her breast.

Her breath came in short, desperate gasps. The air filled her nose with a strange bouquet: the scent of O'Brion tinged with the acrid smell of mule urine. But above all, she smelled her own fear.

Then Old Mule reached over her head and grabbed O'Brion's hat, revealing the features that made O'Brion confident every woman would desire him. Thick, wavy black hair. A well formed nose between a pair of slashing black eyebrows. A thick mustache skirting the top of a sensual mouth. A bone-melting smile aided by a well-placed dimple in the left cheek.

He had used that smile on her. If she hadn't spent her life with a woman who used her looks to get what she wanted, Angela might have fallen for the Irishman's skilled wooing. But Sabrina had taught her how well beauty can hide corruption.

Rather than allow him to use her, Angela had done

a wicked thing. She'd used O'Brion's infatuation to get what she wanted. It had been a heady experience.

"It's the records I checked. Your Major Champion's oath of allegiance wasn't registered. Now, then, I had the marriage as rent me heart in two declared illegal."

She looked into a pair of deep blue eyes glittering with a hungry obsession that chilled her to the bone. He slanted his head. She knew he was going to kiss her. Nausea rolled in her stomach.

"Faith, yourself can marry me."

"Get away from her or I'll shoot a hole in you."

Mrs. Oates! Angela got no chance to savor her relief.

"And wouldn't yourself be risking to shoot Miss Stapleton, too?" O'Brion released Angela as he turned. "It's a risk I don't think you'll be taking."

He pulled his gun from his waistband and fired it. Angela screamed.

The impact propelled Mrs. Oates backward into a heap of petticoats and skirt.

Old Mule kicked, hitting O'Brion in his left thigh and sending him to the ground. The gun flew out of his hand.

"God in heaven! That damn mule kicked me!" Clutching his leg, O'Brion fished for his gun in the straw strewn around the stall.

Angela spotted the gun. Shoving Old Mule aside, she grabbed it.

"Don't move." Hellfire, the gun was heavier than it looked. She held it in both hands and pointed the muzzle at O'Brion. There wasn't much room in the stall, but she kept as much distance as she could between them as she edged her way to the door.

"Mrs. Oates? Are you all right?" She kept her eyes on O'Brion while she called out.

Silence answered her.

"Mrs. Oates? Please, say something." Worried by the silence, Angela risked a glance toward the barn door. The heap of bloody clothing moaned.

O'Brion lunged at her. This time Old Mule kicked with both feet, catching O'Brion in the back of the shoulders and lifting him off the floor. He flew out the stall, ramming his head into the opposite barn wall. With a groan, he sank into a heap.

Old Mule brayed his disgust and trotted out of the barn.

The gun fell from Angela's lifeless fingers. Then she ran to kneel beside Mrs. Oates' crumpled body. Blood oozed from a hole in the woman's chest. Soon it would gurgle out her mouth. The smell of death hung in the night air.

Angela's tears dripped onto Mrs. Oates. "I'm so sorry. It's all my fault." Angela picked up the limp hand, callused by hours holding a plow. "I had no idea he'd follow me."

To Angela's surprise, Mrs. Oates smiled. Her eyes fluttered open. "Please . . . don't . . . fret. I'll . . . be . . . with . . . them . . . now."

The last word bubbled out as much blood as air.

Angela reached up as she had done countless times during the war, and gently closed the unseeing eyes.

O'Brion groaned.

Every muscle in Angela's body tensed. Mind-leaching panic stifled her lungs, locked out even the tiniest breath. Think! She had to think! Hysteria clawed at her. She'd dropped O'Brion's gun near him. Dare she risk going back into the barn?

He groaned again. Louder.

Her father had taught her to remain calm in countless emergencies. Now her life depended upon her ability to remain calm.

She grabbed the shotgun Mrs. Oates had dropped.

She cracked it open. Empty. She tossed it aside and reached for her knife. Pulling it free, she tiptoed back into the barn.

Ransom heard the dairy cow crying with discomfort a quarter mile from Mrs. Oates' farm. Bypassing the cabin, he slid off his horse a few feet from the barn. His feet hit the ground and he pulled his revolver from its holster.

Unable to hear anything over the bawling animal, he pushed open the barn door. He found Mrs. Oates lying a few feet from the doorway. Dried blood had congealed on the faded bodice of her cotton dress. An old shotgun, opened and empty, rested a few feet from her body.

The smell told him she was dead, but he knelt beside her and searched for a pulse. He couldn't find one. Dread seeped into his soul. He couldn't hear anything over the cries of the cow, but he doubted if anyone alive would have left the cow unattended.

Inside the barn, he found a heap of scuffled straw, boot marks, and some cut-up bridle reins. He studied the reins, wondering who had been tied.

Fear. Frustration. Anger. Panic. Despair. So many emotions clamored for release. If he unleashed one, they'd all follow, rendering him incapable of finding Angela. He slammed his right fist into the nearest stall door.

"Sweet Jesu!"

His cry silenced the cow, for a moment.

Find Angela.

The cow started bawling again.

"Damn!" Time pressed against him, but he couldn't abandon the cow anymore than he could leave Mrs. Oates lying on the ground. He milked the cow and set her free. Then, he buried Mrs. Oates.

When he finished, he could smell rain on the air and see its possibilities in the dark clouds scuttling into the distant sky from the northwest. He'd lost precious time, but his years in the calvary had taught him how to track men. With any luck, he'd find them.

Mounting his horse, he started his search.

"You know what Claytor Smith told me?"

The turkey buzzard swooped lower as if to better hear Angela.

"He swore if you saw one buzzard gliding through the sky, you had to watch him until he flapped his wings. And if you didn't see him flap his wings, you'd have bad luck. Well, you better flap your damn wings because I've had enough bad luck to last a lifetime."

The bird sailed endlessly through the sky above her head, his wings held in a shallow vee. Angela frowned. Closing her eyes, she missed the slow flap of the bird's wings.

Why had she run into the night? She'd tied up O'Brion, gathered some food, and left to look for his horse. When she couldn't find the horse, she couldn't return to the cabin.

She was scared her hastily tied knots wouldn't hold. Scared O'Brion had another gun because she forgot to search him. More scared of O'Brion than of walking to Baxter Springs alone at night. Now she was lost, sun-baked with thirst, and her injured leg wouldn't bear her weight any longer.

Here she sat, on the side of a faint track beneath a prairie mimosa. She leaned her head against a tree and inhaled the dust-tainted air. She exhaled a huge sigh. A list of all the things she should have done echoed in her mind.

For starters, she should've held O'Brion at gun point and waited for Ransom.

But no, she let panic rule. Now she'd probably die without telling Ransom she loved him.

These repeated encounters with death were wearing a little thin. And now, she didn't face extradition to Tennessee for trial, she faced a hired killer. As soon as she found Ransom, she would insist they return to Tennessee and clear her name. After she told him she loved him. After she told him about the baby. And after they spent a day tangled together in a soft bed somewhere.

A crow cawed lazily, pulling her sleepy gaze skyward. Much higher than the low-flying crow, the turkey buzzard continued to sail through the sky, sometimes rocking his body from side to side. It had boiled down to her, the buzzard, and God. The odds probably favored the vulture.

The repetitive circling of the buzzard lulled her to sleep.

A scraping noise interrupted her nap. She continued to pretend to sleep. If the buzzards had circled her for the death watch, she didn't want to see them. Nor did she want to see O'Brion if he had gotten loose and found her. Her heart told her Ransom didn't make the noise, because her husband wouldn't tiptoe around her. He'd shake her awake and scold her for scaring him to death.

Metal clinked, ruling out the buzzards.

Curiosity got the best of fear.

Angela opened her eyes to see an archangel. God hadn't deserted her, after all.

Chapter 18

God had sent an archangel to save her. An archangel dressed in buckskin. A pair of wide shoulders blocked the sun from her eyes.

"Take a wee sip of water, lass."

A Scottish archangel. How delightful. She blinked, trying to focus on her angel. A large hand cradled her head and held her steady while she sipped lukewarm water from the canteen pressed against her dry lips.

She stared into beautiful green eyes and a gloriously handsome male face. His features matched the illustrations of archangels in the Stapleton family Bible. She smiled, marveling at the way the sun, snared in the golden tips of hair that brushed his shoulders, haloed his head, A thick blonde mustache grew across his upper lip, curling its way down either side of a finely sculpted mouth.

Oh, yes, she was more than ready to go with this angel wherever he wanted to take her.

"That's a good lass. I'll have you some soup soon."

Angela wondered why he bothered with soup. If he were taking her to heaven, she didn't need to eat. But she was too tired to solve the puzzle and fell asleep, wrapped in a strange sense of security.

She awoke to a cloudy morning, the gentle nicker

of a nearby horse, and the mournful oowoo-woo-woo-woo of a dove. The aroma of coffee tickled her nostrils. It sounded and smelled more of earth than heaven.

She took a quick peep.

"Gude morning to you, lass."

Angela frowned. Her archangel squatted next to the fire, stirring something in a pot. Did angels need to eat?

He poured coffee into a battered tin cup and brought it to her. "Feeling better?"

Angela sat up, brushing a tangle of hair from her face. "Yes, thank you. I'm so glad you found me." She smiled her gratitude.

The angel stopped, cocked his head, then smiled a most beatific smile. Her heart stopped. If she weren't already dead, his smile was enough to kill her.

"They call me the Scotsman." He set the cup on the ground near her. "Careful, it's hot."

Angela wanted to reach out and touch him. Or pass her hand right through him. Then, his name registered in her sleep-clogged brain. "The Scotsman?" She looked into his incredible green eyes. "You're not Michael or Gabriel? I'm not dead?"

A throaty chuckle met her question. "Not quite, lass. The vultures planned for you to be their next meal. But you're alive. Nothing a wee bit of rest and food won't cure.

She loved the way he rolled the "r" in words. His brogue reminded her of Mr. McCloskey, who owned a print shop in Nashville before the war.

The man who squatted before her was too beautiful to look at this early in the morning. He made her conscious of how dirty and disheveled she must be. She picked up the coffee cup and looked around.

They were in a small clearing with his horse hobbled about ten feet from the camp site. She could hear a stream gurgling nearby and even smelled its dampness, but she couldn't see it. The coffee offered to revive her. She tilted the cup against her lips and took a tentative sip. It was the most vile-tasting brew she had ever sampled.

"I'll be happy to take you home if it's on the way to Joplin," the Scotsman said.

She swallowed, the bitter taste forgotten. "Joplin! Hellfire! That's in Missouri!"

"Aye, last time I visited it."

"But my husband is in Baxter Springs. I need to go there."

Did regret shimmer in his emerald green eyes?

"I haven't time to go backward, lass. I'm headed for Joplin. You can go with me, or I'll point you toward Baxter Springs."

"I can't go alone. He's had plenty of time to get free. If he finds me, he'll kill me." A tear plopped into her coffee cup, but she saw only the bullet hole in Mrs. Oates' chest. And smelled the warm stench of blood, not the aroma of burnt coffee.

"Who, lass? Who would want someone as bonnie as you dead? 'Twould not be your husband?"

"Oh no! Not Ransom!" One look into the Scotsman's beautiful, concerned eyes and her story tumbled out. It was a disjointed rendition that started in Tennessee and ended beside the trail in Missouri.

"I can't stay in Joplin alone, either." Desperation chased courtesy from her tone. She tried to soften it by sniffing and wiping her eyes. "If O'Brion finds me before I find Ransom . . ." She sniffed, again.

"I'm sorry lass, I canna take you to Baxter Springs."

"Some archangel you are." The accusation slipped out. She clamped a hand across her mouth.

"Aye, looks can be deceiving. Dinna you sound like the veriest angel when first you opened your mouth. It wanted but six sentences to ruin that impression."

His teasing tone lifted her spirits and helped her corral the panic that fluttered at the edge of her mind.

"We haven't been properly introduced. You probably won't like it, but my name is Angela." She grinned. "Angela Champion."

"Aye. That's the verry name I would have given you if I hadn't heard you swear like a field hand."

She felt her face heat. "Blame my father for my swearing. It was his favorite word and I grew up hearing it. My aunt will never forgive him for teaching it to me."

"Since I canna take you to Baxter Springs, why dinna you come with me to Joplin?"

"I have no money." Panic squeezed her chest as tight as her hand squeezed the coffee cup. "I don't know anyone in Joplin."

"As if Gregor Buchanan would take money for rescuing a bonnie lass such as yourself!"

Belatedly, Angela remembered her manners. "That's very kind of you, Mr. Buchanan, but where will I stay until my husband comes for me? How will I earn my way?"

"Earn your way?"

Interest gleamed in those startling green eyes.

Angela rushed to explain. "I can cook."

The merest hint of disappointment touched his eyes before he smiled. "I have a friend in Joplin who might let you bide until your husband comes for you. She hates to cook, but she loves to eat."

* * *

To Angela's horror, a scantily clad young woman answered the Scotsman's knock upon the door of a large white frame house on the outskirts of Joplin. She stared at the young woman, then swung her glance to the Scotsman.

"Ummmmm, are you sure this is the right house?"

"Aye." He smiled at the young woman.

The young woman smiled back. Angela had seen stiffer butter on a hot summer day in Tennessee than this puddle of femininity.

She tugged at the Scotsman's buckskin clad arm. "I think this is a, a . . ."

"Whorehouse?"

"House of ill repute." Angela failed to keep the censure from her voice.

"Aye." The Scotsman nodded. "Think on it, lass. What better place to hide? O'Brion won't look here."

While Angela tried to absorb the idea of hiding in a whorehouse, the Scotsman smiled at the young woman, again.

"Will you fetch Big Sal, lassie? Tell her the Scotsman's here."

"You're the Scotsman." Awed comprehension bathed the woman's tone, as if she'd heard about the Scotsman, but hadn't believed what she heard.

Angela felt a sense of vindication. At least, she'd been in a state of delirium when she'd mistaken him for an archangel.

"Aye, I'm the Scotsman."

"You can call me Narcissa."

To Angela's relief, Narcissa didn't pull off what few clothes she wore and offer herself to the Scotsman right there in the foyer. Instead, she leaned toward him, displaying her full bosom for all the world to see.

"And anytime you call, I'll come."

"I just bet you will." Angela's mutter earned her a glare from the other woman.

Narcissa shifted her gaze back to the Scotsman. "Why don't you follow me to the parlor?"

Hips swinging, she led them into the parlor. After one lingering glance at the Scotsman, she disappeared. Angela wandered around the room, trying not to trip over one of the five red velvet love seats. A whorehouse. Angela Stapleton Champion in a whorehouse. Yet, she had to agree with the Scotsman. O'Brion would never look here.

The Scotsman sprawled on one of the love seats, his large body dwarfing the small sofa. "Dinna worry, lass. You'll like Big Sal."

"I presume," a voice drawled, "she washes up well."

At the sound of the deep voice, Angela turned from her examination of a small statuette of a man and woman entwined in an unbelievable position doing unimaginable things to each other. A short, buxom woman stood in the doorway looking at her. From the doubt in her dark brown eyes, Angela knew the woman had skimmed her bedraggled, dust-stained person and found her wanting.

The Scotsman smiled. "Aye, Big Sal, that she does."

Angela swallowed the urge to tell this Big Sal person that the Scotsman had never seen her cleaned up.

Big Sal circled Angela as if she were a mare the madam wasn't interested in buying, but was being polite about rejecting, because she liked the owner.

"She's pretty enough, but on the scrawny side." Big Sal stopped in front of Angela, but she spoke to the

Scotsman. "I doubt she'll please any of my customers. They tend to like the ones with big tits."

Angela felt a blush heat her cheeks.

A lazy grin touched the Scotsman's mouth. "I'll grant you she's a wee bonnie lass . . ."

Startled, Angela looked at the Scotsman. No one had ever called her "a wee bonnie lass." All her life she'd been too tall, too slender, and too dark when compared to Sabrina. But situated between Big Sal, who made up in breadth what she lacked in height, and the Scotsman, who topped six feet, she might be considered a wee bonnie lass.

She toyed with the image, liking the Scotsman for giving her another view of herself.

". . . but with a regular morsel or two, she'll fatten up. And you've yet to hear her voice. Aye, that's enough to make a man's blood boil while his soul sings."

Big Sal stared hard at Angela's face as if she couldn't imagine a smile or voice that would make a man's blood boil or his soul sing.

Angela agreed with her. Her voice was a little on the husky side, but she'd never had any indication it made any man's blood boil. The poor Scotsman had been on the trail too long without a woman.

"I hope you've broken her in," Big Sal said. "I've no patience with skittish new ones."

Big Sal didn't think she'd make a good whore! Her dust-streaked cheeks burned with mortification. As if it was difficult to seduce a man. Her experience with men might be limited, but seducing them seemed quite easy.

Hellfire! What in heaven's name was she thinking?

"There aren't many men who'll pleasure you in

bed the way the Scotsman does." Big Sal's soft, brown gaze rested on the Scotsman's handsome face.

From the enraptured expression on Big Sal's face, Angela realized the woman spoke from experience. From the smug expression on the Scotsman's face, he'd heard these words before.

But enough was enough. Angela drew herself up into her best genteel Southern female stance.

"This man has not been in my bed, madam. And I have no idea what type of pleasures he may provide. I happen to be a happily married woman. In a, uh, delicate condition," she added, to clarify the situation.

Complete silence met her announcement.

For about one heartbeat.

"Breeding! My God, lass! I canna believe you let me drag you across Missouri without telling me. What if the bairn had . . ." the Scotsman stuttered to a halt.

"The bairn isn't due for months." Angela rubbed the small mound of her stomach hidden beneath the now-tattered cotton skirt.

Big Sal laughed.

The rollicking, gusty sound startled Angela into a smile.

Big Sal caught her breath long enough to say, "Looks like her voice made some man's blood boil." Her witty remark sent her into another round of laughter.

A scowl marred the Scotsman's handsome face. He waited impatiently for Big Sal to control her laughter.

"She's a bonnie cook," he snapped.

"A cook! Saints alive, why didn't you tell me?"

"I was having a wee bit of a fun."

"I apologize, Mrs. uh, Sal." Angela curtseyed. "We haven't been properly introduced. I am Angela

Champion, lately of Texas. The Scotsman thought you might be able to help me."

"Mrs. Champion needs a place to stay for a few days," the Scotsman said. "You need a cook."

Big Sal looked at Angela with a smile of approval. "He's right. I need a cook." She extended her hand. "If you cook as well as you claim, you can stay."

"She canna go upstairs, Big Sal. She's a real married lady."

"There's a small room off the kitchen."

A brothel. Angela Anne Stapleton Champion was going to live in a brothel. Thank the good Lord, her mother was dead. She consoled herself with the hope that Ransom would understand.

"Come along, then," Big Sal said. "I'll show you the kitchen. The girls'll be glad to have a decent meal."

Angela stopped on the kitchen threshold. Dirty pots, pans, plates, table cutlery, cups, and food debris draped every space of the room. The smell of days-old food and stale cigarette smoke churned through her nose and straight to her stomach. Her midday meal threatened to join the mess.

"It needs a little cleaning up," Big Sal said. "The cook ran off last month with some no-account drifter."

"A little cleaning up." The Scotsman flung his arm out to encompass the whole room. "This is a pigsty."

Angela silently agreed with what he said.

"Don't any of your girls know how to wash dishes?" He frowned. "You can't expect Mrs. Champion to clean this up. Not in her condition."

"Saints alive, Scotsman. She's with child, not dying of consumption."

"Don't worry about me, Mr. Buchanan." Angela patted the Scotsman's arm, appreciative of his disgust but unwilling to antagonize Big Sal. "I spent the last two months feeding a dozen men on the trail. A real kitchen is heaven."

"She'll need help cleaning up this mess." The Scotsman glared at Big Sal.

She glared back at him. "The girls should be awake by now. I'll get her some help."

"And then I'll fix a meal," Angela offered.

Big Sal relaxed. "That'd be nice. We haven't had a good meal in days." She started for the door. "This'll be easy work after cooking for men. The girls only need one hot meal a day, late in the afternoon. They fix anything else they want for themselves."

Angela wasn't sure she liked the idea of letting the women scrounge for food during the day, but she'd deal with that problem later.

"I dinna know." The frown hadn't left the Scotsman's handsome face. "Maybe I shouldn't have brought you here."

"Oh no, you don't." Big Sal went toe-to-toe with the Scotsman. "You can't come in here, promise me a cook, and then take her away."

Angela came between the two. "You did the right thing." She waited for the Scotsman's frown to ease before turning to Big Sal. "I'm not going anywhere, but I can't cook in a messy kitchen."

Within ten minutes, Helen, Athena, Hera, Narcissa, Pandora, and Aphrodite showed up in the kitchen. Angela knew they agreed to clean up the mess they'd made because it put them in the same room with the Scotsman.

Once the pots, pans, dishes, and utensils had been washed and put away, Angela found a well-stocked kitchen. She also discovered a new cast iron stove shipped from Chicago the previous year. After weeks of cooking over an open fire, Angela couldn't wait to use the stove.

She won the job with her cooking, but the first night terrified her. Whoring featured a lot of drinking, swearing, and thumping. She tried to ignore the rhythmic thumping, but she knew what it meant. Alone in her bed, listening to the sounds of lovemaking, she yearned to feel Ransom's hands running across her body.

"Are you gonna cut out those biscuits or stare at the dough all day?"

Angela jumped. "Hellfire, Narcissa. Do you have to sneak around?"

Narcissa held up her slipper-encased right foot. "I can't help it these shoes don't make any noise. The way you were daydreaming, I doubt you woulda heard me if I wore boots and stomped into the room. Worried about how mad that husband of yours'll be when he finds you at Big Sal's?"

Angela sprinkled flour over the dough. "Why would he be angry?"

Narcissa shrugged. "Some men don't like their women seeing other men, that's all."

"What is that supposed to mean?"

"Well, the Scotsman's always here, but he don't see any of the girls." Narcissa draped herself in a chair. "He's always with you."

Angela cut out a row of biscuits, enjoying the doughy smell that conjured up the aroma of hot, baked biscuits. She'd learned not to comment while Narcissa aired her displeasure with the Scotsman.

"'Course, maybe he wants to be first in line when that husband of yourn don't show up." Narcissa held out a hand and examined her fingernails.

Angela positioned the biscuits on the pan. Without bothering to look at Narcissa, she repeated a familiar response. "I've told you, the Scotsman is my friend."

"And I'm Virgin Mary."

Did she hear a note of regret in the prostitute's voice? Angela looked up into a defiant glare that dared her to feel sorry. When she didn't speak, the tense moment passed.

Angela wiped her hands on her apron before grabbing the pan of biscuits and walking toward the stove. "You may think what you will, but my husband will come for me as soon as he knows where I am."

Chapter 19

WITH BIG SAL IN JOPLIN STOP ASC STOP

Ransom read the crinkled telegram again. From the moment he'd received it, hope claimed a corner of his mind. Suspicion of a trap set by O'Brion claimed the rest.

His first stop in Joplin had been the telegraph office. The operator admitted sending the telegram, but not for a woman matching Angela's description.

"I sent that for the Scotsman."

"The Scotsman?"

"He's a scout for the U.S. Army." The man shrugged. "I don't know his real name."

"Tall, dark, Irish fellow?"

"If the man was Irish, why would they call him the Scotsman?" Exasperation colored the man's reply.

Ransom decided not to push him further. "Where can I find Big Sal?"

"She runs a whorehouse on the edge of town." The telegraph operator pointed down the main street. "White wood. On the left. You can't miss it."

Ransom crumpled the telegram and shoved it into his pocket. A whorehouse. The only clue to his wife's whereabouts. If someone had tricked him away from his search for Angela, he would kill.

He hadn't slept in days. Within an hour, rain had

washed away the trail he followed from Mrs. Oates' farm. For three days he searched in an ever-widening circle for any sign of Angela and O'Brion. The third day found him in the Baxter Springs telegraph office. His telegram to Richard had been forgotten when the operator gave him the one from Angela and one from his uncle.

Now he stood on a muddy street in Joplin, Missouri, in front of a frame house that hid its profession behind white paint and fluttering chintz curtains. Although the thought of Angela in a whorehouse sickened him, he could forgive her anything if she were alive.

Hugging that belief, he walked across the street, through the gate and up the steps to the front door of Big Sal's brothel. He rapped on the door.

The woman who answered the door chased away any lingering doubt. Neither the gauzy dressing gown nor the sheer night rail kept any secrets. Rather than lust, the sight ignited disgust. He crushed the image of his wife wearing clothes that made her nipples visible for any man to see.

"Sorry." The young woman surveyed him from his crumpled cavalry hat to the dust coated toes of his boots. "We're not open for business yet."

He pulled his hat off his head. The stench of too much too-sweet cologne coiled off the whore in an invisible cloud.

Her gaze lingered on the parcel he carried under his arm. She smiled with feminine promise. "But I'd make an exception for a handsome man like you."

Ransom swallowed a growl. "Thank you, Miss—"

"Narcissa." She casually loosened the gossamer dressing gown she wore, as if it hid anything from view. "Do you like what you see?" She caressed her breast.

He wanted to shove her aside, stomp into the house and tear it apart until he found Angela. Reaching for the self control so necessary during battle, he smiled an apology.

"Thank you for the offer, Miss Narcissa, but I've come for my wife."

Narcissa closed the front of her dressing gown and jerked the sash tight. "So the Scotsman's harlot does have a husband. I thought she was lying. Come on, I'll take you to 'em."

"You bitch, that's my brooch. You stole it!"

"You gave it to me last night."

"Why you . . ."

Two naked female bodies ran across the second floor hall. A door slammed, shaking all the bric-a-brac lining the whatnot at the bottom of the staircase.

"Let me in!" Whoever was locked out of the room beat a frustrated tattoo on the closed door.

Narcissa ignored the fracas, putting a provocative sway into her walk as she led the way down a wide hall.

Ransom followed her, unable to imagine Angela subjected to such vile women. If she had let another man touch her, he would kill both of them.

Narcissa pushed open a door. The heady aroma of cooking chicken reminded Ransom it had been a long time since he ate. Narcissa stepped to the side, giving him a clear view of the kitchen.

He saw Angela bent over a table, rolling pin in hand. A handsome man dressed in buckskins lounged in a chair beside her.

"You make the grandest pie crusts, lass."

"Aunt Julia would be pleased to hear you say that, she was certain I'd never master the art."

Angela's voice washed over him with warm familiarity. His anger dissipated in a wave of relief. She was alive and well. He opened his mouth to call her name.

Suddenly, she straightened, her hand going to her stomach. "Oh my!"

"What is it, lass?" The man jumped out of his seat. Ransom stepped forward.

"I think it moved." Awe tinged Angela's voice.

What moved?

She took the Scotsman's callused hand in hers and put it on her stomach. "Can you feel it?"

Ransom's relief sizzled into jealous anger. Angela had put another man's hand on her body.

The man closed his eyes for a moment. "I'm sorry, lass. I dinna feel the wee bairn."

Bairn? Shock vibrated through Ransom. Angela was with child?

"Angela?" Somehow she heard his strangled rendition of her name.

She turned. Joy lit her face. In a purely feminine gesture, her right hand flew up to push damp tendrils of hair off her forehead.

The gesture caught at his heart, but he ignored it. He saw only the man's large hand spread over her stomach. A red mist blinded him.

"What the hell are you doing in a whorehouse?"

His cold voice sliced her out of the man's arms.

"Ransom?" Her honey-husky voice tripped over the syllables of his name with disarming innocence. She stepped toward him. Pregnancy had subtly altered the slender contours of her body, giving her a rounded softness he had failed to notice. How long had she been with child? He stared at her abdomen, unable to see anything except another man's intimate touch.

His brain brought out a recent memory to tease him with suspicion. There had been no sign of virginity the morning he found her in his bed. Did she grow heavy with his child? Or another man's?

Perhaps O'Brion had reason to be angry about their marriage.

The man planted himself beside Angela. "Is he your husband, lass?"

"I'm her husband and I'll thank you to butt out of our business. I repeat, Angela. What are you doing in a whorehouse?" He felt the press of female bodies as whores clustered in the hallway behind him. Their cheap colognes assaulted the air.

Angela's tongue darted out to lick her lips. Hungry desire slammed into his gut, its intensity startling him. He wanted to reach out, take her in his arms and brush the sprinkling of flour off her rosy cheek.

"The Scotsman thought I'd be safe from O'Brion here."

The sound of her husky tones sent another shaft of desire winging its way through his body. He stopped it cold. Lust. Not desire based on love, but lust. He'd tried to dress lust up as love, but he couldn't love anyone the way he loved Sabrina. The barriers that kept him sane during the war slammed back into place.

"He killed Mrs. Oates." Angela clasped her hands together.

Their trembling asked for pity; he refused to offer any. "He came after me. She tried to help." Her gaze skittered away from him, lighting on a bunch of dried sage hanging near the oven. "I had to leave her like that."

"She's buried."

Damp relief filled Angela's eyes when she looked at him.

"There's no reason to be angry with the lass. It's not her fault I brought her to Big Sal. I dinna think that mon O'Brion would look here. And Big Sal needed a cook."

"I thought I told you to stay out of this."

"You canna expect me to stay quiet when you blame this bonnie lass for being here."

"I can expect you to remain quiet because this is between my wife and me."

"It's all right." Angela patted the man's arm. "Perhaps it would be best if you and the girls left us alone."

The Scotsman hesitated for a moment, then nodded. "Aye, I'll be in the hall if you need me." One last glare at Ransom and the Scotsman stalked to the door. "Now lassies, away with you. 'Tis none of your business."

The feminine grumbles faded as the door closed.

"Seyler's dead," Ransom said abruptly. "The murder charge has been dropped."

His announcement swung her gaze from the door to him. "What happened?"

"I don't know the particulars. Uncle Richard sent me a telegram. Something about a horse trampling Seyler."

A long-case clock chimed the half hour, its musical notes dulled by the closed kitchen door.

The sound broke the moment of silence between them.

"It's almost time for the girls to eat." She put the work table between them. "I was making a pie." She picked up a rolling pin lying beside a flattened ball of dough.

Restless, Ransom walked around the kitchen. "With Seyler dead, there's no reason for O'Brion to bother you. It's safe for you to go back to Tennessee."

The rolling pin thumped onto the dough.

Ransom stopped next to the work table. "I'll not claim someone else's bastard."

Angela dropped the rolling pin. Confusion trailed across her face. "What are you talking about?"

"You let that Scotsman touch you. A stranger. Or did you nurse him during the war, too?"

She folded her arms over her stomach as if to protect the child from his slashing accusation. "You think I've allowed another man to touch me as you have?"

He steeled his heart against the stricken expression in her eyes. "What do you expect me to think? I spend days looking for you, only to find you in a whorehouse with this man fondling your person."

"He saved my life!"

"And that's reason enough to allow him to touch you?"

The rolling pin rolled off the edge of the table.

"Why the Scotsman?" Raw anger obliterated her usual honeyed tones. "Don't forget Grancer, or how about Malachi? In the hayloft." Scorn ripped through the husky-honey of her voice. "Perhaps he's the father."

"Madam, you go too far."

"Not far enough."

He dreaded what she might say next and shut her up the only way he knew how. "You're nothing like your sister."

She stepped back as if he'd slapped her.

He pressed on with words that would cut her out of his life forever. "You aren't the lady she was and you never will be. Sabrina never would've stayed in a whorehouse. She never would've been unfaithful."

Angela swayed as his words beat against her. Guilt choked him. It wasn't her fault he loved Sabrina. He wanted to soften the blows, but she spoke first.

"You're right." Her shoulders slumped. "I'm not

like Sabrina. And I'll never be like her. You shouldn't have married me."

"I thought Sabrina would've wanted me to take care of you."

His confession jerked her head up. She squared her shoulders. "Sabrina would see me in hell before she saw me married to you."

Her conviction startled him.

"No," he disagreed. "Sabrina had a generous heart. She would've wanted me to protect you."

"Sabrina had no interest in protecting me."

"Of course, she did. You were sisters."

"No, we weren't."

Ransom's world shifted. "Dr. Stapleton was your father, wasn't he?"

"He adopted me. Sabrina and I weren't related."

"You grew up as sisters. Everyone thought you were sisters."

"She played the part of devoted sister to keep anyone from learning the truth."

"Why would she want to keep your adoption secret?"

"She worried someone would realize I wasn't a real Stapleton."

"What difference did that make?"

"My father was a half-breed Cherokee Indian."

How could he have been so blind? The straight black hair, the skin that bore a light tan all year, and the high cheekbones. "You're part Indian."

It wasn't a question, it was acceptance.

Angela didn't hear it, because Sabrina had convinced her no Southern gentleman would accept her. "Everyone thought we were the best of sisters because Sabrina feared social ostracism more than she despised my heritage."

Stooping, she picked up the rolling pin and walked toward the wash pan.

Ransom grabbed her arm and spun her around, the rolling pin went flying. "Why are you saying these things about Sabrina?"

The rolling pin thwacked into the front of the oven. She jumped; he tightened his grip. She welcomed the pain of his fingers digging into her arm. Maybe it would obliterate the pain in her heart.

"It doesn't matter now. Sabrina's dead."

"And can't defend herself from your allegations." He released her, shuddering as if her arm were covered with small pox. "I don't believe you. Sabrina was kind. A generous woman."

In a way, he was correct.

The Sabrina she'd created for him during the war was kind and generous. Angela doubted if admitting she wrote the letters would change anything. Since Ransom couldn't stop loving the memory she'd created, Sabrina would always be between them.

Angela smoothed her hands down the front of her apron, gathered her courage and looked Ransom in the eye. "In a way, I have you to thank for introducing me to Indians. Now that I've met Malachi and Ho-ko-lin-shee, I realize I have no reason to be ashamed of my Indian blood. They're good, honorable men. I'm proud of the Cherokee blood in my veins."

"You should've known by my friendship with Malachi that I wouldn't be ashamed of your Indian blood."

She waved aside his claim. "Perhaps, but you'd spend your life measuring me against an illusion."

He scowled. "Sabrina was no illusion."

She smiled her sympathy. "No, she was a flesh-and-blood woman. No better and no worse than any number of women, but you remember perfection no living woman could achieve. And you've closed your heart to anything else."

Cupping her hands beneath her small, rounded abdomen, she stood a little taller. "I deserve more. And my child deserves a father who isn't suspicious of his parentage."

She'd spoken her heart and her emotions skated from sorrow to joy and back again. The truth cost her Ransom, but she had found herself.

He stood in the kitchen of a whorehouse, his face a study in confusion. She wanted to put her arms around him and tell him everything would be all right. But she couldn't because it wasn't. His devotion to a memory stood between him and love.

She waited, unwilling to be the one to say goodbye.

He turned to leave. She heard the soft crinkle of paper and noticed he carried a wrapped parcel. He swung back around and held it out to her.

"I bought you a dress in Baxter Springs. There's a little money, too."

She hesitated, feeling guilty about taking money from him. What would he do if she admitted she had money? Would he insist she stay with him because he needed it for the ranch? She pushed aside the temptation that given more time he would come to love her. Her newfound self-confidence was too fragile to risk. She'd always love Ransom, but she couldn't live with him.

"I didn't get much for the beeves. The folks in Baxter Springs are dead set against us running them through their farmland." He pressed the parcel into her hands. "But I sold a few head to raise some cash for Harrison and Sawyer. They offered to drive the rest of the beeves to Iowa for a better price."

He stared at her for a moment, as if memorizing her face.

Her soul cried out her despair. She wanted to touch him one last time. To keep her hands from reaching for him, she clutched the soft package to her chest. He looked as dazed as she felt.

"I guess I'll be joining them, now. Or going back to Texas . . ." He shoved his hat on his head.

"Thank you for helping me when I needed it."

When he opened the kitchen door, three whores fell through the doorway. Stepping over the scantily clad bodies, Ransom shouldered his way past the remaining women.

"If you don't want 'im, I'll have a go."

"Saints alive, Pandora, get up." Big Sal waded through the women on the kitchen floor. "All of you. Upstairs. There's no reason for you to be here until Angela calls you for dinner."

Numb, Angela watched Big Sal sweep the women out of the kitchen. One moment she was staring at the kitchen door, the next moment she was staring at the ceiling.

"Open up, lass, and take a wee drop."

"What happened?"

"You fainted." The Scotsman cradled her head in his lap. "Take a swallow. 'Tisn't often Big Sal shares her best brandy."

Angela inhaled the rich aroma of expensive liquor as he pushed the small glass against her lips.

"Just a wee drop to make you feel better."

She took a sip. The brandy burned its way down her throat; tears streamed down her face.

The Scotsman held her in his arms and rocked her. "There, there, lass. T'will be right."

"I'm sorry." She sniffed back her tears. "It's silly of me to cry." He wasn't Ransom, but for one moment she closed her eyes and pretended he was. She listened to the steady beat of his heart and wished her head lay upon another chest.

"I'll be happy to follow the mon and cut out his black heart for you lass."

His offer rumbled through his chest. She jerked away as if the words scorched her ear. "Hellfire, why would I want you to kill the man I love?"

"'Tis as I suspected. But he loves a colleen named Sabrina?"

Her indignation fled. She couldn't stop the downward pull on her lips. Afraid her voice would tremble, she nodded.

"I dinna understand. Why didn't he marry this Sabrina?"

"She's my sister." Angela grabbed the hand holding the brandy glass and helped herself to another sip. Fortified by the warm fuzzy feeling seeping through her body, she said, "She wasn't really my sister. I'm adopted. And she's dead."

"So your mon canna marry her?"

"Noooooo." She took another, larger swallow of brandy. "But he can marry her memory."

"You're a bonnie lass. Yet your husband prefers your sister's memory?"

She took the glass out of his hand and pointed toward the brandy bottle. "More?"

"A wee bit and that's all." He steadied the glass with his hand covering hers while he poured another dab of brandy.

"That's a wee bit, all right." She lifted the glass and tapped it against the brandy bottle. "Here's to a fake memory." She sipped the brandy and leaned against the Scotsman. "The Sabrina my husband loves doesn't exist. I made her up."

"How can you make up a sister?"

"I said that wrong. I had a stepsister named Sabrina. But she wasn't very nice. Beautiful." She nodded her head. "All the men thought Sabrina was beautiful."

She squinted up at the Scotsman. "They never saw the cruel Sabrina. Why, she wouldn't give up one petticoat for the Confederacy."

Twisting the glass, she watched the light play through the amber liquid. "Big Sal has good taste."

"I canna understand how you made up a memory of your sister."

"It was easy. He met her, they got engaged, he left for the war. He didn't really know Sabrina. He didn't know she hated to write." Angela waved her hand in the air. "Terrible penmanship. She didn't want him to know. So I wrote all the letters."

"He doesn't ken you wrote him?"

She put her lips together and turned an imaginary key.

"Ah, lass. What have you done?"

"Created a memory too powerful for my love to conquer."

Chapter 20

A cheery whistle blasted Ransom awake. Something rumbled; dirt pelted his face. He lifted a heavy arm, trying to shield his head while squinting at his tormentor.

A spry, elderly man swept cigar butts, dirt and bits of paper off a wood sidewalk eye level with Ransom's current position. The closer the broom wielding whistler got, the more grit hit Ransom's face.

He tried to roll behind the nearby rain barrel. "Sweet Jesu." His head pounded in rebellion.

"Why morning, Reb. I didn't see ya there."

The cheery words reverberated in his head. Ransom felt as crumbled as the cigar butts the old man swept off the sidewalk. His mouth tasted of stale whiskey, and he hoped the stench assaulting his nose wasn't his person.

He dropped his head into his hands, the past twenty-four hours telescoping into his battered brain. Getting drunk and spending a night in the gutter failed to erase the memory of what he'd said to Angela.

Remorse ate his soul. He'd let jealousy rule his tongue. Being unacquainted with the emotion, it'd taken him three shots of whiskey to name his reaction to seeing the Scotsman's hand on Angela.

How he regretted everything. He didn't want Angela to be like Sabrina. He wanted her to be herself, because he loved her.

Jealousy. He rolled the word around in his mouth, unaccustomed to its taste. Old-fashioned, impossible-to-recognize jealousy, and now she'd despise him forever.

He struggled to prop himself against the rain barrel. The street whirled, then settled into place.

"I cain't believe the sheriff missed you last night. He usually puts drunks in jail to sleep it off."

"Jes' lucky, I guess." Ransom struggled to his feet, wondering if he'd been robbed while he was unconscious. Patting his clothes, he felt the reassuring wad of money. What he needed was a bath, a hair cut and shave, clean clothes, a little food, and a lot of coffee.

And then he'd leave Joplin.

Angela was right, she deserved more than a broken-down ex-soldier with a broken-down ranch. She deserved someone who didn't spend his time mooning over a memory even when love stabbed him in the gut like a wily Long Horn.

He'd lost Angela. And he'd lost the right to put his hands on her stomach and feel her soft curves and the shape of his child.

He looked around for his hat, moving more slowly than the man sweeping the sidewalk. The crown of his cavalry hat peeked from behind the rain barrel. He picked it up, brushed it against his thigh and settled it on his head.

Two hours later, Ransom felt like a new man. His headache had receded to a dull throb, three cups of coffee sloshed around a stomach-stretching breakfast of eggs, sausage, and biscuits. A clean set of clothing garbed his clean body, and as soon as he found a clean pair of socks and put on his newly shined boots, he'd be ready to go.

When a quick search of his saddlebag failed to yield any socks, he emptied the bag on the bed. Ah, he did have a pair of socks. They'd been wedged in Angela's diary. Now they held the first page open. He remembered Shoehorn's pleasure at finding the book intact after the stampede.

"Look, Major, Mrs. Champion's diary. It ain't hardly damaged considering the pounding those idiot beeves gave the camp."

Ransom had stashed it in his saddlebag and forgotten about it. As he reached for the open book, he saw Angela's dark head bent over the pages as she wrote by the flickering light of the camp fire, fussing when a wayward spark snapped too close to her precious book.

A whiff of leather-bound book and the crisp feel of the paper reminded him how long it been since he'd had time to read. But reading Angela's diary wasn't an option. He closed the book, but not before he recognized the handwriting.

He blinked in surprise.

That handwriting had filled the letters written by Sabrina. He stared at the slender volume, seeing the gilt initials inscribed on the leather cover. They gleamed in the late morning sun that slanted through the hotel window.

"A.A.S."

Angela Anne Stapleton.

He reopened the journal and studied the first page. Familiar loops and swirls spelled out Angela Anne Stapleton.

What he saw failed to mesh with what he knew. The handwriting belonged to Sabrina. It was indelibly imprinted in his memory. The letters she wrote might have been destroyed during the war, but he recognized the handwriting.

Only it wasn't Sabrina who wrote these entries. He scanned them. Page after page described the trail drive from Texas to Kansas. He saw concise notes on each injury suffered by the cow herders during the past few weeks.

It was impossible for Sabrina to have written this. There was only one explanation.

His knees buckled. He collapsed on the bed. Angela had written him during the war. She had pretended to be Sabrina.

A wagon rumbled past his opened window. Someone called a cheery "hello." Ransom stared at Angela's diary. How could the world sound normal when it had been turned upside down?

Why had Angela posed as Sabrina?

Sabrina's coy confession echoed in his mind.

"Father says I have the worst penmanship possible. He makes Angela keep all the household accounts."

A confession he'd soothed away with a compliment and a kiss.

He sifted through other memories. The early letters contained stilted inanities and childish pouting because he was gone. Later letters displayed a subtle wit and intelligence that captivated him. He remembered his pleasure at discovering Sabrina possessed a livelier mind than he expected.

Had Sabrina dictated the early letters and then lost interest? Odd such a treasonous thought existed in his heart, but too many snippets of reality nipped at his worn illusion. Angela had been correct. He'd fashioned Sabrina into a perfect memory to protect his heart.

But Angela had let him live with the illusion.

And she was going to tell him why.

* * *

Narcissa opened the door at Big Sal's. "Why if it ain't Mrs. Champion's husband."

"Will you tell my wife I'm here?" Anger clenched his jaw so tight he was surprised the words came out.

"Well now, let me think. Is your little ole wife here?"

Coffee and eggs might have dulled his headache, but he wasn't in any mood to verbally spar with a prostitute.

"Perhaps Big Sal would be of more help."

Narcissa raised her hand and cradled her right breast, pushing its fullness against the sheer fabric of her dressing gown.

Fed up, Ransom pushed past her. "Angela! I want to see you."

"You keep up that yelling, you'll wake Big Sal. She's a real bear when she first wakes up." Narcissa closed the door and leaned back against it. "Why don't you come upstairs and let me show you what you been missing?" She hooked her thumbs in the loose fabric at the rounded neck of her gown and pulled it downward to reveal her breasts.

"I'm not going to ask you again. Where is my wife?"

Narcissa arched her back, jutting her breasts forward. "She's just a pregnant whore, don't ya want me instead?"

Something snapped. Ransom found himself inches from Narcissa's face, her bared breasts almost touching his chest. It pleased him to see her expression reflect fright.

He grabbed a handful of the cloth under her breasts and lifted her off her feet. Pressing her back against the door frame, he raised her until they were nose to nose.

"If you were a man and said that about my wife, I

would call you out. Now I'm not going to ask again. Where is my wife."

Narcissa licked her lips in an entirely non-sexy way. When she answered, her voice held more croak than allure. "She ain't here."

His heart sank. He hadn't considered the possibility she'd be gone.

"You shouldn't be so fast to turn this down." Her voice held a renewed note of cockiness. "With Angela running off with that man, your bed'll be empty."

"Damn that Scotsman."

"Saints alive, Narcissa. Tell whoever it is, we're closed. How can anyone sleep with all this racket going on?"

Big Sal came down the staircase, one hand clutching her calico dressing gown while the other clung to the banister.

"I told you not to wake her."

"It's you! What do you want? If you think I'll let you bother Angela again, you've got the wrong madam."

Ransom released Narcissa, who crumpled to the floor. Three strides put him at the bottom of the stairs. Big Sal stayed on the bottom step. It put her at the same height as Ransom.

"I've come to apologize to my wife." He jerked his thumb toward Narcissa. "She claims Angela ran off with the Scotsman."

"I never said that!"

Big Sal shot Narcissa a pained expression. "That's impossible." A blush tinged her full cheeks.

Before Ransom could ask why, the Scotsman appeared on the second-floor landing, a sheet wrapped around his torso.

Ransom turned around to look at Narcissa. "If she didn't leave with him . . ." Cold fear clamped his stomach.

"O'Brion?" The Scotsman's question rang in the hall.

"He didn't give no name," Narcissa said. "He didn't need to. He had something better than a name."

"If you don't tell us what happened this instant, I swear I'll kick you out of this house."

Narcissa pouted. "Ain't no call to get mean, Big Sal. The man showed me a piece of paper. It were a warrant for her arrest. Said she's wanted for murdering her own sister. In Tennessee."

"Saints alive, Narcissa," Big Sal said. "He could've shown you a playbill. You can't even read."

"I can read a little."

Sweet Jesu, O'Brion had Angela. Conversation swirled around him like the annoying chatter of distant birds while he fought the panic rampaging through his soul.

"Not enough to read a warrant for an arrest. Saints alive, you let a killer take Angela."

"How was I to know? He didn't look like no killer. Handsome devil. With a wonderful way of talking." Narcissa looked in sullen resentment at the two men in the hall. "She gets all the pretty ones. What makes her so damn special?"

"The lass told me the charges had been dropped."

The Scotsman's ringing pronouncement crashed into Ransom's panic, scattering it into manageable pieces.

"Yes. The charge was false. Trumped-up by a man seeking revenge because she spied for the Confederacy during the war. My wife wants to go to medical school and learn how to be a doctor. She's not a killer.

"I'm an Army scout, Mr. Champion. I'll help you find them."

"He's the best," Big Sal smiled up at the Scotsman.

"Now lassie, I dinna ken Tall Feathers would agree with you. He thinks he's the verra best Army scout."

"Don't pay him no never mind, Mr. Champion. He'll find Angela for you."

Ransom wished his conviction was as strong as Big Sal's.

Chapter 21

"Your warrant is useless." Angela's defiant words came out as a dry croak when O'Brion removed the gag.

He held a cup of water to her lips. With her hands tied behind her back, she had to wait until he tilted the cup enough for her to drink. Mastering the urge to guzzle the water, she sipped as if her mouth weren't as dry as the Arabian desert.

For some reason, he'd brought her back to Mrs. Oates' farm. A layer of dust coated the china she'd set on the table that last night, while the faint odor of scorched beef stew told her the stove had burned itself out. The intangible air of human abandonment weighted the one-room cabin with isolation.

The feeling wove its way into her soul, blending readily with the soul-numbing despair she had felt since Ransom walked out of her life.

She was all alone. Ransom had left for Iowa, his love for Sabrina intact. When she refused the Scotsman's help, he'd bid her goodbye.

"'Tis the colonel. He sent a telegram. I'm to leave for Fort Leavenworth with the light."

"I'll miss you," she said.

Ransom had set her free. Nothing stood between

her and medical school. Except her aching heart and a baby.

"Why dinna you go with me, lass? Or I can lend you the money to take the train back to Tennessee."

His offer had touched her.

"Thank you, but Ransom left me some money. I'll leave . . .soon." She'd wanted to leave Ransom from the moment they'd married, and now she couldn't gather the energy to act.

"Aye, lass." The Scotsman hugged her tightly in farewell. "A few days under the hot Kansas sun may well make your husband see the truth."

Was that why she waited? She didn't know.

Now, with the Scotsman on his way to Fort Leavenworth, only Narcissa knew O'Brion had taken her. And O'Brion had paid well for the whore's silence.

Angela licked her damp lips. "Seyler is dead. The murder charge has been dropped."

"Wouldn't I be knowing that."

A frisson of fear cascaded down her spine. He knew Seyler was dead, yet he'd used a bogus arrest warrant to spirit her out of Big Sal's house. "I don't understand. Why kidnap me and bring me here?"

"Kidnap?" He finished off the water in the cup, wiped his sleeve across his mouth. "Well, now, is it kidnapping you think I've done?"

"Have you a better description for taking someone without permission?" She wiggled her hands, which he had tied behind her back. "And tying them up. Keeping them prisoner. Yes, I would call that kidnapping."

O'Brion clutched his chest. "There's a storm of dismay in me heart. Your well-being has always been my dearest wish."

"My well-being? You thought it conducive to my well-being to arrest me for the murder of my sister?"

His expression darkened. "I'm thinking it was a way to stop Seyler from having you killed."

His words startled her. "I don't understand."

"Me plan was simple. Into jail with yourself and safe from Seyler."

"As if Seyler would have let that stop him," she scoffed.

He leaned closer. His breath smelled faintly of tobacco as it warmed her face. "Didn't I have to think fast? It were a play for time."

She refused to cower before him and sat straight in the cane seat chair. "Time for what?"

"To arrange our nuptials."

"You think I would have married you?"

His lips brushed her cheek. "With this love raging in me heart, I'm knowing yourself'll marry me."

His eyes, only inches from hers, glittered. Their single-minded purpose frightened her. Afraid he'd see her fear, she turned her face.

She needed time to think and she couldn't think with him so close. There was only one place on the farm where she'd have complete privacy.

"Will you please untie me? I need to visit the, uh, uh . . . necessary?" She couldn't stop the blush, if she wanted. Only her nursing experience saved her from utter mortification at such a personal request.

"Now, then, is it a monster you think I am? Of course, I'll untie you. And escort you there. And escort you back."

She smiled her gratitude, trying not to hear the threat. Her brain whirled with ways to escape while he loosened the ropes binding her feet and then her hands. Her half boots had protected her ankles, but her wrists burned as if she'd held them over a steaming stew pot.

"Faith, I've gone and hurt your poor wrists."

She pulled her hands around and held them in front of her, palms up. Raw, chaffed skin banded each wrist.

"Is it an apology you want?" He grabbed her hands. "Well, and didn't you leave me tied up like a Christmas goose when you ran away. Still, I didn't mean to make your dear wrists raw."

To her horror he planted wet kisses on each wrist. His mustache prickled the tender skin. She wanted to jerk her hands away, but she feared his temper. No matter how hard she tried, she couldn't erase the image of Mrs. Oates' body being thrown backward as O'Brion's bullets slammed into her. Unwilling to trigger his anger, she swallowed her fear.

"Thank you for your concern. They feel fine," she lied as she gently disengaged their hands. "I need to um . . ."

"Oh, yes." He bowed slightly, sweeping his right hand in the direction of the door.

She walked across the room, wiping the inside of first one and then the other wrist on the front of her skirt. She could hear his boots on the rough wood floor, feel his body's presence trailing behind her in the small room.

When they reached the front door, his arm snaked around her, to open the door. She stepped onto the porch. A forlorn tub of dead roses, born from a cutting Mrs. Oates had brought with her from New England, sat at the top of the porch steps.

"What a glorious day to begin our new life. It's come to me mind as this farm has no one to farm it. Faith and it will make us a good home."

"You want to live here? Pretend you didn't shoot poor Mrs. Oates in cold blood?" The words slipped out in a rush. Horrified, she stopped.

To her infinite relief, he ignored her questions.

"I'm thinking it's a tidy little farm." He stood at the top of the steps and surveyed the overgrown fields that bumped into the wilder prairie. "It calls to me heart, it does. A place where a man can learn how to farm."

Did he expect her to stay here with him? Was he insane?

Perhaps he was. She sifted through her medical knowledge, scant as it was about insanity, finally remembering that some physicians regarded it as a disease affecting the brain. And, dear God, jealousy numbered in the list of causes. Had O'Brion's infatuation become jealousy when she married Ransom? Had his jealousy become so strong it had stolen his ability to think rationally?

O'Brion patted her arm. "Surprised, are you? Can it be an Irishman as doesn't know how to farm. Boston born, the land's a mystery to me. But I'm after thinking an Irishman knows the land. And sure, it's in his blood."

"You want me to live here with you?" She refused to panic, putting a thoughtful expression on her face.

"Is it not destiny as brought us together? Now, you were meant for me. Ours is a perfect love."

"What about my husband?" Once again, her tongue got ahead of her brain. She widened her eyes as if asking an innocent question.

Anger flickered in his eyes and tightened his smile. "Faith and haven't I explained it. I'm your husband now."

"Aye, this is their trail." The Scotsman rose from where he squatted beside the two-lane track they had followed from Joplin.

"Sweet Jesu, I think I know where he's taking her."

Ransom's horse shied sideways, made nervous by his harsh tone of voice. "Mrs. Oates' farm is about five miles west of here."

"'Tis a sad place." The Scotsman swung himself into the saddle. "Angela said she found the graves of Mr. Oates and two bairns. Poor Mrs. Oates went crazy with grieving. Every evening she pretended they'd come home to her."

Ransom grimaced. Another sin for Angela to forgive. He'd left her with a madwoman.

"Ate dinner with them," continued the Scotsman. "Talked about the day's plowing with her husband. Tucked the bairns into bed."

Sympathy for Mrs. Oates filled Ransom's mind. Oh, he might not have pretended Sabrina was alive, but war and death had hacked at his sanity until he found it easier to love an illusion.

But life, led by Angela, beat at his barricaded heart until her generous love shattered the walls.

And now O'Brion had her.

"He wanted to marry her," Ransom said. "But Fletcher convinced her she should marry me."

"I dinna ken what you're saying. The day I found Angela, she told me O'Brion wanted to kill her."

"That's probably what she thinks after seeing him kill Mrs. Oates."

"I thought the mon who sent O'Brion was dead. The charges dropped."

"He is and they are," Ransom said.

"Willna she tell this O'Brion she's no longer charged with murdering her sister?"

"Knowing Angela, she'll use every weapon in her arsenal." Ransom remembered her knife. "That's what gives me hope."

* * *

The three-inch knife blade gleamed in an errant ray of sunshine shining through a knothole in the back wall of the necessary. Angela examined the knife as if she'd never seen it. The walnut handle, carved to fit a small man's hand, rested snugly in hers.

It seemed a puny weapon, but it was all she had. Nor was she sure she could cut through human skin, muscle and tendon to harm, not heal. Yet if she did not incapacitate O'Brion, she would be caught in his web of insanity.

She hefted the knife in her right hand. Grancer, who had judged her incapable of killing anyone, had stressed using the knife as a way to gain time to escape an assailant.

He had been right. She could not kill O'Brion.

But she could injure him.

If she buried three inches of steel in his thigh, and tugged the knife through the flesh, he would go down.

And she could escape.

Relief spun through Ransom when he saw Angela leave the necessary. At the Scotsman's suggestion, they'd left their horses half a mile away and covered the rest of the distance to the farm on foot. They'd made it to the creek when Ransom saw O'Brion leaning against a blackjack oak a few feet from the necessary.

Dropping to the ground, Ransom peered through the underbrush. The tree hid all but O'Brion's elbow; he couldn't get a clean shot. Looking at the Scotsman, he pointed to his rifle, then at O'Brion, and shook his head.

The Scotsman nodded and made a circling motion

with his hand. Ransom tapped his hat in a small salute. Seconds later, he was alone in the trees that trailed the creek. Slowly, the chirrup and chatter of birds and squirrels resumed. An inquisitive blue jay landed on a nearby branch.

Ransom ignored everything, his Enfield rifle trained on a brown-clad elbow.

Angela left the necessary before the Scotsman got into position. Perspiration dampened Ransom's hands as he waited for O'Brion to move into his gun sight. Although O'Brion pushed himself away from the tree, he waited for Angela to reach him.

She said something. Ransom was too far away to catch the words, but the murmur of her honey-husky voice caressed his ears.

"What's this?" O'Brion's harsh question ripped through the quiet afternoon.

He grabbed Angela's right wrist, twisting it upward. Sunlight shimmered off her knife. Fear clutched Ransom's heart. His finger pressed the trigger, he sucked in his breath and prayed for the chance to shoot.

He watched O'Brion wrench the knife out of Angela's hand. Thrown off balance, she stumbled and clutched at O'Brion's arm for support. He backhanded her. The blow spun her to the ground and he was on her in an instant.

Not once did Ransom have a clear shot. The wrestling couple became a flurry of petticoat and skirt. Ransom tossed aside his rifle, splashed across the creek, and ran toward the fight.

O'Brion never heard him coming.

Straddling Angela, O'Brion had her pinned to the ground by the time Ransom reached them.

"Is it me heart you were after planning to carve out?"

"That idea makes me smile." Ransom pulled O'Brion off Angela with his left hand while his right

fist connected solidly with O'Brion's chin. The Irishman flew backward to land in a heap at the bottom of
a small oak tree. Pulling out his Navy Colt revolver,
Ransom walked up to the still body.

He nudged O'Brion with the toe of his boot.
O'Brion didn't move. "Damn glass jaw," Ransom muttered to himself.

"He tore my new dress." At Angela's dazed com-
plaint, he turned his back on O'Brion. She sat on the
ground, fingering her torn sleeve.

"Hush, love." He knelt beside her and took her
hands in his. "I'll buy you another one."

"What are you doing here?"

Her trembling mouth and damp gray eyes ignited
tender feelings he thought he'd never experience
again. He wanted to take her in his arms and never
let her go. But his harsh words stood between them.

"I came to rescue you."

"I thought you went to Ohio."

"I got drunk, first. Spent the night in a gutter re-
penting all those terrible things I said to you." He
grinned his best repentant grin.

She reached up and touched his cheek. Her fingers slid along his skin as lightly as a spider's dance
across its web. Tenderness. Possessiveness. Desire.
She unleashed such a jumble of feelings, he couldn't
pinpoint any one. But he knew he wanted desperately
for her to understand he loved her.

"I went back to Big Sal's to apologize. You were
gone."

"You didn't mean those awful things you said?"

"Not a word."

"Unhand me wife, Rebel."

Angela shrank against him. Ransom shifted, keeping his body between O'Brion and Angela. Worried
about Angela, he'd forgotten to pick up O'Brion's

weapon and now the Irishman pointed a Remington revolver at his head. Behind him, he heard Angela's skirts rustle.

"Is it an engraved invitation yourself is waiting for?"

Ransom eased to his feet. His own gun lay on the ground where he had placed it while he consoled Angela. It might as well have been on the cabin roof.

Not more than twenty-five feet away, he saw the tip of the Scotsman's head as the man belly crawled toward them. As if reading Ransom's mind, the Scotsman raised up and tossed something to O'Brion's left. It splattered against the ground. At the sound, O'Brion turned.

Ransom bent to pick up his gun when something silver flashed past his head. Angela's knife nailed O'Brion's right arm to the small tree behind him. The tableau froze for a heartbeat.

Ransom moved first, scooping up his gun while O'Brion ripped his sleeve free. Turning slightly, Ransom shoved Angela to the ground, aimed and fired.

O'Brion crumpled to the ground, blood gurgling from three holes in his chest.

Angela's soft, "Oh no!" floated from behind him.

"It's perfect." Angela placed a bouquet of wildflowers on the grave at the foot of the new cross. Asters, tansy, verbena and some flowers she didn't recognize mingled their sweet scent with the warm summer air. She ran her fingers across the wood, tracing the rough letters the Scotsman had carved. Charity Amelia Taylor Oates.

Blinking back a tear, she joined Ransom and the Scotsman who stood at the edge of the small family cemetery. "Thank you." She smiled up at the Scotsman.

"'Tis nothing, lass."

To her surprise, the Scotsman blushed.

Ransom extended his hand. "Thank you for helping me find my wife." He glanced in the direction of O'Brion's grave. They had buried him across the creek, out of sight of the Oates' farm. "And for helping us deal with him."

"'Twas a pleasure."

"The sheriff in Baxter Springs will know what to do with these." Angela gave the Scotsman the Oates family Bible. It contained a letter she'd written to Mr. Oates' sister explaining about the deaths.

"Aye." The Scotsman took the Bible, his gaze lingering on Angela.

Was that regret she saw in his incredible green eyes? She reached up and hugged him. "You're a good man, Gregor Buchanan."

"Aye, but not an angel?" His green eyes twinkled with amusement.

"Not for a long time, I hope."

He squeezed her shoulders, placed a small kiss on her forehead and set her away from him. "'Tis time for me to go." He looked at Ransom. "You're a lucky man to have won her heart."

Standing side-by-side, Ransom and Angela watched him ride away.

Ransom draped his arm around Angela's shoulder. "I am a lucky man." He bent his head close to her ear. "I've loved you a long time, haven't I?"

His warm breath sent shivers of pleasure along her spine. "You have?" Her voice held an odd, quivery note.

Ransom nipped her ear lobe.

It made it difficult for her to concentrate.

"I've a confession to make. Shoehorn found your

diary after the stampede. I stuck it in my saddlebags weeks ago and forgot about it. Until this morning."

She knew what he planned to confess, but the silky slide of his tongue on her ear chased away her apprehension.

"Your diary fell open on the bed and I recognized your handwriting. From all those letters you wrote me during the war."

She turned her head to look at him, losing the touch of his tongue. Disappointment tinged the haze of passion he'd created, but she acted out of habit, defending his memory of Sabrina.

"Sabrina had terrible penmanship. I only wrote what she dictated."

"Perhaps that's how it started, but we both know that's not how it ended."

She couldn't look him in the eye and deny the truth. He slipped his finger beneath her chin and tilted her face upward.

"She lost interest in a courtship conducted by letter. But you kept writing."

She nodded.

"The letters changed because you weren't writing what she told you to write. You wrote from your heart."

"It seemed cruel to stop the letters. You said they kept you sane."

"Ah, I did, didn't I." His finger stroked its way along her jaw. "With each letter, I fell a little deeper in love. So you see, I've loved you a long time."

Shivers raced up and down Angela's spine, growing in intensity as she watched his mouth move down to capture hers.

"It looks as if I married the right sister after all," he whispered before his lips settled over her mouth.

Chapter 22

Angela leaned back against Ransom's wet thigh and sighed in contentment. "I'm glad we decided to ride back to Texas."

Ransom trailed tiny kisses from her ear lobe down her neck to her shoulder."

She relaxed, closing her eyes to better enjoy the familiar liquid heat warming her down there.

"Seems a little quiet, don't you think?" He kissed his way to her elbow. "No crazy beeves running away at the snap of a twig." Now his mouth tickled its way across her inner wrist. "No herders pestering you for a cup of hot coffee."

"Mmmmmmm."

"How long has it been since I told you I love you?"

She pursed her lips in pretend concentration. "It's been about five minutes, I believe."

"That long?"

He nuzzled her neck. "We could be Adam and Eve. Alone in the Garden of Eden."

Angela eased her eyes open. "It's lovely, but we'd starve."

They reclined in the shallow end of "their" pool in water warmed by the July sun. An afternoon breeze flirted with the tree surrounding the pool, dappling the water with moving shadows. Angela wiggled her toes. The water wasn't as deep as it had been a few weeks earlier, but it cooled them off.

"I've heard turtle meat is excellent."

Angela looked at the group of slider turtles sunning on a log at the far end of the pool. They seemed unperturbed by Ransom's comment.

"Don't expect me to cook it. I like turtles."

"Then I won't tell anyone this feast awaits when we come this way next year."

"You're planning on another trail drive?"

Momentary silence met her question.

"If Harrison and Sawyer get us enough money to keep the ranch going for another year."

Guilt bit Angela's conscience. She sat up, turned and faced Ransom. "I've got money."

His eyebrows rose slightly, but he didn't say anything. She heard one of the horses snuffling in the grass near the pool. A meadowlark's piercing song eclipsed the warm afternoon drone of insects. Angela had to fill the void of human silence.

"Father invested funds in England. He couldn't get to them during the war." She spoke to the dark blond hairs on Ransom's chest.

"When Sabrina died, I inherited the money." She lifted her eyes to his. "I planned to use it for medical college. Legally, what's mine is yours. To do what you want with it."

A turtle fell off the log with a plop.

Nervous, Angela looked at the log. "I should have told you. Saved you and Richard from worrying about the ranch." She felt a tear dribble down her cheek.

Ransom took her in his arms. She loved the soft-scratchy feel of the light hair that fanned his chest. He nestled her closer.

"It's all right, sweetheart. You did what you thought

best at the time. We shouldn't need the money. And if we did use any, I'd pay it back."

She leaned to the side and looked up at him. "Why?"

"You said it's for medical school, didn't you?"

"But what about . . ," she patted her rounded stomach.

"This fall isn't a good time, but don't they have classes each year? You can go next year."

"You'd do that for me?"

"If men like Sergio, Harrison, and Sawyer are there to help Uncle Richard, I don't see why we can't go to Pennsylvania for a few months. I'd have to be back to hunt beeves in the spring."

"You'd go with me?"

"As if I'd send my wife and child into a Yankee state without protection." His voice held a mock indignation; his eyes lit with amusement.

She kissed his jaw. "Thank you."

Ransom tucked a damp lock of hair behind her ear, pleased to realize her hair tickled her shoulders now. Their wedding day would always be entwined with the memory of cutting off her beautiful hair.

"I'm the one who should be grateful. Even old Seyler deserves my gratitude. If he hadn't been hell-bent on seeking revenge against Fletcher, I would've left you behind in Tennessee."

She smiled up at him dreamily while her left hand smoothed the hairs on his chest. His skin tingled from her sweet touch.

"And I would've gone to Pennsylvania."

He concentrated on their conversation, needing to explain how he felt about her. "Instead, you helped me with my dream. This hasn't been the easiest time for you."

Her hand stilled on his chest. "I only agreed to the

trail drive because I wanted to reach the train at Baxter Springs."

He pressed her closer to his chest, unfazed by her confession. The past no longer held him in its thrall. She was here with him now, that's all that mattered.

"Even in Joplin, I couldn't leave you," she continued. "I kept telling myself I should, but I couldn't."

Curiosity got the better of him. "What made you change your mind?"

She swept her arm outward. "You brought me here. This is where you called me Angela for the first time when we made love."

"Sweet Jesu!" Embarrassment burned through him; she had heard him. He opened his mouth to explain.

Her fingertips sealed his lips. "Don't. I understood. You spent years loving Sabrina. I didn't expect her memory to evaporate because you married me."

He kissed her fingertips. "You are well named, Angela."

She smiled. "Now you're in such a grateful mood, I have a request."

"Your wish is my command, sweetheart."

"Do you think we could find Ho-ko-lin-shee's village?"

Startled by her question, he reeled in his hot expectations. "Maybe." He nudged his thoughts away from sex. "Why do you want to see Ho-ko-lin-shee?"

She hesitated as if weighing her answer. "I'd like to visit an Indian village and meet more Indians. Learn something about my father's people."

He nodded, wanting to show approval but reluctant to interrupt her.

"And I want to invite Ho-ko-lin-shee to Texas." She looked up at him, uncertainty on her face. "Do you think he'd come? He knows so much about healing.

It'd be an honor to study with him. If he would teach me."

"I don't have any answers, but you won't know if he'll agree until you ask him."

"Then you don't mind going to his village?"

"All we have to do is find it."

"Oh, Ransom!" She melted against his chest. "I love you."

From the shining excitement in his wife's eyes, he knew she trusted him implicitly. She believed he would find Ho-ko-lin-shee. He wasn't as sure as she was, but he figured three years in the cavalry traversing a half a dozen states gave him the skill to find an Indian on the prairie.

Not that he had any incentive to find Ho-ko-lin-shee in a hurry. Not with Angela's soft breasts tickling his chest and her sweet lips nibbling at his mouth. No, it would probably take him a few weeks of lustful wandering to find any Indian village at all.

ABOUT THE AUTHOR

Ginger Hanson is a former college history teacher who found writing historical romance a natural outlet for her love of history and happy endings. After a vagabond life as a Navy brat and Army wife, Ms. Hanson convinced her husband to retire to southeast Alabama, where they now live with their two dogs and a cat. Her daughter is a lieutenant in the U.S. Coast Guard.

She loves to hear from readers and can be contacted at www.gingerhanson.com.

Experience the Romance of
Rosanne Bittner